PARIS LIGHTS

PARIS LIGHTS

A HEART OF THE CITY NOVEL

C.J. DUGGAN

hachette
AUSTRALIA

hachette
AUSTRALIA

Published in Australia and New Zealand in 2016
by Hachette Australia
(an imprint of Hachette Australia Pty Limited)
Level 17, 207 Kent Street, Sydney NSW 2000
www.hachette.com.au

10 9 8 7 6 5 4 3 2 1

National Library of Australia
Cataloguing-in-Publication data

Duggan, C.J., author.
Paris lights/C.J. Duggan.

978 0 7336 3665 3 (pbk)

Series: Duggan, C.J. Heart of the city; Bk. 1
Restaurants – Fiction.
Romance fiction.
Paris (France) – Fiction.

A823.4

Cover design by Keary Taylor
Cover photograph courtesy of Shutterstock
Author photograph by Craig Peihopa
Text design by Bookhouse, Sydney
Typeset in 11/16 pt Minion Pro by Bookhouse, Sydney
Printed and bound in Great Britain by Clays Ltd, St Ives plc

For all the dreamers – never wait.

Chapter One

I genuinely believe that aside from your place of birth there is somewhere else you belong: a place you're guided to by your heart. Some people might spend their entire lives in search of such a place, but all my life, throughout my travels, I knew which place was waiting for me.

Paris.

I had fed my love of Paris by having the Eiffel Tower plastered on my bedspreads and cushion covers, by buying kitchen accessories and placemats with *Rue Du Temple* scrawled across them, and hanging a cute *Bon Appetit* sign in my kitchen. I'd tried to explain to my boyfriend, Liam, that it wasn't really an obsession, I had just adopted a French Provincial style of decorating for our home. He seemed unconvinced.

Everyone wants to go to Paris. To fall in love, eat smelly French cheese and drink good local wine while toasting to the Eiffel Tower. It was more than just our home's décor and my Chanel lipstick collection that strengthened my bond.

Paris is the art capital of the world, with tourists flocking from near and far to catch a quick glimpse of Da Vinci's *Mona Lisa* and wander the vast halls of the Louvre. But, while many people believed the Louvre to be the pinnacle of the Parisian art museum scene, there were so many other museums to see. With much excitement, I had rattled off the list of must-see locations to Liam as we'd planned this long-awaited weekend in Paris.

'We could head to the Centre Pompidou, Paris's bastion of modern art. We'll need a good couple of hours to wander through all the amazing rooms with world-famous works of – oh my God, we'll be able to see Picasso, Klimt, Miro and Kandinsky!'

Liam's face had twisted in horror, and he'd said, 'Claire, I would sooner claw my own face off than spend an entire weekend in art museums.'

I had laughed it off, but my heart sank knowing that he wouldn't budge on this. I would have to settle for compromising on the art so we could both enjoy the trip.

Liam had insisted we save the Eiffel Tower until our last day in Paris. He'd said we shouldn't conform to the typical tourist itinerary, that we should discover other parts of the city first. He was so smart, so romantic.

We battled the crowds at the Louvre for a date with Mona Lisa, strolled hand-in-hand through the Jardin de Tuileries, dodged pigeons and love-lock sellers near Notre Dame, and, of course, no trip to Paris would be complete without a visit to the famed Moulin Rouge.

And this morning, stepping from the bus, our heads had craned upwards, my mouth ajar as Liam clicked away on his expensive Canon camera, snapping the iron beast before us. Except it wasn't a beast. The Eiffel Tower was a lady – strong, imposing, beautiful – but I couldn't have said so to Liam. He would have just rolled his eyes.

We'd lingered around the edge of the crowds, taking it all in. It was incredible how something that stood still could evoke as much excitement as a themed rollercoaster at Disneyland. Hordes of tourists surrounded us in a blur of excitement and delight. Despite the wonders around me, though, my attention remained on Liam. I only had eyes for him.

I tilted my head, admiring my gorgeous boyfriend: his dark, unruly hair, his five o'clock shadow, his charcoal-grey jumper and dark jeans that made him look like he belonged here; a true Parisian. Liam had been acting strange for days. Twitchy, antsy, a bit snappy. As he stood beside me, rubbing his unshaven jaw, I could see the cogs turning in his head, no doubt wondering what to say, how to do it. He is such a stickler for details; it's one of the things I love about him.

My chest expanded as I breathed deeply. I tried to hide the knowing smile that twisted the corner of my mouth. *This is it; this is really going to happen.* It was all clear to me now: the impromptu visit to Paris; saving the tower till last.

This is my moment.

Wait until everyone back home finds out about this.

I stood in the heart of the square and waited for Liam to speak. Waited for him to ask the big question, to go down on one knee in front of all these people, and ask me to be Mrs Liam Jackson.

My chest tightened as he turned to me. His focus was on me and me alone. In this moment, under the massive iron structure, the world around us didn't matter. It was as if we were the only ones on the planet and that the tower had been built for us alone. I could feel my skin prickle despite the warm air that swept over us.

'Claire.' Liam swallowed nervously. I could feel my eyes watering as he reached out and grabbed my hand, a hand that had been nervously tapping my thigh.

'Yes?' I breathed out, my heart beating a million miles an hour. *Yes, yes, yes* had been echoing in my mind all morning.

The dark, hypnotic pools of Liam's eyes made me breathless as he gazed intently at me.

This is it! This is what I've been waiting for. The perfect end to a perfect weekend.

He squeezed my hand. 'I think we should see other people.'

I didn't think I'd heard him correctly; the sound of a record scratching in my head might have prevented me from understanding. Or maybe it was the tourists, talking and pointing animatedly as they took selfies with the tower. Even the traffic noise seemed painfully loud right now. I tilted my head as if to listen more intently, my eyes blinking in confusion.

'Sorry?'

Liam's eyes seemed less romantic now, and his face was twisted in pain. But it wasn't pain caused by the inner turmoil of working on romantic perfection like I had thought. It was another kind of pain entirely.

'I said, I think we should—'

'No!' I shut off his words, afraid that he would only repeat himself. 'No, no, no, no!' This was not how it was supposed to go.

I had planned it all in my mind: Liam on one knee, a box appearing from his pocket (preferably from Tiffany), applause ringing out across the square as I cried and said, *Yes, yes, YES!* I had envisioned how to pose with my ring for Instagram, adding the witty caption: 'I said oui oui.' I had even picked out the appropriate filter for our selfie. It was all so perfect – in my head.

'Claire, I'm sorry.' His brown eyes were sorrowful, as though his heart was breaking. It was like I had just said the words that would tear us apart, not him. 'I never meant to hurt you.'

I felt my fists clench. My shock, my disbelief, was morphing into something else, even as the hot tears pooled in my eyes.

He never meant to hurt me.

'You're breaking up with me!'

Silence.

'In *Paris*.'

He looked away.

'Under the Eiffel fucking Tower!' I screamed, attracting the attention of those who were unlucky enough to be standing nearby.

Was there any feeling worse than this? A punch in the face on a gondola in Venice maybe? He might as well have punched me – it felt like all the air had been sucked from my lungs.

My admiration for him, my total and utter besotted and blind obsession with Liam, died. I could feel my heart darken; my soul was so black it scared me. We had been together for eighteen months, had moved from Melbourne to London so Liam could follow his path in life – whatever that had meant; he'd never actually clarified it. If he meant we were both always strapped for cash and working double shifts in the dimly lit London pub, then we were following his path all right. Living the dream! We had been so determined to find our way and make a new life in a foreign land, despite Liam's rather lacklustre path in London. I had been certain we knew each other's dreams and fears. And that's what was burning a hole in my heart, because at the crux of it, I don't actually think Liam knew me at all. Because anyone who ever did know me knew that coming to Paris had been my lifelong dream. I had mentioned it often enough. The city was so close to our new home, but until this weekend we had been too busy to make the trip: there was an excuse, there was always an excuse. So when Liam not only agreed, but instigated this trip, I had convinced myself that this was the moment. Why else would he bring me here?

I shook my head. 'How could you?'

I broke away from his hold. He was trying to explain, but I couldn't listen to his reasoning. I stumbled away, skimming past people as I made my way toward the bus that would take me back to the hotel. Everything was a blur. I sat on the top level of the double decker, my eyes forward, staring aimlessly at a balding Italian man and his wife. I couldn't look back to the tower for fear of catching a glimpse of Liam. I didn't hear Liam calling my name, pleading for the bus to stop as it pulled away. I'm not sure if I was more relieved or hurt by the fact he didn't pursue me, but I guess those kind of dramatics only happen in movies.

The sky was grey and ominous. I swear it had been blue when we arrived. That's how quickly things had changed. My bus rolled on, pausing only to give happy, snapping tourists one last chance to take a shot of the tower. I couldn't even bring myself to look at it, not that I would have been able to see it anyway through my bleary vision.

Maybe one day I would forgive Liam for breaking my heart. But tainting Paris, and ruining my experience of this city, that was something I could never forgive – ever!

~

Apparently Paris is especially magnificent in the rain. I had yet to experience the pleasure in my short stay, but as soon as I stepped off the bus, the heavens opened up, soaking me to the bone. It seemed a fitting finale to my disastrous afternoon. In a moment of complete self-indulgence to my misery, I had refused the complimentary plastic poncho from the tourist bus, opting instead to let the rain pummel me. Ordinarily a person might squeal, laugh and run for cover, delighting in the glorious downpour in a foreign city. It was, dare I say it, romantic. But let's face it, romance was dead, as was my ability to feel anything.

I walked along the pavement from the bus stop to a pedestrian crossing, squelching a slow, sad path in my ballet flats, my pleated skirt clinging to my thighs, my long brown hair plastered to my face. Mercifully, the droplets of water disguised my tears. Our hotel was a few blocks away on Rue Lauriston. We were ideally located between the Arc de Triomphe and the Eiffel Tower. It only seemed like yesterday that we had booked the last room available with great excitement.

Our hotel that *we* had booked.

I guess I had to stop saying things like that now. In one afternoon, the life I'd thought I had had became completely redundant. Was that even possible? Had I stayed to face Liam's explanations I might have found out more. If I'd challenged him, fought, screamed, demanded answers. But 'Let's see other people'? That was like a dagger to the heart, almost as bad as 'I'm seeing someone else'. I tried not to entertain the thought that that could have been the reason behind his decision.

I let my feet guide me along the narrow path, through the neighbourhood that seemed amazingly familiar to me even though I'd only been here for a short time. The past three days I'd been wide eyed, drinking in every detail of the impressive Haussmann-designed apartments and buildings; watching the locals go about their daily rounds to the butcher, florist or bakery in their effortlessly stylish way. The air felt thick. I fixed my gaze on the ground, willing my feet forward, telling myself that my reward would be to lock myself away in my hotel room and let my defences crumble down and scream and cry into my pillow.

The red sign of our hotel was mightier than any beacon. I battled on, each step becoming more perilous as the soles of my shoes fought to gain traction on the wet footpath. It took immense concentration to quicken my pace without breaking my neck, but I was determined. That's when I heard the distant sound of a fast-approaching car.

It slid around the corner, the revving engine of the black Audi echoing in the small street, disturbing the peace and quiet, slicing its way through the dying light. It was enough to distract me, annoyed as I was by the recklessness of its approach as it sped along like a rally car, and in wet conditions too.

I made sure to glare at the driver.

'Bloody maniac,' I grumbled.

Stepping back from the kerb, I gasped as the car sprayed up a wave of putrid gutter water. Now I was mad. Madder than hell.

I watched as the very same car pulled up in front of my hotel.

'Right,' I said. I was in just the mood to give the flashy lunatic behind the wheel a piece of my mind. And sure, there was a good chance that he wouldn't understand a word I was saying, but if all else failed, flipping the bird was a pretty universal gesture. I neared the car, sleek and beaded with droplets of rain, the windows so heavily tinted it was impossible to see inside.

'Hey!' I shouted, knocking on the driver's window angrily.

There was no response; the only sign of life was the heat that radiated from the vehicle itself. I glared at the window where I imagined a person's head might be. Feeling pretty satisfied at showing my displeasure, I sacrificed the unlady-like gesture of flipping the bird and thought it best to just head into the hotel, leaving a watery path behind me.

And I was about to do exactly that when the unexpected happened. The driver's window slowly edged its way down, revealing a pair of intense, angry blue eyes that seemed to stare right into my soul.

Yep, my day was about to get a whole lot worse.

Chapter Two

If I could have, I would have glued all Liam's undies to the floor and set his favourite pair of jeans on fire, all the while tossing his other possessions over the balcony. Instead, with much less drama, I quietly spoke in a croaky voice to the doorman by the front entrance.

'Can you please come and collect some bags from room twenty-five?'

I was wet and deflated and completely rattled from the death stare the Audi driver had given me, which had sent me fleeing into the hotel. Guess I wasn't as tough as I thought. I certainly didn't feel it right now. What's French for fragile?

If it hadn't been for Cecile, the warm, bubbly lady at reception, I would have sworn everyone in Paris hated me.

'Bonjour!' she said, beaming, showing the gap between her extremely white teeth. Her bright blue eyes lit up and I knew I had her full attention like always. 'Oh, Mademoiselle Shorten, you got caught in the rain?'

I sheepishly examined the squelchy footprints I had trekked through reception.

'Next time, take an umbrella by the door,' she added helpfully.

Ha! Next time. There won't be a next time. I am done.

Despite the bitter edge to my thoughts, I smiled. It was strained, but no matter how bad I was feeling I could never take it out on sweet Cecile; she had, after all, been one of the very few highlights of my weekend.

'Merci,' I said, one of the very limited words I knew the meaning of, even after listening to the audio translator on the Eurostar from London three days ago. My memory for language was not great; I had managed to remember that paper in French was 'papier', and the door was 'la porte'. Neither was going to get me out of a bind.

My watery trail followed me across the foyer to the lift. Pressing the button to summon the slowest lift in Paris, if not the world, I brought the edges of my soaked cardi together, the chill from my wet clothes starting to work its way into my bones. The screeching, rackety shoe box–sized lift groaned its way down to reception, the door struggling to open as the tiny cavity of doom presented itself to me. I tentatively stepped in and, like every other time I had done so, I wondered if this would be the time I would be trapped in here. Would today be the day the lift gave up the ghost? With my current track record, I wouldn't be surprised – it would be the icing on the bloody cake.

The lift screeched its way up to level four, its doors sliding painfully slowly to the side, releasing me to freedom on the narrow landing. I couldn't get out quickly enough. I would live to see another day.

I walked down the narrow carpeted hall to our room. The dated, awkward spaces that had once seemed so quaint to me now just seemed dingy. It made me feel less bad about leaving marks on the already worn, rose-coloured carpet. In the short time that I had stayed here, I had realised that our door required a particular lift-twist-and-shimmy action in order to open it. Still, it took me three goes to get it open, with a few swear words to aid the cause. After finally hearing the magical click of the lock, I shouldered my way through, the door hitting one of the suitcases in the light, tidy yet small room. I negotiated my way through the mess of our bags and clothes to the bed. Side-stepping around it I went to the balcony door, wanting nothing more than to let some fresh air in.

As I opened it, the balcony door hit the edge of the bed, allowing barely enough room to go out; it was something Liam and I had laughed about when we opened it the first time. Every new, quirky discovery had been met with carefree laughter because, after all, it was Paris: there could have been a rodent watching TV on our bed and it would have been okay. WE WERE IN PARIS! But now, as I shifted awkwardly through the small opening and onto the little rain-dampened balcony, I didn't feel any form of whimsy or lighthearted joy at all, even though my heart never failed to clench at the sight of the beautiful apartment buildings lining the street. Opposite me, a slightly damp black cat lazily washed himself on the balcony, the window left ajar for him for whenever he was ready to return.

Despite the traffic noise and the sound of a distant police siren, my mind was alarmingly quiet. My legs, which had felt like jelly, no longer shook, and although a breeze swept across me I didn't feel cold. If anything, my cheeks felt flushed and my heart raced; was I getting sick? Was this a normal reaction to heartbreak? I couldn't tell as I had no experience with being dumped, apart from David Kennedy ditching me in Grade Four for Jacinta Clark. Liam had been my first serious boyfriend and heartbreak was new to me, so I didn't know if what I was feeling was normal. I felt like a robot. Was I completely devoid of emotion?

My question was answered the moment I glanced down to the street, my eyes narrowing as I saw the black Audi that was still parked out the front of the hotel. The sudden rage I felt bubbling to the surface proved I wasn't a robot. I was all right, just as furious as I'd been on the pavement, meeting those steely blue eyes boring into me through the slit of the car window. Without apology they'd stared me down, and it had worked.

'Cocky bastard,' I mumbled, my voice causing the cat opposite to pause mid-clean and look at me with his yellow eyes.

'Shut up. I wasn't talking to you,' I said, smiling as he went back to his bath time. My humour was short lived. Hearing voices echo off the buildings, I gripped the edge of the railing, leaning over to get a better look at the commotion below.

A man in a dark navy suit strode out of the hotel entrance. He seemed determined, purposeful and intent on ignoring the struggling doorman who ran after him with an umbrella in a bid to keep him dry. The man ignored him, clicking the button and walking toward his . . . black Audi. He was talking on his phone, loud and robust, as he argued with someone on the other end. He seemed passionate, and manic, his free hand gesturing animatedly, before turning to aggressively wave and dismiss the doorman, who backed away with what looked like a thousand apologies.

The suit, whose face I couldn't see from this angle, opened his car door, ended his conversation abruptly and threw his phone inside.

What an arrogant bastard. I had seen it in his eyes, now I'd heard it in his voice and watched it in his stride. I almost wished that he would look up now, willed him to do so, so I could give him the finger this time, send him a 'screw you, buddy' scowl. The thought of doing such a thing almost made me feel giddy, but of course thinking and doing are two different things, and just as I stared down at him with a knowing look on my face, the last thing I actually expected to happen, happened.

He looked up.

I didn't give him the finger. Instead, I yelped and stepped back so fast I tripped on the lip of the door and went hurtling through the narrow opening, crashing rather mercifully onto the bed, before slipping onto the floor and collecting the side table on the way, pulling the curtain down with me, the rod narrowly missing my head.

I groaned, feeling the sting of carpet burn and a healthy dose of humiliation as I sat on the floor, the sheer fabric of the curtain draped over me like Mother Teresa.

'*Sacré* fuckin' *bleu*,' I said, half laugh, half sob.

Yeah, I showed him all right, I thought gingerly, and picked myself up, using the mattress as support. I hadn't even gotten a chance to really look at his face, all I remembered was meeting those same steely blue eyes and panicking. I heard the loud engine of his car speeding down the narrow road, probably taking out women and children along the way without a care in the world. Men like that belonged on an island; an island that should be set on fire.

I got to my feet, pulling back my curtain veil, and rubbing my arm, wincing at the bruises that were sure to come. I sighed, glancing out the window. The cat was gone. It had probably been spooked by the unco tourist flailing about and disturbing the peace, just as mine was suddenly disturbed by a knock at the door.

'Luggage, mademoiselle?'

Oh shit! Shit shit shit shit.

I stepped once to the left and twice to the right, a dance that continued as I tried to get my head together.

'Ah, just a second,' I yelled a bit too frantically. I picked up the side lamp from the floor, trying to straighten the skew-whiff lampshade and wrestling with the curtain cape over my shoulders. I'm sure I looked like some demented form of the Statue of Liberty. Shoving the curtain and pushing the rod behind the bed, I quickly drew the drapes. *Nothing to see here!*

Flustered, I gave in to the one fantasy I'd had walking back to the hotel: I grabbed every piece of Liam's belongings and shoved them into his bag. Quickstepping to the bathroom I dumped his toiletries into his bag too. It kind of felt good, packing him away piece by piece. By the time I opened the door to the doorman I was breathing heavily, my hair was half dry and fuzzy and my clothes were patchy and creased. If the doorman wondered what a hobo was doing in residence on the fourth floor, he didn't say anything. He smiled and gestured to take my bag, seemingly confused when he looked over my shoulder at where my stuff lay strewn all over the room.

'Ah, just one?' He lifted his finger.

We weren't leaving until tomorrow, heading back to London on the 11.05 train. I hadn't thought beyond just wanting Liam away from me – I couldn't even face him right now. I thought that his bag at the front door was a good enough hint as any; I only hoped he didn't see the need to come and talk to me.

I nodded. 'Just one.'

The door closed behind the doorman, leaving me standing in my room, my heart beating so fast it felt like it was robbing me of breath. I felt hot and manky, claustrophobic, so I peeled my clothes off quickly, hoping that would alleviate the feeling. I sat on the edge of the bed in my bra and undies, hands on my knees, shoulders sagged in defeat. What had I done? A knee-jerk reaction was typical of me, and in this moment a new kind of panic surfaced. Didn't I owe it to us to talk? To try to work it out? After all, the biggest change in my life had been moving to London with Liam. Was I simply going to let everything go?

My thoughts were interrupted by a muffled chime coming from the crumpled pile on the floor. I bent over, searching through the damp mess, feeling the lump in my cardi pocket that was illuminating the thin fabric.

Mum.

Quickly swiping the screen to avoid the loved-up picture of me and Liam, I tapped on Mum's text.

Just saw the pic on Instagram, you FINALLY got to see the Eiffel Tower, more pics please!! Xx.

I stared at Mum's message, confused. I didn't post any –

I froze, a sudden horror looming over me. 'Oh no, he didn't.'

I swiped and tapped the screen urgently, a part of me fearing that it could be true, and just as I tried to tell myself it wasn't, there it was. Loud and proud on Liam's Instagram profile, a picture of the Eiffel Tower – a few, actually, from different angles, different filters.

'You've got to be kidding me!'

He was so distraught at breaking my heart, he'd gone on to take photos, whack a filter on them, even fucking hashtag them: *#Eiffeltower #parislove #wonderwhatthepoorpeoplearedoing*

And he didn't stop there: seemed like Liam had a busy afternoon being quite the tourist, while I sat here in my undies, cold, battered and bruised. I glowered at the screen, tears clouding my vision, barely believing how incredibly selfish he could be.

I threw my phone down and buried my head in my hands. It was over, I knew it was, and more than anything I wished I could bring the numbness back.

I wished I was a fucking robot!

Chapter Three

I woke the next morning on top of the covers, still in only my underwear. There had been no more knocks on my door. No messages, no phone calls, no pleas from Liam for forgiveness or to be taken back. When I dressed, packed and headed downstairs to check out, Cecile at reception told me awkwardly, and with a sad smile, that Monsieur Jackson had booked into another room late last night.

'Thank you,' I said, putting the room key on the counter. 'Has he checked out yet?' I hated to ask but I had to know; I had our tickets for the painful trip back to London, something I could barely think about.

'No, mademoiselle.'

'Okay, well, um . . .' *Leave the ticket at reception and just go.* 'When he comes down, can you please tell him I am in the restaurant?'

Cecile nodded. 'Of course, I am very sorry to see you go. I hope you have enjoyed your stay here in Paris.' Her eyes were kind, and I could tell it pained her to do her usual checkout spiel, knowing full well that Paris was not going to be the city of love for me – far from it. I had hoped to take to the city like a true natural and that maybe Liam and I could return here every year for the anniversary of our engagement. But now I thought if I never saw that tower again, it would be too soon.

'I did,' I lied. 'Thank you for everything. You have been very kind.'

Cecile's beaming smile was back once more, her eyes alight as she stood tall with pride.

'*De rien, merci beaucoup.*'

I smiled. 'Am I okay to leave my bags here?'

'Oui, I'll have Gaston take them for you.'

'Merci,' I said, quietly. I felt like I was annihilating such beautiful words with my accent.

In the restaurant I was greeted by the familiar sight of Simone, a bored waitress from Tottenham who wore her hair in an impossibly high topknot bun. From the intel I had gathered over the weekend, she had been working at Hotel Trocadéro near on three months, didn't speak French but made it work, seeing as a lot of tourists stayed here. Cathy, the other breakfast girl, was a local.

'Fake it till you make it,' Simone said with a wink. 'Where's your man?'

'Oh, um, he's in the shower,' I said, masking my lying mouth by sipping my coffee.

'So you heading back then, to London?' she asked.

'Yeah, and you?'

'Oh, don't even, I'm trying to stick it out just to prove to my ex that I can live without him.'

That got my attention. 'And how is that working for you?'

'He's here every bloody weekend.' She laughed, rolling her eyes.

'Oh.' My shoulders sagged. I had hoped she was about to tell me a heroic tale of girl power and self-discovery, not weekend booty calls, mid-week mind games and text arguments. I zoned out after a while, a glazed look in my eyes, until they refocused on a figure standing at reception, talking to Cecile.

Liam smiled at Cecile, thanking her for what could only be assumed was the message she had passed on for me, then he tentatively turned to the restaurant and approached me. Simone had mercifully moved onto the next table to address a dirty spoon crisis, as Liam arrived before me. His dark eyes glanced at the empty chair, silently asking permission to sit.

When I didn't respond he took it as a yes and pulled out the chair. I looked straight into his eyes with a deadpan expression; I wanted him to feel my pain, my disappointment, my heartbreak.

'I've ordered a taxi for ten fifteen,' he said.

I lifted my chin, giving nothing away.

'Do you have everything?' he asked, like he always did. Always the control freak.

'Of course,' I snapped.

'Well, I think the trip home will give us the chance to . . . talk.'

I shrugged. 'Why wait?'

Liam sighed. 'Claire, please don't be—'

'What? Difficult? Sorry, but you don't get to call the shots, not on this.'

Liam shifted in his seat, smiling painfully at the couple at the next table, before he turned back to me, leaning forward. 'The taxi will be here soon.'

'Okay, well, until then we have some time to kill.' I wasn't backing down on this, no way, no how. I crossed my arms and sat back in my chair, staring him down, much like the suited Frenchman had done to me yesterday. Who'd have thought I would actually be grateful to him for showing me how it's really done? Liam swallowed, shifting once more in his seat.

Ha! What do you know? It really does work!

Truth be known, I didn't really want to talk, not here or on the train. I had nothing in my head, no begging requests for him to take me back, no heartfelt speech to give; nothing. But seeing as the ball was in my court, a situation that was so rare in our relationship, I wanted to at least say something, and the only thing that had sprung to mind was the very same question I had asked myself on the long, rainy walk back to the hotel.

I looked at Liam, my hard stare finally faltering. 'Why?'

It was the simplest of words but held the most meaning, and I knew it was the very question that Liam had been dreading, if the look on his face was anything to go by.

He closed his eyes as if summoning the strength to reply. It made me feel worse that he had to psych himself up to answer me. Surely he would already know why – he was the one breaking up with me. Did he have a gambling problem? A secret wife and kids back in Australia? Did he love listening to Nickelback? How bad could it be?

'I, um – Christ, why is this so bloody hard?'

His big brown eyes looked so pitiful, for a second I actually felt sorry for him; I was ready to say, 'Never mind,' and give him a hug. Until his shifting stopped and he looked into my eyes and I saw it: for some inexplicable reason I knew the answer, I just knew, and all of a sudden I didn't feel sorry any more. I slowly let my arms unfold as the realisation washed over me like a tidal wave. I took a deep, steadying breath.

'Who? Who is she?' I scrunched the serviette in my fist with white-knuckled intensity. 'The girl who's watering our fucking plants?' I said way too loudly – even Gaston from the hotel door turned.

'It's not what you think,' he said. 'Nothing has happened.'

'No, but you want it to.'

He fell silent, unable to even look me in the eyes.

I had been hard-pressed to think of one question, but now it seemed I had a million of them tumbling in my head. *How long? Why her? Why Veronica from upstairs?*

But as the painful silence drew out between us, there was only one question that I really wanted him to answer.

'Do you love her?'

Only then did his eyes look up to my face and in a moment where I felt I didn't know him at all, I found I could read

Liam better than anyone, and I could see the answer in his eyes. It was a crushing blow.

'It's hard to explain. It's different with her. She just . . . gets me.'

I could feel my stomach churning. I seriously didn't want to know the details. I had heard enough.

'Claire.' He took my hand. 'You will always be very special to me.' His face was creased in sincerity, and it took everything in my willpower not to punch him. I might have done exactly that if Gaston hadn't intervened.

'Pardon, your taxi is here.'

Snapping out of my violent thoughts, I pulled my hand away and grabbed my bag. Like a zombie, I weaved around the breakfast tables, following Liam out. It was almost like I was underwater, struggling for breath, disoriented. The smiles and goodbyes from Simone and Cecile all seemed as if they were playing out in slow motion, the sound muted as my foggy mind ran over every horrid moment from the second Liam had dropped a bombshell on me yesterday. Flashing images of our seventy-two hours in Paris pinpointed every time he had rolled his eyes, or argued that I was wrong, or told me not to be stupid; it was a montage of putdowns, something I hadn't even thought about before. His contempt for me hit me like the fresh air hitting my face as we left the hotel.

As the taxi driver loaded our bags into the car, I felt Liam beside me, touching me on the shoulder. 'Claire?'

I blinked, turning to see his concerned eyes, before my gaze dropped to my hand, holding the crinkled train ticket.

'Claire, come on, the taxi's waiting.'

I looked at him, examining his face silently before I smiled slowly and I shook my head. I shoved the ticket into his chest.

'I'm not going anywhere.'

Liam's mouth gaped as he clutched the train ticket. 'W-what?'

'I'm staying in Paris,' I said, lifting my chin. Spinning on my heel, nodding to Gaston, who was already retrieving my bags from the taxi with a big grin, I said, 'Goodbye, Liam. I never did like those fucking pot plants.'

Chapter Four

With every diva moment comes the equally terrifying prospect of reality when you fall back down to earth. In this instance I was standing at reception, feeling utterly nauseous at what I had just done. I had never been anywhere without Liam; he always seemed so street smart, adapted well to foreign environments almost like a shape shifter, and he was so well travelled and confident in the world. I had largely been too, because I was with him. Now I was alone.

'I am so sorry, mademoiselle, but your room has been booked by another. Let me see if there is anything else available.' Cecile's long, manicured fingers danced over the keyboard with urgency.

I could feel myself holding my breath as she examined the screen, waiting for her expression to either lighten with hope or crease in despair. I had no plan B; everything in my life now was an utter unknown.

Then her face creased in despair. 'I am so sorry. We are fully booked.'

I felt the world turn; my head was light and I didn't know if I had even answered Cecile or just gripped the side of the desk to stop the room from spinning. I felt hot, white spots dancing in my vision. *Okay, breathe, Claire, just breathe; we can figure this out, no problem.*

I heard Cecile's panicked cry – 'Gaston! Gaston!' – and then blackness descended.

The next thing I felt were the waves of air hitting my face as I slowly blinked my eyes open. I felt a strong grip around my shoulders, sitting me upright on the cool marble tiles. Cathy from the restaurant was frantically waving a newspaper in my face.

'What happened?' I tried to break from Gaston's hold but he was adamant to keep me still.

'*Ne bougez pas!*' he said, which, at a guess, meant 'stay put'.

'You fainted,' said Cathy.

'I what?' Oh God, it was mortifying.

'Do not worry, Mademoiselle Shorten, just get up very slowly.' Cecile moved to my other side, helping me to my feet. I had never been so grateful to them for being an anchor as the room continued to spin. Little did I care; dignity was severely underrated anyway. They guided me to a chair near the tourist brochures, where they made me sit before a glass of water was thrust into my face.

'Thank, ah, merci,' I corrected, taking the glass with a shaky hand.

I grounded myself with that glass of water, sipping on it as chaos swarmed around me in a flurry of French words that I had no hope of understanding.

The conversation died, and now they stood around me. It was like they had no idea what to do with me. I had to get my shit together. A few more moments and I would be fine; I would work it out. I was a big girl. There had to be somewhere they could recommend.

Gaston turned to Cecile, his expression uncertain. '*Le sixième ètage?*' he said. I didn't know what that meant but Cecile's eyes widened, like whatever he had just asked was completely ludicrous, and yet her mind seemed to be ticking, as her gaze drifted from Gaston to me. I no doubt looked a sorry sight: bloodshot eyes, white as a ghost, nursing my glass of water; all I needed to do was tremble my chin and I would be truly pathetic.

Cecile's mouth curved into a small smile. 'Gaston, grab Mademoiselle Shorten's bags.'

Cathy gasped, stepping forward. 'No, Cecile.'

Cecile cut her a dark look; it was the first time I had seen anything like that from her, but she was definitely not to be trifled with.

Gaston smiled, going to the front door to gather my bags, but instead of taking them outside to be unloaded into the next taxi like I expected, he carried them in my direction, coming to stand beside me. I blinked in confusion.

Cecile's blinding smile was back, shuttering over any darkness from a minute before.

'Gaston, please escort Mademoiselle Shorten to the sixth floor.'

My last glimpse of the reception area was of Cathy's horrified expression, then the door of the lift blocked my view of her. I suddenly felt very nervous – was Gaston leading me to certain death? Could this elderly lift possibly handle two more floors? Me, Gaston and my luggage in this confined space was enough to make the dizzies kick in again, but I stayed the course and pushed my mind forward. *Stop being such a bloody sook, Claire.*

'You will like the sixth floor,' Gaston said.

'Well, I don't think Cathy was too impressed about it.'

Gaston laughed, but said nothing more.

'Does she want to stay on the sixth floor?' I said, mainly to myself, as I tried to wonder why Cathy had taken it almost personally. The lift came to a shunting stop and the number six was illuminated above the door. The door opened, then Gaston stepped onto the landing with my bags.

'No one stays on the sixth floor. It is forbidden,' he said cryptically.

I swallowed, almost tripping as I followed Gaston down the long hall. 'Um, then why are you bringing me here? I don't want to be in any trouble.'

'Well, it wouldn't be a good turn to send a girl who has fainted out onto the streets of Paris, would it?'

'I feel much better,' I said, taking in the vast differences of the sixth floor to the one my previous room had been on. It was flooded with natural light from a large window, which shone onto a small, ornate table set with fresh flowers. The floor was a beautiful herringbone French oak parquet, unlike the other floors' crusty, worn carpets, and the walls were all painted a crisp blinding white; framed black-and-white pictures of Paris lined the halls, pops of black and grey against the stark white. It was almost as though we were in a completely different hotel altogether, like a secret world at the top of the building. Not only was it seemingly forbidden to others but I certainly felt like an imposter.

'Ah, Gaston, I am honestly so grateful, but I don't think that I am going to be able to afford the nightly rate here.'

Gaston laughed; for all I knew I was about to be entrapped in a twenty-year time-share lease.

He stopped before a door, placed my bags on the ground, and retrieved a key from his pocket.

'Get some rest. Cecile will stop by at the end of her shift to check on you,' he said, unlocking and pushing the door open. He stepped to the side, allowing me to enter first.

I entered the room tentatively, my eyes widening at the unexpected grandeur inside. We definitely couldn't be in the same hotel.

The room was like a mini apartment. There was actually space to move and there was no carpet stained by a leaky old AC unit, or mission-brown built-in wall desk. The room was only partially painted and exposed electrical wiring dangled from a wall light. A picture leaning against the wall next to a power tool suggested that they weren't exactly expecting company.

Gaston scoffed with embarrassment. 'Ah, yes, the room is undergoing some improvements,' he said, quickly moving to pick up the drill. Seeing as I had been homeless I wasn't about to complain – even in its unfinished state, the room was glorious.

To my left there was a large marble-tiled bathroom, with a shower and separate bath, which I was already fantasising about submerging myself in. The room was bright and white like the hall, with accents of black and gold from cushions and fabrics. Even the curtains were plush – I vowed to keep away from them. Well, I would just be more careful, I thought, as I was instantly lured to the double balcony doors. I peeled the lace curtain across to reveal a patio, complete with table and chairs and—

'Oh God.'

Gaston came to stand beside me. 'Nice view, eh?'

There she was, in all her glory: the Eiffel Tower. Most people would kill for a view like this; I wanted to recoil and draw the curtains.

'It's beautiful,' I stammered, not wanting to seem ungrateful. I was waiting for the massive catch, like having to sign a contract in blood. I wondered if in future I should faint at airports to get an upgrade?

Either way, there was one thing that I knew: despite all the foreign words exchanged, I knew it was Gaston who had suggested the sixth floor, and I had never felt so grateful in my life. Considering the way the day had started, he would never know just how he had saved me.

Gaston was probably in his thirties, dark skinned, slender, yet not much taller than me. He had been my first introduction to the hotel, and he had been a champion in looking after me since.

'Merci beaucoup, Gaston,' I said, trying not to smile.

Gaston nodded, looking suitably impressed. 'Make yourself at home. If you need anything, dial nine for reception,' he said, handing me the key before heading to the door and leaving me standing in my own little piece of Parisian paradise. I dug my nails into the palm of my hand, hoping that I wouldn't wake up from my dream, but the sixth floor was very, very real.

Chapter Five

I f just for the night, I was going to make every minute of this count.

After a long, hot shower, I engulfed myself in the fluffy white robe and complimentary slippers that were at least three sizes too big for me. I raided the minibar, hitting on all the things not provided in my old room. This really was the penthouse experience, despite its half-finished state and the fact I could smell the paint fumes. The linen was so silken and smooth to touch, I was almost too paranoid to sit on the bed out of fear of wrinkling the expensive fabric.

Oh, who am I kidding? I dived onto the bed, sinking into the plush, feather-top mattress, and rolled over onto my back, punching the feather pillows into the right shape to lounge against. But the instant droopiness of my eyes failed me.

Maybe I dozed for an hour, maybe five, I couldn't be sure; all I knew was that the sun had dipped and a darker shade of daylight filtered through the window. Much like the day had changed yesterday, a storm was brewing. I looked at my watch, and the first thing that came to mind was that Liam would be back in London by now, back to his thoroughly watered pot plants, back to *her*. My chest tightened and hot tears welled in my eyes as Liam's betrayal boiled my blood. As much as I'd tried to mask it by burying myself in the luxurious pleasure of the sixth floor while sipping on mini bottles of alcohol, there was no escaping it – Liam had smashed a hole in my heart the moment he had confessed the reason, the *real* reason, we were through. Oh God, I couldn't even think about it.

I groaned, rolling over to bury my face in the pillows. The hungry growl of my stomach was almost as loud as my muffled voice. I pulled myself into a sitting position, thinking of my next plan of attack. I was almost afraid to go down to reception out of fear that there had been such a huge mistake – what if they told me to pack my bags and get out? – but even I knew ignorance was not always bliss.

I didn't know when Cecile was due to finish her shift, but now I was rested and somewhat less manic than this morning, I owed it to her to go down and see her. Work out a plan, though I had no idea where to begin. All I knew was, I didn't want to go back to London, not yet. How could I? Face him, face her: it was the last place on earth I wanted to be. I would sooner head home to Melbourne, which was a definite possibility. But more than that, I really didn't want to leave Paris like this, I didn't want to give Liam the satisfaction of tainting the one place I had dreamed about since I was a little girl. As much as I didn't know what I was doing, there was a fire in my belly to find my way – or wait, was that hunger?

No, it was definitely determination.

A true sign that I was making myself at home was the unpacking of my toiletries in the bathroom. I brushed my teeth, looking at my puffy eyes. I barely recognised my sullen reflection.

Come on, Claire, time to put on your brave face.

I gathered my hair up into a sweeping ponytail. Dressing in my navy linen shorts and white sleeveless blouse, I stepped into my ballet flats and grabbed the room key and my turquoise bag. The afternoon deserved an umbrella and a stroll to a nearby café; if that wasn't enough to give me time with my thoughts, then nothing would be.

Walking into the lobby, there was a different kind of buzz about the place. There seemed to be more staff swarming in their burgundy vests. Cecile, who wore a burgundy jacket thanks to her manager status, stood next to a burgundy-jacketed man, one I had not seen before. He was rummaging through papers as Cecile spoke, quickly and frantically down the phone, in French. Cathy and Simone were busying themselves in the restaurant, Gaston was cleaning the front door with a rag and a cleaner was busy buffing the polished tiles in reception. I didn't know what was happening; maybe this happened every Sunday before the beginning of a new week?

I couldn't gain Cecile's attention, she seemed so stressed and anxious about her task, another side of her I had never seen, that I thought it best to catch her on the way back.

I tiptoed around the buffer, careful not to leave any marks. This time I made sure to reach for a complimentary umbrella as I stepped into yet another cloudy, grey day in Paris.

'Bonjour, Gaston,' I said, opening my umbrella and resting it on my shoulder.

'Bonjour, Mademoiselle Shorten,' he said.

I winced at the formality. 'Please call me Claire.'

'Oh, well, bonjour, Claire.'

'So, what is with all this? Is the queen coming to town?' I laughed, waiting for Gaston to laugh too. Instead, he straightened, his brows furrowed as if he too was worried, preoccupied somehow. He went to speak, but was drowned out by a fast-approaching London accent – Simone.

'I don't give a shit. I am going for a smoke before I bloody claw someone's face off,' she yelled behind her, bringing out her packet of cigarettes.

Gaston gave her an annoyed look.

'I don't care, Gaston. It's bloody bullshit. I should have knocked off four hours ago, I didn't sign up for this,' she said, leaning against the hotel exterior, taking a deep draw. In the natural light, Simone wore heavy, unblended makeup, with black eyeliner arcing up at the corner of each eye. She looked like and kind of sounded like the love child of Amy Winehouse and Adele; her voice definitely cut through the air in the Paris street.

'What ya reckon, Claire, do you think it would be a bit sus if I fainted in the kitchen to get out of work?' She said it with a wink, aiming for a joke.

'Well, I don't recommend it,' I said quietly.

'So how's life on the sixth floor?' she asked, waving the excess ash from her cigarette. 'Can't say I've had the pleasure.'

'It's lovely. I had a good sleep. I feel much better now.'

'Yeah, well, lap it up, luv, because you see that cloud creeping in over your head?'

I followed her long-nailed finger to the clouds above us.

'That ain't nothing compared to the black cloud that's coming over this place tomorrow.'

I looked back at her confused – was she giving me a weather report?

'Shouldn't you be helping Cathy in the restaurant?' Gaston said, his tone firm.

'Ha! There ain't no amount of help going to save our necks,' she said, throwing her cigarette into the gutter. 'You can scrub all you like, it won't make any difference.' She spun on her heel and headed inside.

Gaston glared at her. I felt like a massive third wheel; perhaps I should have stepped away from the conversation, but it had certainly intrigued me.

'What does she mean, there's a black cloud coming? She's not referring to the weather, is she?'

Gaston shook his head, turning his attention back to the glass pane. 'Not exactly,' he said. His mood seemed to be dark now, as if he was weary and the lighthearted welcomes and smiles of hospitality had all but dried up. Or maybe I was just a part of the furniture now and he didn't see the need to put on his professional face with me.

I wanted to press further, but thought better of it. 'Well, I'll see you later. If Cecile is looking for me, can you just tell her I've gone to get something to eat? I won't be too long.'

Gaston grunted, and I was suddenly glad I hadn't pressed for more information. Whatever Simone had alluded to only seemed to add to the stress of what was going on. Whatever it was, it was none of my concern; I would reside quietly on the sixth floor until I worked out what I was going to do next. I would catch Cecile in a better moment when I returned, plus I would be more nourished and clear-headed. I hoped.

~

One comfort I had was my very vivid memory. The first morning of our stay, as Liam grumbled over the mystery of how to connect his laptop to the wifi, I had taken my first solo expedition to hunt and gather breakfast for us. It had been a welcome distraction from our cramped quarters and Liam's outbursts. Today, the sun was still battling the clouds, as I turned right, following the path I'd taken a few days ago, making my way into one of the busier avenues. I felt a certain power, knowing where I was going and what I wanted, instead of seeming like a confused tourist aimlessly wandering the streets.

I took note of the street sign: Avenue Kleber. It seemed important to know these things, seeing as I was on my own now. I waited to cross the busy road to one of the best patisseries I had ever been to. When once again I stood in front of the window of the boulangerie patisserie, the enticing treats displayed behind the glass made my stomach rumble. Having had nothing more than a cup of coffee and a dry piece of toast for breakfast at a time when my appetite had well and truly deserted me, my focus was now on a crispy French baguette spread with camembert, then I'd stray to other delights: croissants, pains au chocolat, chausson aux pommes, pain viennois, brioches; so much goodness I didn't think my heart could take it. Mercifully there was a smaller line on a Sunday afternoon, and I hit the counter to point and mime my requests in no time. I was soon sitting at one of the small outside tables facing the street, watching all the late-afternoon traffic go by.

I inhaled and watched a French flag above my head furl and unfurl against the wind. I heard my coffee and plate touch down on the table and my mouth instantly watered. I bit into the dense bread and creamy goo of the cheese and closed my eyes, euphoric, as I enjoyed the solitude of a place that bore no memory of Liam. This was mine, and I felt a lightness in my heart knowing that I had made it so. For as long as it took to eat the baguette, I could almost forget why I was here and why I had chosen to go for a walk and get some space.

Oh yeah, that's right. I had to think about what I was going to do with my life, that's all. Nothing heavy, just my entire future rested on this baguette. So far it was making me very happy indeed. Now all I had to do was think.

What the hell am I going to do?

I flipped the serviette over. I would write a list of options; lists were always good. Rummaging through the never-ending depths of my bag for a pen, my fingers brushed against a crinkled, folded-up piece of paper. Yanking out the paper my eyes locked onto it – a folded-up map of Paris. Placing my bag aside and thinking nothing more of the pen, I unfolded the map, taking note of all the scribblings at each location. Manic, excited scribblings from a pre-Paris Claire, who'd had all the hope and wonder of too much to discover in a short amount of time. But now there were no time restrictions, no deadlines and nothing and no one holding me back. My trip planning had always annoyed Liam, but it really was an occupational habit. Back in Australia I had worked as an events coordinator, a time that seemed like a lifetime ago. Then I'd taken a rather large pay cut to work at a small London pub. I had never resented giving up my career so Liam could find his – my sacrifice was a part of the bigger picture. Now the bigger picture was a really murky one.

But as I studied the map before me, there was a sudden clarity, a new realisation that seemed to give me the answer without even having to make a list or think it over in any great detail. If there was one saving grace in all of this, it was my British passport, allowing me to work anywhere in Europe without a visa. How lucky was I that my mum had emigrated from England when she was a teenager? If I was going to do this, I needed more time, and all that was dependent on one small detail. I wrapped up the last of my baguette, plunged it into my bag, and sipped my coffee, before snatching up the map and heading back down Avenue Kleber, toward my hotel, to speak to Cecile.

Chapter Six

Something was definitely happening. Hotel Trocadéro had gone from chaos to ghost town. The reception was unmanned and even Gaston was nowhere to be seen as I slotted my umbrella back into the stand near the door. Maybe everyone had been fired, having let the neurotic, light-headed Aussie camp on the sixth floor. *I have to find Cecile.*

I tapped the bell at reception and cringed. I felt bad having to stop anyone from what they had been doing. I kind of wanted to just slip seamlessly back up to my room, but until I sorted out the finer details, I wouldn't be able to relax. If I could swing it, I wanted to stay here for a few days longer, just until I had enough courage to take the next step in my plan.

The high-pitched ring of the bell lingered in the abandoned reception area. The staff had done well to have all the surfaces polished and shiny; the lounge area was pristine, with not a magazine, book or cushion out of place. The room was quite quirky and eclectic and despite the typical black-and-white Parisian prints on the wall, the décor was

striking and vibrant. A large purple lounge was the star of
the room, framed by two blood orange–coloured armchairs.
A black oval coffee table divided the seating and sat on top of
a black-and-white striped carpet – it was kind of like *Alice in
Wonderland* meets Paris. An old-style typewriter propped up
a selection of books on a shelf. I would certainly be happy to
rest here for a while until someone appeared, but just as I was
about to make myself at home on the lounge, the door into
the restaurant was flung open, causing me to stand quickly.
The burgundy-jacketed man I'd seen with Cecile appeared;
I would have thought he was frowning at me until I realised he was sporting a monobrow that never seemed to alter
his expression from looking anything other than annoyed.
Despite his murderous eyes he smiled, quite genuinely, as
he approached.

'Can I help you, mademoiselle?' he asked, with an air of
courteous professionalism.

'I'm sorry to bother you, I was just wondering if Cecile
was available?'

'I am sorry, she is in a staff meeting. Is there anything I
can help you with?'

I paused, feeling kind of funny about speaking with – I
looked at his name badge: Philippe. It was ridiculous but it
kind of felt like me staying on the sixth floor was a secret
between me and Cecile, and that, based on the reaction of
the other staff, maybe I shouldn't have been telling anyone,
especially someone in a burgundy manager's jacket, where

I was staying. The last thing I wanted was to get Cecile into trouble.

'Um, no, thank you. Maybe if you could please ask Cecile to contact me once she is available?'

'Certainly,' he said, making his way back to reception in order to take note of my message. 'You are a guest here at the hotel?'

I swallowed. 'Yes.'

'Your room number?' he asked, pen poised and looking up at me expectantly.

'Oh, um, can you just tell her Claire Shorten would like to speak to her. She'll know what it's in regards to,' I said.

'Ah, Claire Shorten,' he said, moving to the computer and tapping in my name before I had a chance to say another word. His gaze fixed on the screen, and his monobrow dipped so low I thought he might have been able to shoot laser beams out of his eyeballs.

'There seems to be some mistake: it says you are on the sixth floor,' he said, mainly to himself.

I shifted anxiously. I was starting to get worried. What was so horrifying about the sixth floor? Maybe someone was murdered up there and no one in their right mind would want to stay there. He looked at me, waiting for me to confirm that it was a mistake, but I didn't. I couldn't.

'It was the only—'

'Excuse me, Mademoiselle Shorten, I will just have a word with my colleague,' he said rather curtly before heading back to the door that led to God knew where. My stomach churned, certain that Cecile was going to get into trouble.

I was all but ready to go pack my bags when Philippe appeared again, the same dreaded look on his face until he reached me, only then did his face lighten in a smile, but this time it didn't seem so genuine.

'Cecile said have a good night's rest and she will see you in the morning.'

'Oh, um, I just wanted to confirm the rate of the room, just so I can—'

'It will be all sorted in the morning, mademoiselle,' he said, cutting off my words. He seemed eager to return to the staff meeting, and I was just as eager to let him.

'Oh, okay, well, merci beaucoup,' I said, heading quickly to the lift, praying that it would make the rickety journey to the sixth floor.

~

Don't do drugs, kids. But if you get dumped in Paris, by all means, pop a valium.

Sunset saw the return of my misery, tears streaming down my face and tissues strewn about my luxury apartment as I ordered room service for dinner. More tears flowed after I called work back in London and gave notice. It went down like a lead balloon.

My spirit was at an all-time low; it took every ounce of energy I had to Skype my mum and lie about how everything was going fine. I had known within the first two-point-five seconds of speaking to her that she was none the wiser. Besides, I doubted there would be any loved-up selfies of Liam and the pot-plant whore for a long while. In this scenario he was most definitely the bad guy, so it wasn't like he was going to advertise our split to my family, which for now served me just fine.

I raided my small stash of valium, reserved for flying and underwater trips via train from London to Paris, hoping it would help me sleep in my new room in my plush bed . . . on my own.

~

By morning I was in a much better headspace after a deep, drug-induced sleep and I was ready to face the world. I wasn't taking any chances, however. I packed my suitcase and sat it by the door. I took a sweeping look around my luxury pent-house, taking in every detail and committing it to memory. If they hadn't found me another room, I doubted I could stay here, on the forbidden sixth floor. I sighed. Well, it was nice while it lasted.

On my way down for breakfast I came up with a theory: I must have been staying in quarters that belonged to the owners; maybe they were out of town and my staying in their residence was a big no-no. Despite this, I was confident that Cecile would be able to point me in the right direction for alternative accommodation. But as the door to the lift opened, there was just no way of preparing for what was about to greet me.

My heart sank so low and so fast I swear I heard it hit the polished reception floor. Cecile was sobbing, sobbing and ranting in French so quickly I could tell even those who spoke the same language were struggling to keep up. Even Philippe's monobrow seemed concerned. Gaston was there, taking charge, escorting Cecile from reception to one of the orange chairs in the lounge, leaving Philippe to deal with a couple of confused tourists standing at the counter.

I didn't wait for answers, thinking that poor Cecile's meltdown was directly linked to me. I followed them into the lounge, hoping that standing before her would block the view of the ogling breakfast guests.

Cecile buried her face in her hands, her shoulders shaking with sobs.

'What's wrong?' I asked Gaston, who was crouching by Cecile's side, offering her a box of tissues.

'Simone quit this morning,' he said with a glum expression.

I wasn't going to lie, I was flooded with relief that the answer wasn't, 'Cecile has been fired for putting you up in the penthouse on the sly.' But then confusion set in: was Simone such a great loss? Was there some hidden, irreplaceable talent of hers I was unaware of? Because all I had witnessed was gossip and laziness. She was definitely not a team player. Maybe Cecile was just a sensitive soul.

'Of all the days for her to do this. I could kill her!' Cecile burst out angrily, grabbing violently at the tissues and blowing her nose.

Okay, not such a sensitive soul then.

'What are we going to do? Who is going to serve?'

I turned to see the restaurant less than half full. Cathy was rearranging the fruit display with ease; I really didn't see what the fuss was all about.

'Is Simone quitting really that bad for business?' I asked tentatively. Only yesterday the whole place had been unmanned altogether for their staff meeting – is that when all hell broke loose?

Gaston shook his head. 'This is the worst possible thing that could have happened. Any day but today.'

Okay, I know I didn't speak French, but I was having a hard time deciphering English these days. Mysterious sixth floor; Simone saying a black cloud was descending over the hotel; now she had quit, causing teary hysterics – what on earth was going on?

'Forgive my ignorance, but why today of all days?' I asked, bracing myself when both sets of eyes looked up at me in distress. Cecile's bloodshot ones welled once more as her chin trembled.

'Because, because . . .' She couldn't hold it together, she started to cry and rant in French again, burying her face in a fistful of tissues. Gaston was comforting her, rubbing her shoulders. He let out another weary sigh.

'Because?' I asked, ever so gently.

Gaston met my eyes; his seemed to have traces of something that almost looked like fear. It was enough to make me swallow in anticipation as he worked up the nerve to speak.

'Because, today *he* is coming,' he said, a darkness falling over his usually bright and cheery face.

I froze, barely able to draw breath when I pressed further. 'Who?'

'The devil; the devil is coming.'

Chapter Seven

It was not a time to laugh, although my instinct had been to do just that.

'Sorry?' I asked, thinking I had misheard him, but then Cecile, wiping the smudges of mascara from her cheeks, spoke.

'Louis Delarue is coming to lunch.'

They both looked at me expectantly, ready to witness my own horror register at the mention of his name. Instead, the only thing that swept across me was complete blankness.

'Oh, okay.'

'This afternoon,' she said in clear, slow English as if to emphasise the gravity of the situation.

I nodded, still with a vacant look in my eyes.

Cecile and Gaston looked at each other again, seeming rather disturbed by my reaction, or rather non-reaction.

'You do know who Louis Delarue is?' Cecile asked. Her sobbing had morphed into complete disbelief.

'Uh, I can't say as I do,' I said, trying to lighten the mood with a bit of a crooked smile. It didn't work. At all.

Gaston was aghast. 'You do not know who Louis Delarue is?'

'Nope, sorry, should I?'

Cecile shook her head. 'He is only one of the most renowned chefs and restaurateurs.'

'He comes to failing businesses and critiques them; he can make or break livelihoods with a single look,' added Gaston.

'Oh, so he's coming to critique the hotel?'

'He is meeting with his production crew here and starting his evaluation today. We cannot afford to be down a single staff member.'

Again I thought back to the calibre of Simone's skills and I couldn't help but think that her quitting could only be a good thing. And then I looked at Cecile, and her stricken, worried demeanour; she was near to having a nervous breakdown. I didn't know who this Louis character was, but I could see that his visit was important, that he could make or break the hotel, and if the likes of the foul-mouthed Simone were required to help out, then the stakes must have been high – really high.

'I can help,' I blurted.

That got their attention. Their silence was unnerving, their shocked faces the only sign that they had heard me. Gaston slowly stood.

'I'm serious. I am happy to help in any way I can. I might not be able to speak the language, but I'm guessing Simone wasn't exactly fluent, and I worked in events management back in Australia, so I can definitely think on my feet and stay calm in a crisis, and as far as I can tell, this is a pretty big crisis.'

Cecile stood too. She seemed afraid to hope that I was speaking the truth. 'You would do that?'

'If it wasn't for you, I would have been wandering the streets of Paris, or worse still, fainting in the gutter.'

Cecile smiled, and a glimmer of her old self was there again. 'I was happy to help.'

I nodded. 'And so am I.'

~

Cecile flung the kitchen door open so fast I had to stop it flinging back into my face as I followed her through.

'Gather around everyone, we have a new staff member.' Cecile beamed. If it wasn't for her flushed cheeks, you might not have guessed that only moments before she had been a hot mess. I stood by her side, smiling at everyone who gathered – three people.

'Is this everyone?' I murmured out of the corner of my mouth, trying to be discreet but probably failing miserably.

Cecile frowned, as if annoyed by the question. 'Oui, this is everyone.'

The hotel boasted forty-four warm and welcoming rooms, so at full occupancy I guess there wouldn't be a real need for an army in the kitchen, which was probably just as well as you wouldn't have been able to fit one in here. It was the tiniest, messiest kitchen I had ever seen. You couldn't see a scrap of the bench, and empty boxes were piled up at the back door. My eyes moved to the open coolroom door, glimpsing a continued mess of boxes and chaos. A beanpole of a boy diced carrots on the central island. He awkwardly chopped, keeping his elbows tucked in so as not to knock into anything and he was slightly hunched so as not to bang his head on the pots hanging from the rack above.

'This is Francois – he helps with the preparation and dishes and general kitchen maintenance.'

Francois wiped his hand on his grubby apron, and offered it to me. 'Bonjour.' He looked at me expectantly as he shook my hand, once, twice, three times.

'Oh, um, Claire, my name's Claire.' What I was really thinking was, what kind of maintenance had Francois been doing?

A shorter man wearing a stained white chef's top stirred a clear liquid on the stove; he seemed unkempt and disinterested in my presence.

'This is Gaspard – he is our head chef.'

Gaspard abandoned his duty and turned to me, giving me a moist handshake and a curt head nod.

'Hello,' I managed, feeling strangely intimidated by him.

'And of course you know Cathy.' Cecile smiled, turning to Cathy, who stood to the side, watching on with interest and very little emotion.

None of them seemed happy I was here. I don't know what I expected really: to walk into an industrial kitchen with big open spaces, lots of stainless-steel benches, and a conga line of people in crisp white chef's uniforms and puffy white hats?

I thought that maybe they might rejoice that help was here, that they weren't a man down any more, and with a joint effort we could show this Louis Delarue what Hotel Trocadéro was made of. But as the reality, or rather the enormity, of the situation washed over me, I came to realise that Simone quitting, that being a man down, was the least of anyone's problems.

I turned to Cecile. 'Can I have a word with you for a second?'

'Of course.'

I smiled at the team, feeling slightly awkward as I backed out of the swinging door and into the restaurant, to stand in the little alcove where excess cutlery was stored.

'Cecile, when is he coming?'

'He is coming for lunch.'

'So, what, in four hours?' I asked, panic spiking my voice.

'Oui, he is meeting with his counterparts to review the profile of the hotel and see if he will take it on for his show.'

'His show?'

'You have not heard of his show?'

'I don't even know who he is.'

Once more, Cecile looked at me as if I was slightly mad. 'He has a reality show called *Renovation or Detonation*; he goes to hotels and decides whether he can save them or not.'

This was not good at all, because based solely on that kitchen I knew exactly what he would be inclined to do. A world-renowned chef was about to cast his perfectionist eye over Hotel Trocadéro and even though I didn't know who he was, I was terrified for them.

'Cecile, you have to put me in charge of that kitchen.'

'Pardon?'

'Not as cook or chef or anything, but you need to put me in there not just as a Simone replacement, which I will totally do all of what she did, but you need to put me in there to light a fire under them, because if I don't, this Louis guy will, and you don't want that.'

'They have been cleaning all week.'

Oh my God, they had? I visibly recoiled. If that was an improvement, I would hate to think what it had been like. I felt my stomach turning at the thought of their complimentary breakfast.

'Cecile. Four. Hours.'

I could see her finally thinking, really thinking, as though what I was saying made sense.

'Cecile, the place looks amazing, the restaurant, the lounge reception, it all gleams, and you and Gaston and even Philippe are all so welcoming, but it can't just be smoke and mirrors. It has to be across the board, and this big-shot chef is going to have Terminator vision for that kitchen.'

I am not sure that Cecile actually understood all of what I was saying, but I think she got my meaning.

She sighed, as if defeated by the logic. 'Gaspard will be so mad. We cannot afford to lose him.'

I placed my hands on her shoulders, imploring her to look at me.

'Trust me, Cecile, if you don't do this then everyone loses.'

Chapter Eight

In order for a good deed to be done, it had to start with a little white lie.

If I was to stand any chance of actually influencing an already established team that was obviously set in its ways then I had to appear as someone with power and knowledge, not merely as a blow-in who would start dishing out orders. I had to be firm but fair, a precarious balance; it would all be in the introduction, the rather fake introduction.

Cecile stood stoically in the kitchen, her back straight and her chin lifted with an air of confidence. We'd had only a few minutes to run over a vague backstory for me, but she'd winked and said, 'Leave it to me.'

'Okay, everyone, I want you to officially meet Mademoiselle Claire Shorten. Claire was good enough to come all the way from Melbourne, Australia, to assist us in preparation for one of the most important episodes in Hotel Trocadéro's existence.'

I breathed in; this was an excellent start.

'Mademoiselle Shorten has overseen some of the leading restaurants in the world.'

Okay, that's a bit much, just tone it down a little.

'She has just come from London to bring her knowledge to you and train you on how to use the best practice in a professional kitchen. I have hired Mademoiselle Shorten because she aims to show Louis Delarue exactly what Hotel Trocadéro is all about.'

Cecile's speech had them all listening, glancing at each other and straightening. Their expressions went from contempt to something resembling hope, as though I was here to solve all their problems. I felt sick.

Oh, Jesus.

'So what is it that you will do here? Will you take over Simone's duties?' Cathy asked.

I opened my mouth, ready to say yes, but Cecile cut me off.

'Claire will be our maître d'.'

My head snapped around to Cecile.

'What?' I asked quietly.

'After Claire helps you in the kitchen, she will be at front of house with Cathy to greet our VIP guests for lunch.' Cecile looked at me, as if pleading with me not to disagree.

Shit.

I smiled.

'Okay, well, I will leave you to it, Claire. Remember, work together and let's show them what we are capable of.'

Cecile's departure was met with guarded silence, then all eyes rested on me.

The one thing I was grateful for was the apparent understanding of English all round. I cleared my throat to speak.

'Are you a chef?' Gaspard demanded.

'No, not at all; maybe you can teach me a thing or two in the kitchen because I am flat out boiling water.'

Francois glanced at Gaspard, seemingly alarmed that I was unable to do something so simple.

'You cannot boil water?' Gaspard questioned, equally horrified.

'Oh, yeah, of course, it was just a joke. I am no chef,' I stumbled. Christ, I sucked. I calmed my nerves. 'Listen, I'm not here to tell you what to do, or to try to turn your world upside down. I'm merely a fresh pair of eyes that can help you make things a little easier. It might not get us entirely over the line with the likes of Louis Delarue, but we have to start somewhere.'

'Like where?' Francois asked.

'Well, to start, those boxes behind you, by the door. I think if we collapsed them, stored them away for recycling, there would be a huge amount of space created.'

'Mademoiselle, this is a French kitchen, we do not have big, fancy spaces,' said Gaspard.

'Absolutely, this kitchen is tiny, and that's not going to change, but we can change how we use the space, and this is where you are going to have to trust me.'

The shuttered look of unease swept over their faces again. *Oh boy, this is not going to be easy.*

'Okay, what do we know about Louis Delarue, can someone tell me?'

'*Il est un salaud.*' Cathy laughed, causing the others to titter like school children.

'Okay, help me out here, pretend you are translating for Simone,' I said, trying to keep things light.

'Half the time we didn't translate for her,' said Francois with a boyish smile.

Cathy sighed. 'It means, "he is a complete bastard".'

Just like I'd feared.

'And how do you think he would react, coming in here and seeing the kitchen like it is now?'

'We are cleaning out the cool room,' said Francois.

'Which is an excellent start, but we have to do more. In less than four hours he will be here and he will be eating and no doubt bursting through that kitchen door to meet the staff who have just served him lunch. Gaspard, do you have a menu set for him?'

'Oui.'

'Good. Cathy, is the room prepped – fresh linen, polished cutlery, wine glasses?'

'The last of the breakfast guests have left. We have to clear it.'

'Okay, well, we need lunch to be off limits to the public and available only to this VIP luncheon. Is there a way to close off the restaurant to the lounge?'

Cathy straightened, a light shining in her eyes. 'Oui.'

'Excellent, let's do that; it's only for the day. Can you go run it by Cecile and tell her what we have planned?'

Cathy didn't hesitate, brushing past me to push through the door. I let the feeling of adrenalin wash through me as my rambling directions seemed to be producing action.

'Francois, we'll work on cleaning out the last of the breakfast stuff; we'll start there and then finish with the cool room.'

Francois moved and I could feel my heart soar. It was now just me and a none-too-pleased-looking Gaspard. I steeled myself, walking over to stand before him.

'Gaspard, let's put your kitchen on the map.'

Something lit in his eyes, taking the darkness away, replacing it with something very sincere. He cared, I could see it; for the first time in possibly a long time someone was challenging him, ever so softly, but it was a start. All he had to do was work with me.

'You ready?'

'*Plus que jamais*,' he said with a little smile.

I stood there trying to read if what he had said was a good or bad thing until Francois came to stand beside me with a handful of plates.

'He said "more than ever".'

And with that translation, I knew that this was definitely the start of something.

Chapter Nine

There was a tiny, murky window in the swinging kitchen door that I had to stand on my tiptoes to see through into the restaurant. It was how I had planned to view the entire lunch. Cecile may have painted me as a maître d' extraordinaire, but I was nothing of the kind. I wanted to empower Cathy to take the lead: she spoke the language and this was her world. I was happy to help with keeping the benches clear so Francois could be Gaspard's right-hand man. I knew that when the heat was on there would be no time for translating for me; they just had to do what they had to do in order to get the food up to the pass. The kitchen was almost unrecognisable in that there was now bench space, and a good mopping of the floor had made it look ten shades lighter. A bit of elbow grease and some tough-love decisions to clear out the cool room had really decluttered the space. Cecile came to inspect the final product, and by the look on her face, I think she most definitely approved.

I vigorously rubbed a stain off the counter. 'Cecile, are we able to get some fresh flowers from nearby? I think it would really enhance the linen.'

She smiled. 'I will see to it,' she said, disappearing.

As far as the lunchtime menu being any good, I couldn't say; the extent of my food knowledge from the kitchen had been a continental breakfast. Still, the pistou soup Gaspard had been working on smelt delicious. With a new plan put in place, I could tell his spirit had been lifted. He'd even helped take out the boxes. He now stirred his soup, humming a tune and lightheardly tapping the edge of the pot. Francois seemed suitably nervous, continuously wiping down surfaces and looking at the clock. Even Cathy seemed quiet, thoughtful. Nerves were a good sign: it meant they cared.

'Now, remember, it's VIP only so we have to serve – how many, Cathy?'

'Six are coming.'

'So that's eighteen meals, tops. You got this, eighteen's nothing, you probably do twice that for lunch every day.'

'Actually, we don't do many lunches, or dinners. Most people choose to eat out,' added Francois.

Okay, now was not the time for him to be telling me this. I really didn't want to think about how unprepared they really were.

'Well, now's our chance to really put on a show,' I said.

'Well, Mr Flash Man better not come into this kitchen insulting my food, otherwise I will sit him on his back-side,' Gaspard said, waving his wooden spoon. Gaspard was probably five foot three at most; I doubt he would be sitting anyone on their arse, wooden spoon or not.

'Remember, Gaspard, even if he comes in saying the nastiest things about your great-great-grandmother's secret recipe, you will be nice, polite and courteous.'

Francois smiled at Gaspard, who waved me away.

'I mean it, I want you all to be nice. Francois what is "nice" in French?'

'*Agrèable.*'

'*Agre-a-ble,*' I repeated in my worst French accent.

Francois nodded. '*Bien joui* – well done.'

I lifted my shoulder like it was no big deal. I could get a handle on this whole French language, I thought, feeling a new level of confidence surge inside me, until the swinging of the kitchen door collected me and a breathless Philippe appeared.

'He's here. Louis Delarue is here.'

'Oh God.' I swallowed, turning to the equally frozen, wide-eyed staff. 'If we get through this – I mean, when we get through this, remind me to get you to teach me some swear words in French.'

Gaspard laughed. 'Mademoiselle Shorten, something tells me you are going to know a few before the day is out.'

'Of that, Gaspard, I have no doubt.'

None whatsoever.

~

'Battle stations, everyone' seemed like a bit of a dramatic thing to announce, but it's exactly what it felt like: a battle.

For me it was a faceless battle; I'd convinced myself it was an advantage to not know who the hell this tyrant Louis Delarue was. I was nervous because the atmosphere not just in the kitchen but in the entire hotel had been so toxic. I could see the fear in their eyes, the anxious glances at clocks and the shifting into panicked chaos, knowing he was here. That Louis Delarue had arrived.

I asked Cathy, 'Are you okay to do this?'

She nodded a bit too eagerly, then took a deep breath and squared her shoulders.

'You got this, Cathy; remember, this is your restaurant, you know it better than anyone. We're all here behind this door ready to do whatever you tell us, and remember, he's just man, a normal man underneath the act. Just be cool.'

She looked at me as if I were a raving lunatic. 'He is not *just a man*, Claire. He is a god,' she said, shaking her head. She took a moment to calm herself before pushing through into the restaurant. There was nothing I could do or say now, to her or anyone; the chips would fall where they would fall.

I wanted desperately to look through the window, but knew that was very unprofessional. With only the quiet bubbling of the soup pot on the stove, I could hear the muffled voices in the restaurant – more importantly, I could hear the upbeat welcome of Cathy's voice, so light and breezy. I swear she never spoke to me that way at breakfast. She was really turning on the charm – excellent.

Francois and Gaspard were wedged right next to me at the door, trying to listen in.

'Okay,' I whispered. 'In this *Renovation or Detonation* show, what usually happens? Does he come into the kitchen and introduce himself or does he eat first?'

'Well, they don't show him meeting like this, but when the show happens he always eats first,' said Francois.

'Okay, and are there times when the food is not to his liking?'

Francois eyed a grim-faced Gaspard before looking back. 'He never likes the food.'

'What? Like, *ever*?'

'Ever.'

Okay, probably not the best conversation to kick things off with.

I swallowed. 'Well, there's a first time for everything.'

And just as I was about to give them another 'you got this' speech, the kitchen door was flung open, affording me the briefest glimpse of suited men and one woman seated at the table.

Cathy came into the kitchen, her cheeks flushed and her hands shaking as she held her notepad – a blank notepad.

'You haven't written any orders down?' I asked.

'He said I shouldn't use a notepad, that it screamed of incompetence,' she said, trying not to let the tears well in her eyes.

'What, does he expect you to memorise their order?' asked Gaspard, outraged.

'I can't memorise them now: the menu has just changed,' she said, on the verge of hysteria.

'Okay, Cathy, listen to me. This is a test, he is testing you, pushing you, okay? Write down the orders, and take every bit of criticism on the chin and smile like you mean it. Thank him for any piece of wisdom he parts with. The sooner you get the orders, the sooner we can get them fed and out of here.'

Cathy listened to each of my words in a way she had never done before. I was proud that she was becoming more visibly calm.

'Here, Cathy.' Francois passed her a basket of bread.

She took it, brushing her fringe out of her eyes and straightening her spine.

'Good girl, now go get those orders,' I said, rubbing her shoulder as she pushed back into the restaurant; this time I made sure to get a better look at the table. Even at a glimpse I knew which one Louis was – I could tell merely by the body language. He sat at the head of the table, his back toward the kitchen; every other person at the table was turned to him, captivated by his presence. He waved his hand animatedly in conversation, and the door closed just as laughter erupted, no doubt from a witty little anecdote about his life. I rolled my eyes. *What a bunch of kiss arses.*

I didn't know exactly why his reputation preceded him, but the fact that he had everyone so rattled was enough for me to despise the man. And then I had to remind myself, be nice – be *agre-a-ble* – and I had almost convinced myself that I could be just that, until Cathy walked back through the door and burst into tears.

Agre-a-ble was about to go out the window.

Chapter Ten

ow was this happening? How was the ship sinking so fast? Not one order had been taken, not one ounce of food was being prepped.

'He wants to know where the fresh fish is from.'

'Oh, for God's sake,' I said under my breath. It was also a detail that had me kicking myself; of course he wanted to know about the produce. I had been so determined that the kitchen not be a health violation there had been no time to talk about memorising menus or where produce came from. Turning to Gaspard, I said, 'Where do you get your fish from, Gaspard?'

He shifted, as if deeply uncomfortable by the question.

'Do you get it from the local fish monger or the market? Where?'

'It gets delivered.'

'Okay, by whom?'

'I can't remember the name.'

I felt dread building inside me. 'But it's fresh, yeah? Where is it kept? I didn't see it in the cool room.'

'It's in the box freezer in the courtyard,' added Francois, rather sheepishly.

'*What?*' I said, snatching the menu from Cathy's hands and reading what I was afraid of reading. 'It says fresh fish on the menu.'

'Oui, it is fresh when it is frozen,' defended Gaspard.

I closed my eyes, turning away, only to open them and stare at the kitchen door. 'My God, we are going to be absolutely crucified.'

'What do I tell him?' asked Cathy, her eyes wide with panic, as she was the one who had to face the firing squad.

'Tell him the truth.'

'What? That I don't know where it comes from?'

A chill ran through me, hearing her saying it out loud.

'Why does he need to know the specifics?' asked Francois.

'Because something tells me he is the kind of man who would have great pleasure in finding out the truth behind a lie.'

Cathy's hand rested on the door; she was looking at me as if she was waiting for me to change my mind. I shrugged. 'Tell him.'

Poor Cathy entered the firing line again, and again she was sent back with a question about the menu. Each time she returned, a little piece of me died. The morale in the kitchen was at an all-time low. I was preparing myself for Gaspard, who was taking his rage out on his pot set, to untie his apron and tell Louis Delarue exactly where he could shove his questions.

'Keep it down,' I told him. 'If you have anyone you want to be angry at, try looking in the mirror. If your staff aren't trained because you don't know the answers to *your* menu then don't go chucking a hissy fit. You're the one who is responsible.'

I regretted the words the moment they came out of my mouth. Gaspard looked at me as if he wanted to cut me into tiny pieces, and with his access to sharp knives I thought he might do just that, before the door opened once more. We all turned, almost accustomed to the dread of Cathy's next question, but there was something different this time; she was almost smiling as she waved the forbidden handwritten order in her hand.

'Order up!' she called, drawing a unified sigh of relief.

Relief was short lived, though, as reality sank in. Now was the time to worry. Now was the time to cook.

~

I didn't know much about commercial kitchens. Unlike the picture Cecile had painted, I didn't have international knowledge of the hospitality industry, I wasn't a messenger from God here to save the day. All I did know was gained from binge-watching the Lifestyle channel when I was hit by a head cold my first winter in London. I had learned enough to at least pretend I knew what I was talking about.

'Come on, guys, communicate with each other. Francois, I want you to say, "Yes, chef!" when Gaspard asks you a question, okay?'

'Yes, chef!' Francois said, panicked.

I smiled. 'Excellent, now to Gaspard.'

I turned to check on Cathy, who was placing a water jug and six glasses on a tray for the table. She slowly picked up the stainless steel platter, the glasses rattling as she barely controlled her trembling hands. Water spilt over the lip of the jug. She set it down twice, shaking her hands out to try again but it was no use, the jingling became louder, the spillage bigger. I grabbed a cloth and helped her mop the tray.

'Here, I can take it,' I said.

'Really?'

'If you want me to, I will. It's only water, unless he asks me if it's from the foothills of the Himalayan Mountains. Do you know where it's from?'

Cathy laughed. 'From the tap.'

'Well, not exactly the Himalayas,' I said, taking the tray from her.

'Thank you, Claire. I will be okay to deliver the food,' she assured me.

'Of course you will,' I said with a wink. 'Hey, you want to top me up with more of that tap-water goodness before I go out there?'

Cathy obliged, grabbing the jug and plunging it under the tap.

'Merci beaucoup, wish me luck,' I said with my back to the door, taking in a deep breath just like Cathy had done a million times before. Now it was my turn to walk into the lion's den.

Be nice, be nice, be nice, I chanted in my head. Now was not the time to adopt my usually fiery behaviour that I blamed my hot-headed mother for; now was the time for calm, for zen. *I've got this.*

I pushed against the swinging door and turned steadily to face the restaurant, plastering on my best smile. With each step I took toward the table, I projected warmth and confidence.

I treated the table as a whole, choosing to place a glass down for the person next to Louis Delarue, a stocky, pale man with glasses. I didn't dare try to be clever, so I simply mixed my limited French with English.

'Bonjour, would you like some water?'

His eyes lit up. 'That would be lovely, thank you,' he replied in a delightful if not a bit posh English accent. It somehow put me completely at ease, to move around the table and place glasses down in front of each person, ever aware of Louis Delarue watching me intently. Keeping him as a blur made him less real to me, and I managed to work my way around the table without a tremor or fault until inevitably I came to the last glass, and the last place, standing next to a man in a blue suit, his arms resting on the table, his expensive watch glistening under the light of the chandeliers.

The last one: place down the water and head back to the kitchen.

With the assumption that he wanted water just as everyone else had, I confidently began to pour his water, my hand so steady I felt my heart swell with pride, a small knowing smile curving the corner of my mouth, until I made the biggest mistake of my life.

I looked up.

A familiar pair of steely blue eyes locked with mine, the same eyes that had stared me down through the open window of a black Audi as I stood heartbroken in the rain; the same eyes that had lifted up to me on the balcony from the street below; the same angry, hard, hypnotic eyes pierced through me like a lightning bolt, pinned me in place and instantly turned my blood cold. I was completely transfixed until the English man coughed, startling me and snapping me into realising that I had completely overflowed Louis Delarue's glass with water.

'Oh shit!' I cried, stopping so quickly I bumped the table, knocking the overflowing glass on its side and dumping a deluge of cold water directly into Louis Delarue's lap.

'*Putain de Christ!*' he screamed, leaping up from his seat, surveying the damage to his now drenched crotch. My mouth was agape, a mirror image of the other guests, who looked on in horror, but not as much horror as the three little faces pushed up against the kitchen window, watching the nightmare unfold. I wanted to die, but never more so than when my eyes met Louis Delarue's. All of a sudden I would have given anything for that cocky kerbside death stare, because the look he was giving me now and the sound of Cecile's quick-stepping heels approaching on the tiled floor meant I was in so much trouble.

Chapter Eleven

'I am so, so sorry,' I stammered, putting down the jug and, because I'd obviously left my brain back in the kitchen, dabbing at his thigh, thinking, hoping, it wasn't that bad, but of course it was. Louis Delarue snatched the serviette out of my hand.

'I've got it,' he snapped in his creamy accent as he started brushing down his expensive trousers.

This was a disaster. In order to prevent this from happening to Cathy, what did I do? I spilled cold water on Louis Delarue's crotch.

Cecile rounded the corner, her eyes widening before she quickly masked her emotions. To my utmost relief she didn't ask what happened. Ever the professional she simply asked, 'Is there anything I can do?'

'Oh, I think we have everything under control,' said the only woman at the table, her red hair cut into a bob, and a scarf tied around her neck. She was ever so chic, minus the heavy eyeshadow that highlighted her cat-like eyes. She was

the kind of woman you could envision smoking a long cigarette at a café somewhere. She seemed somewhat delighted at
the spectacle unfolding, but her demeanour didn't make me
feel any more at ease.

'I am, again, so sorry. I will get you some more water,'
I said, giving any reason to excuse myself so I could bury my
head in my hands and give into a moment's mortification.

'No!' he said, holding up his hand. 'You have done quite
enough. Where is our waitress?'

'Oh, Cathy, she will be delivering your meals,' I assured.

'Well, thank God for that.'

'Just be grateful that it wasn't a scalding cup of coffee,'
said the pompous grey-haired man opposite the Englishman.

'Oui, darling, maybe you stick to the buttering of the
bread, yes?' said the woman.

They all laughed, almost as if I wasn't standing there while
they discussed how utterly useless I was.

Louis Delarue had sat back in his seat, grimacing and
shifting in discomfort. I was going to offer him a hair dryer
but that would no doubt make them laugh all the more.
I glanced at Cecile, who seemed deeply worried, shaking
her head at me as if warning me not to say another word.

'Well, if you need anything, please feel free to ask me or
any of the staff,' she added politely.

'How about a dry cleaning service?' said the brown-haired
man who hadn't uttered a word so far, his lips pursed as he
delivered what he thought was a killer line. His eyes flashed

around the table for approval, but his companions didn't seem to find it as funny.

'Of course, we will happily take care of any laundering needs,' answered Cecile, panic underlining her voice, no matter how she tried to disguise it.

Louis Delarue rubbed at his eyes, running his hands through his thick, dark hair; it was like he was on the edge of an outburst he was desperately trying to curtail. With Cecile now gone, I took my cue to go while the going was good, only to be stopped before I had a chance to move.

'What is your name?' he asked, his tone bored, his face tired.

I stood still, looking down into his eyes; they weren't angry now but it didn't make them any less intimidating and for a split second, I swear I'd forgotten my own name until his brows rose. I cleared my throat, turning directly to him as I clutched my tray to my chest like a child hiding under their blanket from the bogeyman.

'Claire,' I said, lowly. Hating how small it sounded, hating how insignificant he made me feel.

'Claire?' But it was almost like he was rolling my name around on his tongue, testing what it felt like, what it sounded like – and coming from him it sounded dark, smoky, with a hint of something else, but that something else was a secret, only for him to know.

I thought he might press more, question the twang to my accent, grill me on water-pouring knowledge or just basically tear me apart in front of the table of bigwigs for my raging incompetence; instead, he turned away, dismissing me.

I allowed myself no time to feel the shame of him ignoring me and walked as calmly as I could back into the kitchen. I had gone from feeling completely in control and unflappable to red-faced and humiliated. A wave of nausea came over me. I felt like nothing else mattered now. I had completely blown any chance of Louis Delarue wanting to help this hotel. Not only had I abused him and called him a maniac yesterday, but I was also caught spying on him from my window, and now I had soaked his genitals in cold water, the ultimate cherry on top. I'd completed the trifecta of fuck-ups.

I pushed through the door, fighting not to crumble to the floor; instead, I tossed the tray into the sink and clasped my hands against my cheeks as I tried to still my whirling mind. The tiny, cramped kitchen was silent, and I could feel all eyes on me, drilling into the back of my skull. I lifted my hand in defeat, turning to face them.

'I'm so sorry, guys.'

Cathy frowned. 'Don't be sorry. It was an accident.'

'Yeah, a big fucking accident,' I agreed.

Gaspard's brows lifted, as if he was completely taken aback by my language – quite rich coming from a chef.

'Are you okay? You went white, like you'd seen a ghost,' Cathy said, placing her hand on my shoulder.

I shook my head. 'I know him!'

'What?'

'He's the same jerk that went speeding past me in the rain and splashed gutter water all over me.'

Cathy's brows arched in surprise. 'Well, it looks like you got your revenge.'

'What? Oh God, no, I didn't mean to do that. I mean he totally deserves it, but it was definitely unintentional.'

Gaspard looked on, crossing his arms over his chest as if he highly doubted me.

'It's the truth,' I insisted.

'Well, I would love to offer you counselling sessions, but I am ready to plate up. Francois, I need those croutons ready.'

'Yes, chef!' Francois said, jumping into action.

One by one, dishes of hot soup came to the pass. The potential damage I could do with those was terrifying.

'It's okay, Claire. I will take these out.'

'No, I'll help,' I insisted, grabbing two bowls.

'Are you sure?' Cathy seemed uncertain, worry in her eyes.

'If I don't go back out there now, I'll never be able to show my face again.'

Cathy nodded. 'Okay, let's go.'

We carried our bowls to the door, stopping for a second to give one another a look of dread.

'Cathy, can I ask a small favour?'

'Oui.'

'I'll deliver Louis Delarue his soup, okay?'

Cathy clearly knew what I was getting at – I needed a moment of redemption.

Gaspard crossed his heart and said a silent prayer. I didn't know if he thought I needed it or if he did.

Pushing our way through to the restaurant with the grace and professionalism of staff you would expect at the Ritz, we delivered the food without issue. I placed a bowl down in front of Mr Snarky Grey Hair and then one in front of Louis Delarue. As I placed his bowl down, my eyes lifted up to again meet his ever-watchful stare. He showed no emotion whatsoever as he eyeballed the pistou soup, until he looked back up at me. There was definitely an emotion there: a deep-seated contempt, one that made my heart pound against my chest, and not in a good way. Now I knew that it didn't matter what the soup tasted like; it could be the most magnificent soup ever created, but he was going to be brutal. I saw it in the cold depths of his eyes. I could see how he intimidated and belittled people, bullied them into thinking they were not worthy of his presence. There was something in the challenge of his gaze that made my insides burn in anger; I'd never much liked bullies and in the short amount of time I'd had the displeasure of being in his lordship's presence, I didn't much appreciate being treated like I was beneath him.

Instead of scurrying immediately back to the safety of the kitchen, I lingered, maintaining eye contact with him, unblinking, until I glanced at the stain on his trousers, reminding him of his discomfort. I gave a small smile as I nodded my head.

'Bon appetit,' I said to him.

He cocked his brow, amusement sparkling in his eyes, but I couldn't be sure if it lingered for long before I broke away from the table and followed a horrified-looking Cathy back to the kitchen.

Now we had to wait for the verdict.

Chapter Twelve

As predicted, the pistou soup was unseasoned and uninspiring. The duck breast stuffed with sugared almonds was overcooked and inelegant, and the mixed berry mille-feuille was sloppy and too sweet. Cathy and I decided to spare Gaspard comments such as 'Wouldn't feed it to my dog' and 'Is this a joke dish?' Each blow we delivered was like a wound to Gaspard's soul. By the time we'd finished, his complexion was a deep red. I seriously hoped that he didn't have a blood-pressure problem, but more worrying was his close proximity to sharp things. If Louis Delarue thought he would wander in here to meet the staff and offer a parting blow, I don't know if I would be so inclined to stop Gaspard reaching for a knife – it might be something we all wrestled for.

I had wanted there to be an air of relief once we had brought the dessert plates to the sink, that we had survived, and that a weight had been lifted, but it didn't feel like that at all; the atmosphere was still intense. The VIP party retired into the lounge to continue their meeting, no doubt discussing the fate of Hotel Trocadéro. If they thought it not worthy to save, the hotel would remain the same: untouched and unloved. If they took the Trocadéro on, the Louis Delarue name was apparently enough to breathe new life into it. This was what the staff had been hoping for – the hotel to be brought up to scratch. But as I washed the dishes in the tiny sink, thinking back to how Louis Delarue had been humiliated in front of his colleagues by the girl who had abused him merely days before, in my heart of hearts I knew he would punish me by punishing the hotel. I felt utterly despondent; here I had been entrusted to help them out as a way to repay their kindness, and what had I done? Completely sabotaged their chances. I should have gone back to London and left well enough alone, but of course that wasn't my style, was it? I cringed as I wiped down the sink, recalling my smartarse *Bon appetit.*

It took all my courage to plaster on a smile and turn to face the others.

'You did a great job today, guys! No matter what the outcome, you all tried really hard.'

My pep talk fell on deaf ears. It seemed morale was at an all-time low and after my water-spilling antics, I'd lost some serious street cred. It was like they were able to see straight through my facade now, and I didn't feel as confident as I had before. I urgently wanted to speak to Cecile, and apologise for failing her. But in order to do that I would have to walk through the lounge, and while they were in there, relaxing with their smug, full bellies, we were all prisoners in the cramped kitchen, scrubbing benches and pots and awaiting our fate.

Finally the kitchen door swung open and there, tall and foreboding, stood Louis Delarue. The entire kitchen froze almost comically still. Not one person moved a millimetre, it was like we were all suspended in time, or at least that's how I felt, looking into Louis Delarue's stone-cold gaze. I was anxious for Gaspard and Francois: were they going to feel the wrath of this tyrant of a chef? He looked as if he might tear them to pieces, run a white glove over the shelves and get a UV light to trace over the cupboards.

A black cloud had descended on the kitchen; a beautiful, stylish black cloud. It was undeniable – Louis Delarue would turn your head in the street. He wasn't classically handsome, but he held himself with great confidence. I stepped away from the sink toward him, intent on taking the brunt of his displeasure. His lean, six-foot-tall frame towered over me; if I'd found him intimidating sitting down, he was absolutely overpowering standing. Just being near him made me wish that the ground would open up and suck us all through a whirling vortex.

But his eyes shifted from me and I felt my blood run cold as his attention turned to where Gaspard stood with a ladle in his hand. Francois looked equally worried, paused mid-wipe of his work station. Louis stepped into the kitchen, letting the door swing closed behind him, like a jungle cat and we were his prey. He took in Gaspard's stained chef's jacket; the chef certainly wasn't the healthiest-looking specimen with his three-day stubble and his nicotine-stained fingertips. He was pretty much a PR nightmare, and standing next to Louis Delraue, well, there was no comparison. I wouldn't have been surprised if Louis chose to shut this kitchen down and make everyone unemployed without so much as a blink of an eye. I could tell that he would look on such a thing as sport, so when he actually stepped forward and stuck out his hand to Gaspard it took us all by surprise, especially Gaspard, who tentatively held out his hand.

'I just had to say congratulations,' Louis said, his eyes almost twinkling with delight.

Cathy and I looked at each other. My heart soared as we watched how relief washed over Gaspard before he squared his shoulders in pride.

'Consistency is not an easy thing to achieve,' Louis added. Francois was now grinning ear to ear, getting caught up in possibly the most incredible career highlight of his and Gaspard's lifetimes. I felt completely giddy and so incredibly proud. All the hard work had paid off, and I could almost cry I was so happy. And then I saw the good humour fade from Louis's eyes.

'And you consistently managed to under-deliver with every under-seasoned, flavourless meal I had the unfortunate task of eating.'

My mouth fell open.

When I saw the hope diminish in Gaspard's eyes I knew I hated Louis Delarue, that he was a soulless bastard.

'Monsieur Delarue, I am saddened to have disappointed you,' said Gaspard. Long gone was the big-noting, grumpy chef who had threatened violence if Louis Delarue so much as stepped into this kitchen and said a bad word against his cooking. In his place was a quiet, sad old man and my heart broke for him.

'And are you always so consistently an arsehole?' I said.

Cathy's head swung around so fast I thought her neck might have snapped. Her reaction was nothing compared to the way my breath had stopped as soon as the words had unintentionally tumbled out of my mouth. Still, I had no choice but to face the music now, squaring my shoulders and holding my ground as Louis turned to frown at me, as if he could not believe what he'd just heard. I could barely believe it myself, even more so when a wolfish grin spread slowly across his face.

'The girl who lives on an island far, far away,' he said, turning fully to me. He had obviously pinned my Aussie accent.

'If you're about to make a joke about Australia being built by convicts, then spare me, I've heard nothing but that for the last two years in London.'

Geez, Claire, overshare much?

Louis looked at me as if I was a piece of mould growing in an abandoned Tupperware container. He stepped closer to me, standing just to my side, forcing me to crane my neck to meet his eyes.

'I am meant to make my decision on whether I can put my efforts into saving this hotel and bring it into the leading category of fine dining and luxurious accommodation. The Trocadéro is one of hundreds of applicants striving to be chosen to be brought into the twenty-first century; it makes for a very difficult decision.'

I tried to swallow discreetly, but I was having a hard time concentrating on staying calm and keeping my breath even while his rich accent rolled over me like thunder. I dared not blink as he spoke to me. His cocky grin was back in place, curving the corner of his mouth as if he had a dirty little secret. It would be absolutely hot, if I didn't want to punch him in the face so badly.

'Your point being?' I could hear the words come out but I was powerless to stop them.

'The point is I am eternally grateful to you, Claire.'

My name on his lips sent warmth through me, and I didn't quite like to admit the feeling.

My eyes narrowed, and my silence urged him to explain himself further.

He smiled then, delighting in the fact I didn't follow. 'Because you have just made my decision a whole lot easier,' he said, before he turned his attention to the others and gave a nod of approval. '*Au revoir et bonne chance,*' he said, before casting me one last 'fuck you' look and pushing through the kitchen door, leaving us in shock.

'What did he just—'

'He said "goodbye and good luck",' said Francois, who threw his dishcloth across the room into the sink. Taking in the looks of anger and despair, I realised that I may not have understood the language but I sure got his meaning. Louis Delarue would not be helping us, and it was all my fault.

Chapter Thirteen

Death by minibar.

Downing the last of some booze whose name I couldn't even pronounce, I chucked its teeny-tiny bottle onto the bed next to me. It clinked against all its empty brothers and sisters, as it landed beside empty chocolate wrappers and packets of chips. If I was going to be checking out in the morning I might as well have a huge blowout tonight, I thought as I opened the very last mini bottle of alcohol and saluted to my laptop screen.

'Cheers, Paris, it's been real,' I announced, taking a big gulp, before spluttering and choking on the vile amber liquid. 'Oh, sweet Jesus, fucking shit.' I cringed, examining the bottle that sat snugly in my palm. *What the hell did I just drink?*

I checked the label to make sure it didn't say Le Draino or have a mini skull and cross bones on it. That's all I needed to top off my Paris experience: jilted tourist dishwasher found face down in Parisian penthouse suite. Well, at least the penthouse part sounded impressive. And it would certainly be a relatively painless death, unlike the poor people I was bearing witness to on my computer screen. In my tipsy, self-pitying state, I had taken it upon myself to Google who exactly this Louis Delarue joker was. And it had taken me all of two-point-five seconds to come to the conclusion that he was a big deal, a really big fucking deal.

What have I done?

Louis Delarue was an author, a restaurateur, a TV celebrity and revered as one of the most highly acclaimed chefs of his generation. Not only was he a regular judge on a BBC cooking show, but he was also the co-creator of his own widely successful show *Renovation or Detonation*, the very show I had been binge-watching for the past hour. The formula was pretty much the same: he would rock up to some struggling hotel, check in, critique the accommodation, eat and bag out the food, then yell and scream at the staff until they were at breaking point.

There was a moment where I actually felt relieved that I had saved the Trocadéro staff from such bullying. It was hard to watch, hard to imagine him yelling at Cecile until she crumbled. But to my horror there was also a common theme in the show: the staff always responded to his tough love; they begrudgingly respected him and listened to him, and he actually made a difference to these businesses. His unpacking and repacking of the hotel's issues transformed the hotel, each change and suggestion made sense, and the transformations were something to behold. He used his own money and his own team to renovate key spaces in the hotel to show them their potential. Every show ended with teary, thankful staff, and a glimmer of humanity in Louis Delarue. He was a cantankerous bastard, but he knew what he wanted and regardless of how he got there, he drew out the best in people.

I spiralled into a deep depression. I felt terrible, not only from the contents of the minibar swimming around my insides, but because I had completely sabotaged any chance the Hotel Trocadéro had of Louis Delarue taking on the hotel for a project. I hadn't even had the nerve to meet with Cecile after lunch; I had disappeared to the sixth floor in order to digest what the hell had just happened. There was no doubt in my mind that Cathy and the team would have Cecile filled in by now. My mind flashed to me calling Louis Delarue an arsehole, and I died a thousand deaths, throwing myself backward on my pillow and wishing that when I woke up in the morning it would all be a dream, or rather, a big, nasty nightmare. But every time I closed my eyes I saw him looking at me through the car window, up from the street, at the table in the kitchen; he was everywhere, taunting me.

I pulled myself up with a groan; the circle on the YouTube screen was whittling around, loading the next clip, and there he was again, but this time he was sitting down, a beautiful garden the backdrop as he was interviewed by a woman off camera. The whole interview was in French, but I didn't need subtitles to pinpoint his charisma. He was almost unrecognisable, and his manner seemed light, even playful. I could hear the effect he was having on the interviewer as she laughed. His eyes twinkled as he squinted against the sunlight. I almost caught myself smiling at the screen as he burst into laughter, and then I cursed myself. *Don't be fooled, Claire, this man is like a spider, luring prey into his web before striking a deadly blow.* It was the kind of thing that made him an A-grade villain, a man you loved to hate – or was it hated to love? Either way, I was equally relieved and horrified. All I could do was catch the next Eurostar to London and go back to tampering with my own life, which was just as big a mess. Me and misery were becoming fast friends.

There on my plush bed, legs crossed, staring blurry-eyed at the laptop screen, I had never felt more alone, until, in what seemed an act of divine intervention, my Skype icon flashed with an incoming call. I flinched, fearing it was my increasingly and alarmingly tech-savvy mother, who had tracked me down on yet another platform, but much to my relief, it was my sister Sammi. I couldn't click the accept button fast enough to see her bright, sunshiny smile pop up on my screen. I screamed, clapped and cried.

'Hee-eey,!' I sing-songed, waving at the screen.

'Hee-eey,' she sang back, laughing at my enthusiasm. 'Or should I say, "Bonsoir"?'

The twang of her Aussie accent saying bonsoir rather unconvincingly made me think that was what I must sound like.

'What time is it there?' I asked.

'It's one am . . . again.'

I shook my head. 'Bingeing on Netflix?'

Sammy sighed. 'The struggle is real.'

I breathed out a laugh; despite sitting in my Paris penthouse I felt seethingly jealous of my sister and her simple pleasure. Netflix bingeing in her daggy PJs on Mum and Dad's couch sounded glorious.

'What's wrong?' she asked.

'Huh? No, nothing.' I was taken aback by how she could tell so much from my expression, even through a fuzzy Skype connection.

'Liar!' she said, shifting on the couch as if settling in to drill me.

'Seriously, all is well, I'm staying in a really nice place,' I said, trying my best to highlight the good things.

'Oh sweet, what does Liam think of Paris?'

Fuck! 'Yeah, good, um, hey, have you heard of a chef called Louis Delarue?' I asked, quickly shifting the conversation.

It worked, judging by the rising of Sammy's perfectly manicured eyebrows. 'Are you kidding? You would have to be from Mars not to know who Louis bloody DeLaHubbaHubba is,' she said.

'Okay, so that's a yes then?'

'Ah, yeah, a big hell to the yes. Not long ago I finished all seven seasons of *Renovation or Detonation*. God, I love that show.'

Was it possible to feel worse? That my hopes of being cheered up by my beloved sister were futile?

'Why do you ask?' she said, grabbing for the remote and turning the volume of the TV down to hear me better.

'Oh, no reason . . . he came to the hotel today.'

Sammy did a double take. '*What?*' she said, suddenly muting the TV and adjusting her screen so I had her undivided attention. 'Speak! Tell me every minuscule detail,' she said very seriously.

I sighed, fighting against rolling my eyes. I really didn't want to bring down the pedestal Louis Delarue was sitting on for my sister, but if I didn't vent to someone I was going to develop a stomach ulcer. What was a girl to do? If I was going to slash down her vision, I was about to do so with a chainsaw.

'Okay, then, you asked for it.'

~

Sisters. Always there for you. To listen, encourage, support with an unwavering love and fierce loyalty. Or at least that's what I had thought.

For a moment it seemed Skype had frozen, that Sammi's face was permanently stuck with a confused scowl. I told her exactly what had unfolded in these past few days – minus the whole Liam fiasco. I told her I had chosen to stay on for a few days because I had been given an opportunity of a lifetime, until I had accidentally poured cold water on Louis Delarue's crotch and called him an arsehole. I had thought that Sammi might find it funny, but she had covered her mouth in shock, which made me feel really shitty, and even more so now I was squaring off with her disapproving sneer.

'Are you fucking crazy?' she shouted.

'Sorry?'

'People would give their eye teeth to get an opportunity even to breathe the same air as Louis Delarue, and you have managed to assault him and insult him in the space of a few hours.'

I rolled my eyes, suddenly finding my chipped fingernail fascinating. I was starting to regret having told her anything at all.

'He's like restaurant royalty.'

'Yeah, well, I'd never heard of him.'

'That's because you are too busy skipping after Liam and playing housewife.'

Ha, if only she knew how that had changed. Then it occurred to me – until tonight I hadn't actually thought about Liam, not once. I had been too busy. It may have been the day from hell, but as far as my heart went, I was kind of proud of myself.

'Claire, you need to go and apologise.'

'I'm going down to see Cecile in the morning,' I said.

'Not to Cecile, Claire. To Louis.'

I scoffed, laughing at the absurdity of her words, until of course I realised she wasn't joking. She was deadly serious.

'I will not!'

Sammi threw up her hands in despair. 'You are so bloody stubborn, just do it!'

'No!'

'Claire, this is bigger than you. You have to apologise to him, and you better hope that your begging skills are good enough for him to change his mind and reconsider helping the hotel.'

Her words hit a nerve, and I hated her for that. My pride would fight every step of the way, but my guilt was definitely overriding any other emotion. *Damn her!*

'I've gotta go,' I said, afraid that if I kept hearing her out I might be persuaded.

'Don't be like that, Claire. Christ, anyone would think I was the older sister, the way you chuck a tantrum.'

'I am not chucking a tantrum!'

'Oh right, let me guess, you're off to raid the minibar and eat all the chocolate then.'

'Don't be ridiculous,' I said, slowly extending my leg and sweeping the empty liquor bottles well out of view. 'Goodbye, Sammi!' I said in my no-nonsense, older-sister voice.

'Apologise, Claire!'

I waved. 'Night-night.'

'Claire,' Sammi warned.

'Byyyyeeeee.' And I closed the lid of my laptop, leaving me in complete blissful silence.

But the problem with silence was the freedom it afforded my mind to wander, and guilt to hook its clutches into me. By the time I had made myself comfy in my bed, ready for a much-needed sleep after the exhaustion of the day, I had half convinced myself that come morning, I would work on trying to fix things with Louis Delarue and see if there was any chance of him coming back to transform the hotel. In a way I hoped that maybe I would wake up and find that it had all been a dream, but as I closed my eyes and was once again haunted by Louis Delarue's cold, hard blue eyes, I knew that it was unlike any dream I had ever experienced before. No, it was more than that. It was a bloody nightmare.

Chapter Fourteen

My ears were ringing so insistently the sound woke me up. It wouldn't stop no matter how I tried to bury my head underneath the feather pillow. As the piercing sound continued, the more alert I became, and I lifted my head and squinted toward the sound. I realised that the ringing was coming from my bedside. The ornate old-fashioned gold-and-floral phone was rattling with every ring. If this was Sammi, ready to give me my early morning wake-up call and guilt trip, I would murder her.

I clawed my way over the king-sized bed and scrambled to reach the phone, to put a stop to the sound.

'Hello?' I croaked.

For a moment I thought it might have been a heavy breather on the other end, but then the distracted person at the end of the line must have realised I was there.

'Claire? Claire, is that you?'

I frowned, hearing Cecile's manic question. 'Well, I am the only one on the sixth floor, aren't I?' I know it was first thing in the morning, but I would like to think that my sleepy voice didn't sound too masculine.

'Ah, well, maybe not for much longer. Claire, you have to come down to reception right away.'

Uh oh. I sat bolt upright. 'Is everything okay?' I asked, my chest starting to pound at a hundred miles an hour. The people who really stayed up here, the actual owners of the hotel, were they back? Did they plan to kick me out after the disaster of yesterday? Would I be suddenly on the street? I couldn't exactly blame them.

'Claire, please hurry, you must come down right away.' The line went dead, and foreboding swept over me.

I washed my face, brushed my teeth and chucked my hair up in a topknot, working my fingers through my fringe and trying for that whole messy bun look, but somehow not pulling it off like most of the cover models would. I straightened my navy pleated skirt and polka-dot blouse, wedging my feet into my ballet flats, and gave myself the once over. I'd never been called beautiful, always falling more on the pretty or cute side. My eyes were far too big, and my chestnut-coloured hair was more kinky than curly. I sighed; at least if I was heading down to the firing squad I wouldn't look hideous, and my dad had always said that my big blue eyes made him crumble any time I turned the sads on. Maybe I could use them to my advantage now.

I had been practising saying sorry as I got ready; it had to be convincing, authentic, had to have an ounce of emotion, seeing that somewhere between sleep and waking

I had decided that the only way to make it up to Cecile and the others was to swallow my pride and apologise to Louis Delarue for how I had treated him yesterday. It almost made me ill thinking about it, but of course with Cecile's sudden panicked beckoning, tracking down Louis and doing the right thing might be the least of my worries. I shut the door behind me feeling nervous, and made my way down the hall to meet my fate.

I didn't know what would greet me in reception: maybe a revolted look from Gaston, or Philippe lowering his monobrow and shaking his head in disgust. Or would I get the cold shoulder from Cathy? So when the lift door opened and the first thing that greeted me was Cecile's blinding smile I was never more confused.

All air was knocked from my lungs as I stepped out of the lift and Cecile wrapped her arms around me in a powerful bear hug. Maybe I had been right last night: maybe saving them from the bad-tempered, soul-destroying chef would be better for them all?

'Are you hungry? Come, sit with me,' she said, hooking her arm through mine and leading me in the direction of the lounge like we were two Victorian ladies on a Sunday stroll. 'Philippe, can you look after the reception for a while?'

Philippe winked and nodded, just as high spirited as Cecile was. Oh God, did they not get the memo? Surely Cathy or Gaspard had updated her on yesterday; oh, please, tell me they had. But as I took a seat next to Cecile in the lounge, Cathy miraculously appeared with a basket of pastries and a pot of coffee and put them on the coffee table in front of us. She too seemed all smiles and winks. Was I living in an alternative universe, I wondered, because none of this made any sense. I had prepared for the world to hate me, not usher me into the lounge and offer me baked goods.

'So, you wanted to see me?'

'Oh, Claire, I don't even know where to begin,' Cecile said, taking my hands in hers. The shininess in her eyes made me uncomfortable.

'How about you begin from the beginning,' laughed Cathy, who was busy topping up someone's coffee at one of the breakfast tables.

'No, no, be quiet,' Cecile insisted, holding her finger to her lips. Whatever the cryptic nature of our meeting might be, she wanted to be the one to tell me.

'Cecile, you're kind of freaking me out.'

Cecile laughed. ' I'm sorry, Claire, please do not worry. I bring most excellent news.'

I straightened in my seat.

'Louis Delarue's production team contacted us this morning, and they unfortunately can't fit us into the schedule for the television series.'

I blinked, completely confused by Cecile being happy about this. Maybe she had misinterpreted the meaning and gotten her English mixed up. Maybe I had saved the day and they really didn't want Louis Delarue here.

'And this is good because?'

'Oh no, it is terrible news, the worst!'

Okay, I really would never get my head around the cultural divide. I shook my head. 'I don't understand.'

Cecile could barely contain herself, leaning forward as if to share a secret. 'They can't fit us in, but Louis has insisted that they make it happen.'

My eyes widened. 'He's going to help?'

'Oui, he is coming back.'

'Wow,' I said, remembering yesterday, thinking maybe our exchanges hadn't been that bad, but of course they had. Maybe he wasn't that big a tyrant after all; he clearly didn't hold a grudge. I could almost feel my shoulders sag in relief, knowing that these wonderful people were going to get the opportunity of a lifetime to not only learn from one of the greats, but to bring the Hotel Trocadéro into the modern day. I was excited for them and so utterly relieved that my idiotic actions yesterday had not completely sabotaged them, and better still, I didn't even have to apologise to Louis Delarue. If I never saw his face again, it would be too soon.

'It sounds amazing, almost too good to be true.'

Cecile's smile faltered, the sparkle in her eyes dimming. 'Ah, well, there is one thing.'

Oh, here we go. I crossed my arms. 'What? He wants you to pay him? Or wait, he wants his initials embroidered into the bed linen, or his name embossed into the hotel letterhead. Gosh, I just knew there would be something with him; please tell me you haven't sold your soul in order to work with the devil.'

'Well, not exactly,' she said, looking at her hands clasped in her lap.

I stiffened, suddenly unnerved by Cecile being unable to look at me.

'Well, what's the catch then?'

Cecile finally lifted her eyes to meet mine. 'There was a stipulation.'

'Yes?'

'Louis requested he work exclusively with the hotel's maître d'.'

I watched her carefully until suddenly it became blindingly clear. And before my jaw hit the floor the severity of the situation sank in.

They hadn't sold their souls to the devil – they had sold mine.

Chapter Fifteen

What is French for 'over my dead body'?

If Sammi thought me capable of throwing a tantrum, then the staff of the Hotel Trocadéro and their big, hopeful eyes were about to witness one of epic proportions, as soon as my voice came back. My mouth gaped and the connection of obscenely knitted together sentences in my head failed to make it to my tongue.

Cecile shifted nervously, glancing at an equally worried Gaston, who hovered, pretending to straighten tourist pamphlets.

'You are probably overwhelmed, Claire. It is a great honour.'

I breathed out a laugh, probably the only time I'd breathed at all in the last few moments.

'That's not exactly the thought that went through my mind,' I admitted grimly.

Cathy was standing nearby, looking at me warily; in fact, everyone seemed to be on tenterhooks. Surely they weren't surprised by my less-than-thrilled reaction? Seriously, had they not seen Louis Delarue on YouTube? I would sooner be back in London watering Liam's pot plants while he went on a date with the hippy upstairs.

'It would be a great experience for any maître d',' added Gaston encouragingly.

'That's the thing, I am not a maître d'!' I insisted. The closest I'd come was pouring a pint at the Gloucester Arms Hotel near our London home. This was something else altogether.

'It will only be for two weeks,' Cecile insisted. 'Think of all the sights you can see in that time.'

Oh, she was good: clever and cruel, using the lure of Paris to make me stay.

I shook my head. 'I can't afford to—'

'You can stay on the sixth floor.'

I laughed. 'Like I said, I can't afford—'

'You will be our guest. I can't pay you a full-time wage as such but I can offer you board and food in exchange for your help. Work with Louis and you can stay in the heart of Paris for as long as you like.'

Oh, she was really, *really* good.

Arrogant monster chef aside, the time away from the perils of my less-than-ideal reality called to me. A chance to keep busy and time to work out what I was going to do. Two weeks rent free in a luxe Paris hotel room bigger than most apartments I had seen. I could get properly acquainted with Paris, this time on my own terms. I could tick all the art museums off my list, all the ones Liam hadn't wanted to see. I felt a little anxiety spike in my chest thinking about what it would mean to make a decision that was fully my own. I had been so dependent on Liam thinking for me on so many things, I barely knew how to clearly function without him. It was . . . overwhelming.

Cecile tilted her head to the side, trying to peek under the lashes of my downcast eyes as I sat, far away in thought, biting my bottom lip. She smiled, because she knew her words had made me really think.

I squared my shoulders, sweaty hands resting on my knee-caps. 'Two weeks?'

My question caused Cecile to break out in a bright smile, one that she tampered down quickly so as to not seem overly confident. Then she plastered an all-business glower across her face as she nodded.

'Oui, two weeks.'

I sighed deeply. I was defeated, and she knew it.

'I don't want to be featured on the show,' I said adamantly. I could actually think of nothing worse than having to be humiliated on national television. 'I'll do behind-the-scenes stuff but I cannot be held responsible for what comes out of my mouth when dealing with that man.' *That impossible, infuriating, arrogant, control freak of a man.*

'Okay, I will let Louis know,' said Cecile. 'Just act exactly how you did yesterday, it obviously was enough to impress him into coming back.'

I laughed. 'What? You want me to pour cold water over his genitals?'

'Actually, I would prefer if you didn't,' said a masculine voice from behind me.

My head spun around so fast I swear I nearly pulled a muscle, but any pain was completely forgotten when I saw who that voice belonged to: Louis DelaHubba-Hubba, as Sammi put it.

He looked like he was about to walk the runway, not conduct business in an aged hotel in urgent need of a makeover. He stood in the archway connecting the foyer to the lounge. Gone was the formal suit, instead he wore dark jeans and a white shirt, his collar open and casual underneath his navy jacket. The shiny tips of his expensive brown leather shoes made the entire outfit scream well-groomed wealth, and the devilish smirk on his face was the mark of a confident man.

I, on the other hand, had just been caught out talking about his genitals, so my confidence was not at an all-time high.

'Oh, Monsieur Delarue, we weren't expecting you until tomorrow.' Cecile stood, smoothing the invisible creases from her skirt as she walked quickly to where Louis stood. His attention remained on me, a knowing smugness entering his eyes upon seeing the red tinge to my cheeks. I wanted to look away, but mercifully I didn't have to as he lazily turned his attention to Cecile. She was a little slip of a shadow next to him; even in heels, her petite, feminine frame was overshadowed by his lean, graceful stance, his shoulders square and proud.

'Is there somewhere we could speak in private?' he said to Cecile. Apart from his little dig at me, he hadn't so much as acknowledged anyone else's presence in the room. Even the people at their breakfast tables in the restaurant seemed to gawk and whisper in wonder; none of them dared approach for a selfie or autograph. They weren't that dense; Lord Louis's vibe was anything but approachable. Even Cecile seemed frazzled by being asked to speak in private.

'But of course,' she stammered, trying to get her bearings as to where to lead him, accidentally heading in the opposite direction to where she actually wanted to go before realising and doubling back, almost bumping into Louis, who seemed vaguely annoyed at her lack of composure. Cecile escorted him to the door near the lift, which led a small office where you would catch staff munching on snacks in their break.

When the door closed everyone took a collective breath, but relief wasn't afforded yet – that wouldn't come until the sound of Louis's Audi disappeared down the street.

Cathy came to stand beside me. 'I wonder what he is doing here so early?'

Maybe he was requesting that he didn't want to work with me after all, I thought hopefully, maybe he was in there demanding that unless I was gone he would not offer his services. It would be awkward for Cecile to have to ask me to leave, but I would happily do so. It didn't matter that the thought of having to go back to London to face the music didn't exactly thrill me, nor that the very brief daydream of living in that plush apartment was still vivid in my mind.

Although, if anything bad was going to happen, let it be now and not later. The suspense was killing me, killing all of us. I was suddenly grateful that Gaspard and Francois were locked away in the kitchen, although I did hope they wouldn't mind if I was sticking around to help out. From what I could gather, Cathy didn't seem to – if anything, everyone seemed excited about it.

Then it dawned on me – was I going to be Louis's punching bag? The decoy for rants and forked-tongue accusations? Maybe they had thought I could handle it. But I didn't want to be treated like that again. Sure, Liam hadn't been a celebrity chef–level tyrant but he sure as hell was a control freak, eager to tell me what to do and how I should feel about something. And now what? I was expected to take another dose of that multiplied by a million? *I don't think so.* Now was my time, for *me*, and as much as I liked the people here and appreciated how they had helped me, it was time to start helping myself. And to do that, I didn't want to be bowing down to the likes of Louis Delarue and praying that I wouldn't be responsible for whether he helped or not.

My mind was made up; the message clear. I was not going to be anyone's doormat any more. I stood from my chair and marched a determined line to the closed office door.

~

Tears – Cecile was in bloody tears!

They had barely been in the room for two minutes and Cecile was a blubbering mess. I stood in the doorway, my hand still clasping the door handle, my accusing stare shifting to Louis, who sat on the opposite side of the desk, sighing heavily. He leaned forward and drew a tissue from the box by the computer screen. He seemed merely inconvenienced by her emotion, I thought, until his gaze turned to me. It was not clear if he was actually annoyed with me and my seemingly unprofessional, unannounced entrance. His brows rose in a silent question – *What do you want?* I almost faltered, feeling rather foolish and embarrassed because he could cut me down with one angry look. And then my attention went to Cecile blowing her nose and my anger mirrored his.

'You just can't help yourself, can you?' I said, crossing my arms.

This time only one of his brows cocked but again he didn't speak. If I hadn't known better, I would swear he didn't speak English at all; his broody, stone-cold silence was infuriating.

'You just don't seem to operate without somehow demeaning someone else. Tell me, Monsieur Delarue, does it make you feel almighty and powerful to make a woman cry?'

'Claire.' Cecile sniffed, but her words were cut off by Louis raising his hand. He didn't even look at her; it was a manoeuvre born from complete and utter disrespect for anyone or anything. I didn't care that he was impressive on paper – I'd be damned if I would be intimidated by a bully like him. The speech inside my head seemed so impressive, I was as fierce as Beyoncé, until Louis stood, casually buttoning his jacket.

I braced myself for retaliation, a dressing down, a dismissal at least. He stepped forward to stand before me, and I looked defiantly up at him; by now I was somewhat of an expert at looking into those eyes, I had memorised them – dreamed of them even.

'You could be a problem,' he said, a small twitch to the corner of his mouth.

'I've been told that before.'

'Do you always jump to conclusions?'

'They are rarely wrong.'

'So you think you are a good judge of character?'

'I am an excellent judge of character,' I said.

'Well, that's something we have in common then.'

I breathed out a laugh. 'I seriously doubt we have anything in common.'

Louis smirked. 'Don't be so sure,' he said, bowing his head ever so slightly before glancing at a red-faced Cecile.

'A demain,' he said.

'Oui, see you tomorrow.' Cecile gave a small smile.

I stepped aside, letting Louis brush past me in the small space. The lightest touch of his jacket skimming across my skin felt strangely intimate, as did the musk of his cologne that lingered with a trace of vanilla and cedar. He had good taste, I'd give him that.

I wasted no time shutting the door behind him and closing the distance to the desk, taking the very same seat Louis had sat in. My manic thoughts ran through a number of scenarios. Had he wanted to see the books? Had he been horrified by the state of this squashed and chaotic space? Had he changed his mind, insulted her intelligence – what?

'Are you okay? What did he say to you?'

'I am just . . .' Cecile's chin trembled.

'Go on,' I encouraged.

'I am just so happy,' she said, passing a piece of paper across the desk, which was, surprisingly, not smudged by her tears.

I looked down at the expensive paper with a gold embossed L at the top. My confusion was present even after briefly skimming it and giving it back to Cecile. I shrugged. 'It's in French.'

Cecile laughed, taking it from me. 'Oh, pardon, I forgot. Monsieur Delarue has organised a private fitting for all staff to be clothed by Madame Delair.'

Cecile turned the paper and tapped a sentence; I tilted my head to the side to best see the cursive writing.

'Rue du Faubourg Saint-Honoré,' I read in a painfully horrific French accent.

'Do you know what that is?'

'What?' I laughed, her transition from tears to smiles was contagious.

'La Rue du Faubourg Saint-Honoré is a long and narrow street bordered on both sides by the most luxurious shops in the world, art galleries, nice cafés and restaurants. It is everything you can't afford all in one place.'

'Sounds dreamy,' I mused. 'So this letter is like a golden ticket?'

'He has set up an account for us.'

I frowned, thinking it all very reminiscent of the *Pretty Woman* plotline.

'Oh, Claire, it has begun: Hotel Trocadéro is going to be everything we ever dreamed it could be.' Tears began to well in her eyes again. I really respected her passion. Cecile *was* Hotel Trocadéro, as much as Gaston, and Gaspard were.

And then something really awful twisted at my insides as I stared at the letter.

'What is it, Claire?' Cecile must have read my grim expression.

'So, in other words—' I lifted the letter '—Monsieur Delarue did a very nice thing just now.' My shoulders slumped.

'He is a very generous man.'

I closed my eyes, wishing she hadn't just confirmed the very thing I feared. I would have given anything for him to have come in here and been the absolute villain I had pegged him as. My sudden dramatic outburst and sarcastic accusations were once more out of line. I had yet again humiliated myself in the most epic of ways.

I sighed, slapping my hands on top of my knees. 'Well, it seems utterly clear then.'

'What is that?'

'I am a dreadful judge of character.'

Chapter Sixteen

There was no talking myself out of it this time.

I, Claire Shorten, was going to do it. I was going to apologise to Louis Delarue.

He was due to show up at some point today to check in and take stock of the hotel before the camera crew arrived next week. I didn't feel anxious about this visit, because I had seen a glimmer of humanity in him, even if it had been dished out in the dingy back room for no one else to see. Perhaps his ogreish outbursts were reserved for the cameras? Maybe he saw real promise in the hotel, in the staff, and maybe this was going to be a painless, flawless expedition into change?

Oh, how wrong I was.

Louis Delarue arrived in the evening, descending on the hotel like a cloud of doom. I wish I could say I was exaggerating, but I'm not – Louis arrived in a big, bad way. Storming through the foyer, straight past a welcoming Gaston, he ran his hand through his rain-dampened hair. His jacket collar was turned up to ward off the evening chill, the jet black really setting off his dark demeanour as he aggressively slammed his hand on the reception bell, even though Philippe and Cecile were close by. It was like he hadn't seen them.

All I hoped in that instant was that he hadn't seen me. My eyes peered over the top of the *Vogue* magazine I was reading as I slunk down in my chair in the lounge. I had a clear view to where he stood in reception.

'Bonjour, Monsieur—'

'What is this?' Louis snapped, motioning to the bell he had just rung.

Cecile's mouth was agape, her eyes darting to the gold bell on the counter top.

Philippe quickly took the lead. 'That is for guests to ring if the reception is unattended.'

'Why would you leave the reception unmanned?'

'Well, sometimes we need to go and help other guests and sometimes there is only one of us at the desk and, and—' Philippe was flailing, and I felt so bad for him I just wanted to give him a hug.

'This reception is never to be left unattended, do you understand? I don't care if a fire burns beneath your feet: during business hours you are here to welcome and greet guests *always*.' Louis scooped up the bell and chucked it into the waste basket behind the counter. Even Philippe looked impressed. 'No more bells,' he added with a no-nonsense intensity to his voice.

Cecile gathered herself again, continuing as if nothing had happened. 'Welcome to Hotel Trocadéro, if you could please fill in this form, I will have Gaston collect your bags and show you to your room.'

'Are you not going to tell me about the hotel facilities?'

Oh my God, give her a bloody chance.

Cecile faltered. 'Oh, facilities?'

Louis scribbled his details on the paper manically, not even looking up as he spoke. 'What time is breakfast? Is there room service, wifi, a turn-down service, laundry, minibar?'

Cecile seemed flustered; it was as if I could see the inner workings of her mind, and it was screaming at her for being so stupid.

Louis violently signed his name and passed the form back over to Cecile. 'Let's make one thing perfectly clear,' he said, his eyes shifting between Philippe and Cecile. 'I don't want to be your friend.'

Whoa. I couldn't clearly see their reactions, but if they were anything like mine, I'm sure they would have wanted to hide behind a magazine too. I had absolutely no intention of apologising, not to this version of Louis. This was the ruthless businessman I had seen on those frightening YouTube clips, and although he wasn't being a screaming tyrant, he was nevertheless extremely blunt and severe. I swallowed, gripping the edges of my magazine with a white-knuckled intensity.

Please don't see me. Please don't see me.

Mercifully, Gaston lingered anxiously, if ever so patiently, behind Louis. He picked up his luggage and took him to

his room. The Hotel Trocadéro had officially checked in Dr
Jekyll and Mr Hyde.

I watched Louis disappear from sight and let the clock
tick over a few minutes before I left the sanctuary of the
lounge and headed to the foyer. I exchanged looks with Cecile
before heading to the lift and pressing the button, waiting for
the agonisingly slow numbers above the door to click down.
Just as the lift dinged its arrival, the door to the small office
opened, and out came a flustered Gaston.

'I will bring your luggage up as soon as you are settled,'
he said, turning to Louis, who followed him out to the foyer,
only to pause when he saw me standing there. The lift's door
had barely opened before I jumped into action, diving inside,
pushing the button incessantly for the doors to close. It made
no difference – they closed oh so slowly, as they always did.
I exhaled in relief as the strip of light across my face dimin-
ished as the door closed me off in the relative safety of the
tiny lift, ready to lock me away from those eyes. Until of
course an arm jammed itself into the gap.

I yelped at the unexpectedness of it and the door retracted,
revealing Louis. He quickly pushed into the lift, standing by
my side. So fast did it all happen he even beat me to selecting
which floor to hit, making me blink and shoot my hand out
to hover over the lit button. Louis had selected the sixth floor,
the very same floor I was staying on.

Oh shit.

I pulled my hand away as if I had been electrocuted.

'Coming for a ride?' he said.

I suddenly felt hot and claustrophobic in the tiny space with Louis's arm touching mine and that same, undeniably decadent, cologne in the air. I had to remind myself to take deep, calming breaths so as not to totally freak the fuck out as the pained screeching of the lift shuddered its way upward. *This could not be happening, he could not be my new neighbour; I had wanted to avoid him, not as good as shack up with him.*

After what seemed like an eternity, the lift shunted to an abrupt halt, opening its door to release me from my holding cell. We both stepped onto the landing. I'd thought the opening of the doors and stepping out into a vaster space would kill any awkwardness between us, but I was so wrong. I knew that in order to get to his door – directly opposite mine – Louis would have to walk the same long, narrow hall. A long, long walk – was it too late to jump back into the lift?

I thought Louis might extend his hand and offer a gentlemanly 'After you', but he did no such thing, and why should he? He was no gentleman, and as far as being wooed by custom-made, designer staff uniforms, I think perhaps Cecile was a bit overexcited. After all, that hadn't been from the kindness of his heart – this was business, something he intended to rule with an iron fist. It was evident from when he had stormed in here this evening that there was no Mr Nice Guy, if there had ever been a glimmer of such a man.

I don't want to be your friend was as warm as he was going to get. And if I was going to be working alongside him, practically living beside him for the next couple of weeks, then maybe I would use some initiative and try to get off on the right foot, because all other attempts had certainly been a disaster.

Louis walked past me, but instead of going down the hall, he stood in front of the window that led out to a tiny terrace with a view of the buildings across the way. There he stood, seemingly not even giving a single thought to me lingering awkwardly in front of the lift as I stared at his back. His arms were crossed, his stance wide as he glowered down at the street. A king overseeing his kingdom, his mind ticking over with all the thoughts of a business proposal and the trauma that he was no doubt planning to put everyone through. Yep, I definitely had to start this off right.

I tentatively went to stand at his side. A silence hung in the air, interrupted only by the sounds of a distant siren and traffic. I almost let myself get lost in the view, almost completely forgetting what I was standing there for. I breathed deeply to calm myself before gathering enough nerve to turn my head and look at his strong, manly profile, his brooding stare emphasised by the darker lines of his concentration.

This is it, this is the moment you've been looking for, and now is the perfect time to redeem yourself. Do it, Claire, and then you'll know that you've done the right thing.

That one inner voice cut through the others screaming at me to run to my room and lock the door, I shut the fear down and dug my nails into the palm of my hands, no doubt leaving half-moon crescents in my flesh.

Now or never.

'Louis . . . I'm sorry.'

Louis's head snapped around so fast it took all my will-power not to break into a smile. I couldn't help feeling completely smug at the sheer surprise in his expression as he stared down at me. I had never felt more powerful.

He seemed confused but didn't ask me any questions; I guess based on our exchanges you wouldn't have to be a genius to know why the word 'sorry' was coming out of my mouth. He also looked annoyed, which wasn't the easiest thing to pinpoint because that's the way he always looked, like he had a bad taste in his mouth.

'Who knew an apology could be taken so badly?' I said, thinking maybe I should have just kept it to myself. I don't know what I expected really, maybe a curt nod of acknow-ledgement, or him waving my words away. I certainly didn't expect barely any reaction at all.

I don't want to be your friend. That's what he'd said to Cecile and Philippe – clearly it went for everyone. Right. Got it. I had said my piece. I wouldn't push it while I had my pride semi intact.

I peeled away from him, making the journey along the narrow hall, thinking at least there wouldn't be an awkward walk together to our bedroom doors, until of course I pulled up in front of mine to take out the room key and noticed Louis approaching. Mercifully there wasn't a trick jiggle and twist with this door, but still, the quicker I tried to slot in the key and turn it, the more clumsy I became. It wasn't long before Louis was at my back, sliding in his own key and unlocking the door with ease. I couldn't help but glance at him, smugly pushing through his door, a knowing smirk the last thing I saw before he let the door slam behind him just as my lock clicked open.

Bastard.

Chapter Seventeen

It now made sense that rendezvous was a French word. It was made specifically to describe the way terrified staff of hotels assemble in secret. The staff of the Hotel Trocadéro called it a 'crisis meeting'.

In the four hours that Louis had been in the building, he had gone down to reception three times, and rung down six; needless to say, Cecile was a bit frazzled. I hoped they planned to enjoy their designer uniforms, because something told me that you got nothing for nothing when it came to Louis.

'Claire, why are you subjecting yourself to this madness? You can leave at any time,' Cathy asked. Her question seemed a logical one.

'I suppose I should be out seeing the sights, being a tourist,' I agreed, as I glanced around the cramped office. Francois was biting his nails. Gaspard rubbed his belly, his white T-shirt stained with something orange. Philippe ran a trembling finger along his monobrow, attempting to smooth away his stress, I suppose. Even Gaston's lightheartedness was noticeably absent. There were other faces I had not seen before, the cleaners. The whole atmosphere was enough to give anyone a stomach ulcer, so why was I here when I could be cruising down the Seine?

And then I realised.

'I guess I have nowhere else to go.' My words may have sounded sad, but I was okay. The distraction of all the drama had me not so much worried like the rest of the staff, but somewhat . . . entertained. Yeah, I was a bad person. Not to mention I loved a good challenge, something I hadn't really been faced with recently, and when it came to degrees of difficulty, Louis Delarue was a bloody eleven out of ten.

'The man is mad!' Gaspard declared.

'The man is a genius,' corrected Francois.

Gaspard slashed a hand through the air, wiping Francois's words away. 'So, he's a mad genius then, I don't care.'

'I don't know about any of that, but he scares me,' said Sophie, one of the cleaning ladies.

'Well, try being neighbours with him, that's not much fun,' I said.

'I told you not to put her on the sixth floor,' Cathy said to Cecile.

'Wait, is that the reason why? Because he was going to stay on the sixth floor?'

Cecile's mouth became a grim line.

'Okay. That makes sense,' I said. Then I thought of the care they had taken to make the world-renowned chef comfortable – they renovated the sixth floor but couldn't clean out the bloody cool room? It seemed the staff of Hotel Trocadéro had gone all out only in some aspects to reduce the fallout from Chef Louis, but as far as I could see they had a long, long way to go.

It was then I knew what the challenge was, why I was here in this tiny, claustrophobic room instead of wandering the streets of Paris and Instagramming my adventures. I had something far more valuable than anything anyone in this room had: I was a tourist. Staying in the hotel, experiencing every aspect of service before I became a part of the team. I could pinpoint it all, and if I was to help them, I knew exactly how. I had to make them aware of the things they could not see.

I smiled to myself, revelling in the wicked way my mind worked.

'What's so funny?' Cathy asked, nudging my arm.

All anxious eyes turned to me, intrigued at how well I was handling the pressure.

I gave them a knowing smile. 'Madames and monsieurs, if you bear with me, I think I might have some game-changing advice.' I grabbed a pen and notepad. I couldn't have had any more power even if I'd had a pointer and overhead projector. I was in the zone, scribbling profusely.

'Now the main objective will be to work with him, not against him. Agree with kindness and acceptance.'

'Does that go for you too?' mused Gaspard, earning him a snigger from everyone surrounding me at the desk.

I couldn't help but smile. 'Yes, even me.' I looked down at my paper with its growing list of dot points. 'He is probably going to want to see all the rooms. Are there any that are really bad?'

Sophie said, 'Rooms eleven and fourteen are our worst, the air conditioner leaked and stained the carpet in eleven, and fourteen has hole in the wall behind the door.'

'Okay, well, he is going to be asking why it hasn't been fixed, so we all need to know the answer, and we all need to have the same answer. Nothing will infuriate him more than a blank look.'

'So what else can we do to not make him so angry?' Cathy asked.

'We can't redo his first impressions, unfortunately, but I can tell you what my first impression was when I came here.'

Philippe shifted uneasily, almost like he wasn't prepared for the truth.

'It was really lovely: the décor is dated, the hotel is a bit rundown, but I saw past all that, and you know what the most important thing was?'

Everyone seemed to shrug.

'It was you guys: the staff were helpful, friendly, welcoming.' I looked at Gaston, whose chest puffed out a little. 'It wasn't enough to avoid being kind of disappointed by my room, but it made a huge difference. The aesthetics of the hotel – the décor, linen, food, all that can change; all that can be fixed, but if you don't have the right staff with the right attitude, then all the thread counts and fancy wallpapers in the world mean nothing. Let him take you into the twenty-first century, and even point out the things you think will benefit the hotel. Remember, he is going to respond better to passion than fear.'

'How do you know so much?' asked Gaspard, who seemed rather unconvinced.

'Look, I'm not saying he's not going to chew you out in every department and tear shreds off us, all I'm saying is be prepared. Don't fight the obvious or offer excuses. Agree that it's unacceptable, and move on toward a solution.'

'Anything else?' asked Francois.

I thought for a moment. 'Don't apologise.'

Cecile was confused, ready to challenge me.

'Don't apologise,' I repeated. 'Remember, we can reconvene at any time, but just try not to worry, I am so sure everything will be absolutely fi—'

My words were cut off by the loud, insistent sound of a bell ringing, as if someone was slapping it, again and again and again.

We looked at one another.

'Who is covering reception?' I asked urgently.

Cecile and Philippe stared at one another, their horror paramount.

Everyone scrambled for the door, pouring out of the small room and into the foyer. Our shoes squeaked inelegantly along the floor, and as soon as we had rushed around the corner into the lobby, our fears were realised.

There, standing in reception, was an irate-looking Louis Delarue, slamming his hand on the reception bell repeatedly, the very one he had thrown into the wastepaper basket earlier. We stood there, a hovering school of fish waiting to swim into shark-infested waters.

Cecile marched forward, taking the bell from the counter, and glorious silence fell. 'I am so sorry, Monsieur Delarue.'

I closed my eyes, dread sweeping over me as Cecile did the very thing I had asked her not to.

Opening them, I could see a vein pulse in the side of Louis's neck, his expression incredulous as his attention skimmed over the rest of us. We dispersed like rats in an alley, all quickstepping to our appointed places, except for me – I stood in the foyer, being stared down by Louis's murderous blue eyes. He seemed about to explode.

Instead, without taking his gaze from mine, he stalked toward a visibly shaken Cecile. He held his hand out to her, but kept his eyes on me. I wanted to look away, but I knew this was not how the game went. Cecile didn't need Louis to put it into words. She placed the bell into the palm of his hand, waiting for the onslaught, ready to duck when he hurled the bell across the room to smash it into a million pieces. Instead, he finally looked at Cecile.

'I want to meet with all staff in the morning at six, in the restaurant. I wouldn't want to miss out on anything.' His words dripped with sarcasm.

'Pardon, Monsieur Delarue, but tomorrow is my day off,' said Philippe, who stood behind the reception desk.

Louis looked at him, cutting him down with his eyes. It was almost like a superpower.

'But of course I will be here,' Philippe stammered. It was the right response, seeing as Louis Delarue seemed less angry and more bored now, turning his attention back to Cecile.

'I'll conduct one-on-one interviews tomorrow with every staff member,' he said, stepping away from her and walking past me as if I was invisible, playfully throwing the bell up and catching it like a ball. We were all so relieved and ready to let him go back up to his lair, we thought we might be home free, and relatively unscathed. He pressed the button, and the lift door automatically opened for him, as if it too was afraid to mess with Louis Delarue and dare keep him waiting. He stepped in the lift and turned.

'And I will want to see all the rooms tomorrow,' he said.

Oh boy, tomorrow was going to royally suck.

Chapter Eighteen

had been so confident.

I had even managed to lift the spirits of the staff momentarily, but now as I sat on my bed, legs crossed, I felt deflated, glaring at my door and kind of horrified about what lay just beyond it. So close, too close. When looking for any kind of distraction or pick-me-up, I thought I would most likely find it in the email that sat in my inbox from my sister, subject: winky face.

'This ought to be good.' I sighed, double clicking on the email.

Now are you sorry? it said, next to a link.

Intrigued by Sammi's cryptic message I clicked onto the link that led me to *GQ* magazine.

'Wow!'

There on my screen, bolder – and dare I say more beautiful – than real life was a picture of Louis, mid-stride, buttoning up his suit jacket and looking directly at the camera with his bedroom eyes. The photo was so striking, so stunning,

I swear I felt my breath catch. He had never looked at me with anything other than contempt, but I would defy any woman who was on the receiving end of such a gaze not to fall in love with him. I swallowed, glancing at the door, hardly believing that he was only in the next room.

I scrolled down the article to other pictures. The next was of him leaning against a sports car, hair in slight disarray, looking off into the distance, one too many buttons undone on his shirt. Free to openly stare at the image of Louis, I was able to examine him like I never could in person. He wasn't classically handsome, with thick, dark, wavy hair that was greying at the temples; it offered him a real distinction, as did the way he held himself: even in a photograph he was straight, proud, like a dancer. It almost made me think even his way of storming from one place to the next seemed graceful. He had beautiful hands, long and slender with impeccably manicured nails. His heart-shaped face and broad-set eyes, his prominent nose: he was the epitome of classic European beauty.

If I didn't know who he was he would most definitely be turning my head in the street, and that really annoyed me. He had an ugly personality, it was just a shame his looks did not match it. A fine-looking specimen of a man, until he opened his mouth. There would be no use trying to tell Sammi; she could go on fantasising about the man being a saint. I snared the last of the chocolates and idly read the article with a smile on my face, but halfway through my smile completely evaporated.

'You've got to be kidding me.'

As it turned out, Louis really was a saint; despite his bad-tempered, rock-star attitude, he was a huge giver to charity, aiding the homeless, literacy for children, cancer research and a foundation that raised money for children's wards. Millions upon millions: donations from his own fortune, not to mention what he had funded using his celebrity status. By the end of the article I didn't hate the man, I was damn well in awe of him. Louis Delarue was not to be feared: he had a tremendous amount of humanity in him. And wasn't that why he was here, to save the flailing Hotel Trocadéro?

I closed my computer, an inner peace settling over me along with a new optimism about meeting with him tomorrow.

~

While the others acted like they were marching to their death, I was light on my feet, bright eyed, my ponytail swinging as I entered the restaurant to see all the glum, worried faces.

'Bonjour!' I sang, sitting next to Cathy, ready with my pen and notebook. She looked at me like I was a freak and turned away. I was ready, almost giddy, to look at Louis in a new light, see past the mean-man facade and just not be so uptight about him any more.

I heard Cecile's heels on the tiles, quick, determined steps followed by heavier steps. I knew who they belonged to, and sure enough, right after Cecile came into the restaurant, Louis appeared, his face its usual stone, a few days' worth of stubble on his chiselled jaw a stark contrast to the clean-cut, black-and-white images I had seen last night. Unbeknown to me I had straightened; a huge, goofy smile spreading on my face as he came closer to stand at the head of the room. He glanced my way and frowned. My eagerness faltered a little, and I felt a bit silly that I had been staring at him like that.

'Are you feeling all right?' Cathy whispered, leaning over to me.

I cleared my throat and plastered on my poker face, distracting myself by dating the top of a fresh page on my notepad. 'Yeah, fine.'

Cecile's usual cheery demeanour was nowhere to be seen. Her eyes were cast down, her face flushed – had she been crying again? I felt my blood boil underneath my skin, caring little now of Louis's sainthood; I just wanted him to get on with weaving his magic.

Louis stood at the front of the room. He clapped and rubbed his hands together expectantly as his eyes skimmed over us. 'Okay, are we ready?'

The room was silent as we all looked at each other, seeking the answer. Some nodded, but rather than let the silence drag on I blurted out the first thing that fell into my mind.

'Yes, chef!'

I inwardly cringed the moment the words fell out, but much to my surprise I wasn't met by the usual darkened stare; instead, a crooked little smile appeared across Louis's face, but it was gone so quickly I thought I had imagined it. Only the spark in his eyes told me I hadn't.

He nodded to me in acknowledgment. 'Tres bon,' he said, which I knew meant 'very good'.

What had been a knee-jerk reaction had paid off. I sensed good vibes about today. I thought if we showed respect, he would give respect, and I was suddenly confident in the advice I had given the staff last night. *He will respond to passion, not fear.*

I felt a new hope swell in my heart. Cathy smiled at me and I knew she felt it too. We were going to be all right; we could do this; we were all going to be all right.

Louis walked casually to the side of the room, his hands in his pockets, his demeanour lighter than I had seen before, as he sighed and turned back to us.

'First things first.'

Everyone straightened expectantly in their seats, ready to carry on the good vibes.

And just as I felt the butterflies swirl in my belly with the new-found hope of what was to come, Louis turned toward Philippe.

'You're fired!'

Chapter Nineteen

He couldn't do that! Oh my God, could he do that? He totally just did that.

All hell broke loose – heated words were exchanged in French between Louis and Philippe, with a surprising interjection by a very upset Cecile, followed by Gaston grabbing Philippe by the arm and guiding him away, until Philippe snatched his arm away and stormed out. Of all the times I needed to understand, I couldn't, and there was no time to translate.

'Claire.' Louis was saying my name. 'Will you show me the rooms, please?'

My mouth was still agape; was he serious? Fire someone, then business as usual?

'Um, do you think now is a good time?' I said, hoping the others would back me up on this, but they seemed resigned to their own thoughts. The good vibes had gone out the fucking window as soon as Philippe had exited the building. I glanced at Cecile, who was heading back from reception. She stood before me and handed me a key. My eyes dipped to the key, confusion lining my face.

'This is a skeleton key designed to open every room,' she said, a vacant look in her eyes. 'Start on the first floor.'

I slowly stood, lowering my voice to speak to her. 'Cecile, Philippe just got fired, do you really think that we should be doing this right now?'

'Oui,' she said, and I suddenly felt terribly sad. Was Cecile really prepared to sacrifice anyone to keep Lord Louis happy? Her attention turned to Louis.

'Once you have inspected the rooms I will organise individual interviews to take place.'

He nodded, seeming pleased with the arrangement as he walked out to the lounge, only stopping to look at me quizzically, as if to say, *Aren't you coming?*

I was so upset I could barely believe what was happening. When I'd told the staff last night to be agreeable, I hadn't expected them to shut down altogether. I feared that my advice was doing more harm than good. And just like the obedient zombies they had become, I found myself walking out of the restaurant and following Louis's long strides. I almost crashed into his back when he stopped abruptly, pressing the lift button. I couldn't believe how calm he was; he had just fired someone and done so without even blinking, and now he wanted to run a white glove over window sills and inspect the rooms. I wanted to kick him.

'You are unbelievable,' I said, shaking my head.

'Why, thank you,' he said, looking at the numbers above the lift door.

'It wasn't meant to be a compliment.'

'I'm sorry, but you are going to have to speak a little slower, your accent is very thick.'

The doors opened and I followed him into the lift. 'I can't believe you're joking at a time like this.'

'I am deadly serious.'

'How can you ruin someone's day, potentially their *life*, and then go on like nothing has happened?'

Louis rolled his eyes; it was reminiscent of how Liam would respond to me if I questioned something, and despite my soapbox moments with the staff about being nice and collaborative, something inside me snapped just as the doors opened to the first floor.

'You know what? Why don't you just save the really dehumanising, humiliating stuff for the cameras, you seem really good at that,' I said, making my way straight to room one.

'Pardon?'

'Oh, I'm sorry, is it my accent?' I asked, slotting in the key, twisting and unlocking it first go. Pushing inside, I switched on the light, thinking I couldn't care less if he followed me in or not, until my foot kicked something. A shoe, lying on its side next to a bra . . .

Oh my God.

I looked up to see a man standing frozen in the bathroom, a towel wrapped around his waist, toothbrush in his mouth as his widened eyes gawped at me. The frightened scream of a woman covering herself up in the bed drew my gaze to her.

'Oh, I am so, so sorry, pardon, pardon.' I held up my hands, backing out the door so fast I don't think my feet touched the floor. I slammed the door behind me, to find Louis standing casually to the side, leaning against the wall – no, make that using the wall as support to keep upright because he was laughing so hard.

'It's not funny!' I screamed, my hands balled into fists.

'This would make for great television.'

Oh God, all the more reason to not have any part of this.

'Yeah, well, I'm having no part of that so . . .'

'Ah, what a shame.' Louis wiped a tear from under his eye as he tried to regain his composure. 'Please tell me you have a list of the vacant rooms?'

'Vacant? Cecile just gave me a key and said to go to the first floor.'

Louis shook his head. 'Shall we see what lies behind door number two?' he said, his eyes alight with mischief. God, how I hated him.

'I think this little adventure is over, don't you?' I said, walking back to the lift.

'On the contrary, I was just starting to enjoy myself.'

'Oh, I'm sorry. I thought you got your kicks from firing staff members,' I threw over my shoulder, startled that he now stood at my side.

He had finally sobered, this time not looking at the illuminated numbers above the lift, but down at me.

'He was not a good man, Claire.'

I blinked, somewhat taken aback and a little unsettled, hearing my name from his mouth; his creamy accent saying my name did funny things to my tummy.

'W-what do you mean?'

Louis remained guarded, but said, 'Leading up to deciding whether I wanted to choose this hotel, I looked over the financials, did a case study of the business: the incomings, the outgoings. The business is a failing one at best: competition is fierce and the financials were a disaster. I asked to review the security footage to see how the staff operated, more so to see the comings and goings for a day, not to actually catch someone stealing from the business.'

'Philippe was stealing?'

'Pocketing money from the safety deposit box and writing it off.'

The lift doors opened, but I didn't want to move, mainly because I was in shock, and also because Louis was actually giving me some candid information.

He moved first, and I followed him.

'So is that what was being flung around in French, the actual truth of what he had done? He seemed pretty angry.'

'A defensive man is usually a guilty man.'

'So everyone knows?'

'Everyone who can speak French,' he said, glancing at me with a cocky, crooked grin.

It all made sense now: Louis must have given Cecile the heads up, that's why she couldn't look at anyone. He had wanted everyone to be present when he fired Philippe so they were aware that such deceit would not be tolerated.

I blew out a breath. 'Well, hopefully that will be the last of the surprises for a while.'

And just when my thoughts seemed a million miles away the lift door chimed open and much to my confusion I looked out to the landing and then to the number lit up inside the lift. *The sixth floor?*

I had been too shocked to even realise that Louis had pressed the button. He stepped out onto the larger, more modern landing and placed his hand on the door to prevent it from closing me in.

'Well, aren't you going to show me your room?'

'My room?' I said, perhaps a little too sharply.

He shrugged one shoulder casually. 'At least we know it's vacant; it is, isn't it?'

'Well, yeah, but . . .'

He headed down the hall, ignoring my stammering, until he arrived at my door. He turned to look at me expectantly. I was less concerned with having Louis in my room than scrambling to think what state my room was actually in. Had I left my undies on the floor in the bathroom? How badly were clothes flung all over the place, and takeaway containers stacked in the little bin? Oh God, there was a trail of empty minibar bottles and chocolate wrappers near the bed – classy.

Louis leant against the door frame, his hands in his pocket, seemingly enjoying my discomfort. 'Something wrong?' he asked.

'I just don't think there's any point; my room is obviously the same as yours,' I said.

'Have you seen my room?' he asked.

'Well, no but—'

'Well, I'll show you mine if you show me yours,' he said. There was an element of tease behind his words, and a boyish grin spread across his face and I couldn't help but smile a little. It was short-lived, however, as I slotted the key into the door and said a silent prayer before I pushed it open.

The room was a disaster. The bed was unmade with clothes strewn over the end of it. Luckily there were no undies on the floor, but there was a bra hanging on the door handle that I quickly unhooked and shoved into my pocket before he saw. The only thing he really looked at was the line of empty mini bottles on the bench above the fridge, but I couldn't see the expression on his face as he continued to walk into the dim room. I didn't put the light on, I really didn't want to highlight the mess, but then of course Louis walked over to the curtains and drew them open, flooding the room with natural light.

'It seems a crime to leave the curtains closed with a view like that,' he said, tilting his head to the impressive sight of the Eiffel Tower in the distance. I casually scooped things into my suitcase and pulled up the covers on the bed. I knew what he was saying: the view was the best part of this room. For someone who had dreamed of Paris all her life and was blessed with that view, the golden twinkling of the city lights were pure magic at night, it was a shame I couldn't bear to look at it now. For me the Eiffel Tower meant heartache, and try as I might to push my reality down as deep as possible, I really didn't need a reminder of Liam's betrayal.

'You have something against the view?' he asked, turning to me.

'It's lovely, but can you please keep them closed?'

Louis looked at me like I was mad and instead of doing what I asked, he pulled the curtains wider and opened the door out to the balcony.

I had momentarily forgotten that you didn't tell Lord Louis what to do; he was worse than a child. I scooped up the last of my clothes and hid them under the blanket, then went to the open balcony door, stepping out to stand beside Louis and watch as the morning sun sparkled across the roof tops. Seeing the tower in the distance wasn't as crushing as it had been the first time, although there was something rather surreal about standing in the morning sun next to Louis, in silence, watching the world go by, brushing the hair from my eyes, and feeling so calm. I really was denying myself a lovely view, something I had let the ghost of Liam ruin for me.

'See, you don't know what you're missing,' Louis said.

'Some kind of tourist I am, huh? Repelled by the Eiffel Tower.'

'It offends you that much?'

I sighed, clutching the edge of the curved iron railing, thinking I really didn't want to get into this, but also not exactly wanting to come across as a complete freak. 'My boyfriend broke up with me under the Eiffel Tower a few days ago.'

Louis's expression didn't change; he still just stared at me like I was a lunatic, like my reasoning made no sense. Most normal people might say something comforting or say that they were sorry, but not him. I straightened, thinking maybe he didn't understand the significance of how traumatic it had been. I felt angry at his indifference.

'I had dreamed about coming to Paris all my life, and the one weekend he brought me here I was certain he was going to propose to me, not break up with me,' I said. For some insane reason I wanted Louis to understand. 'He took the one place I loved and tainted it.'

Louis looked into the distance in silence, but I could see he was thinking, probably of a way to escape this conversation: a girlie deep and meaningful was clearly not within his realms of expertise.

'There's really only one thing you can do,' he said eventually.

'I know, I know, open the curtains wide and get on with it,' I said bitterly.

'Perhaps, but I was thinking more along the lines of burning down his favourite pub. Opening curtains is easier.'

I burst out laughing, which earned me a lopsided grin. I don't know what was more unexpected, my deep-bellied laughter or his smile.

'That actually is the best idea ever. He would be lost without the Gloucester Arms.'

The banter ended, and silence fell; it felt strange to have shared a moment like that with this aloof man, to have made him smile.

'Your turn, show me your view,' I said, stepping back into the room, waiting for Louis, who took one last breath of air before returning inside. I shut the balcony door behind him, pausing as my hand instinctively went to reach for the curtains. I could feel his eyes on me as my fingers fell and I let the curtain be, leaving them open. Without looking at Louis I went to the door, proud of my little victory.

Chapter Twenty

There wasn't a thing out of place in Louis's room: the bed was made; his shirts hung in the wardrobe with his neatly tucked-away suitcase; his toothbrush, razor and Matador Louis Feraud cologne were all set out, perfectly aligned on the marble counter in the bathroom. If it weren't for those items you would think no one had checked in at all. Louis was a perfectionist and paid attention to the detail of every aspect of his life. And his curtains were definitely open. The room itself was similar to mine, though with more masculine art selections and scatter cushions, not to mention one very obvious difference: the renovation in Louis's apartment had been completed, no half-painted walls or rogue wires. It occurred to me that Louis hadn't had anything negative to say about the general décor or arrangement on the sixth floor, which was a good sign, but I knew that wouldn't be the case on the other floors.

'Can I use your phone for a minute?' I asked, not waiting for the response as I picked up the receiver and dialled for reception.

'Bonjour, Monsieur Delarue, how can we help you?' said a cheery Cecile. She was faking it well because I knew that after this morning's events she would be anything but cheerful.

'Oh, um, Cecile, it's Claire.'

There was a long pause at the other end of the line. She was no doubt wondering what I was doing in Louis Delarue's room.

'I forgot to ask you which rooms were available to show Louis?' It felt strange referring to him like that, considering everyone usually called him Monsieur Delarue while bowing before his feet. The fact I could also see him watching in my peripheral vision was a bit unnerving too.

'There are only three rooms available: four, fourteen, and twenty-three, two of them are our worst.' Cecile's voice had altered somewhat. 'I would start with twenty-three, that is the least worst.'

Oh goody, it was all downhill from here, and then I remembered my own advice. *Just be honest.*

I hung up and thought better of trying to get out of what we had to do. Louis wouldn't be kept away forever.

I turned to face him, taking in a deep breath. 'Okay. There are three rooms to show you, and they are not going to be the best; in fact, they are pretty rundown, so before you go screaming and ranting about how awful they are, I just want to give you the heads up.'

Louis blinked. 'Well, I was going to skip the rooms but now I really want to see them.'

Fuck.

'Look, I know you're here to ultimately help the hotel, so I think seeing the worst will be for the hotel's benefit.' Wow, I even surprised myself with how diplomatic I sounded.

Louis cocked his head. 'How long have you been working here, Claire?'

Uh oh. 'Not very long.' I tried to word it in a way that sounded better than 'Oh, about, three days!'

'And you know much about the hotel industry?' he asked, working his way casually around the room, his hands in his pockets. Holy crap, my greatest concern was him seeing the rooms and now I was in the spotlight.

I lifted my chin. 'I have worked in hospitality.' After-school part-time job at the corner store and a stint pouring beers at the local, but surely we didn't need to go into specifics. 'I was an events manager for about two years. I might not have a Wikipedia page, but I like to think that I have a good head on my shoulders.'

Louis paused, his mouth twitching. 'So, you have read my Wikipedia page, have you?'

Oh, kill me now.

The look on my face must have completely given my guilt away.

He broke into a broad smile. 'You googled me.'

'Only because I didn't know who you were.'

He folded his arms and shook his head in disbelief. 'Such a stalker.'

'I wouldn't get too big an ego about it – like I said, I had never heard of you before.'

'Sure you hadn't.' His words were laced with sarcasm.

'I did some research and I have to say that, yeah, you have an impressive curriculum vitae.'

Louis smiled, seemingly pleased by the admission.

'But apart from that, your attitude kind of sucks.'

His smile fell away as his arms dropped to his sides, the same thunder returning to his face. Yep, that would be my usual 'not knowing when to shut up' problem that had followed me around most of my life.

'Do you think I have gotten where I am and achieved all that I have through being nice and agreeable?'

I shrugged. 'I just don't know why you can't be both.'

Louis scoffed. 'This isn't about making people happy, this is business, and if you can't separate the two and make the hard calls, then you might as well have dated rooms and stained carpets and bad reviews, and yes, I have read them all, and seen the photos.'

'I just think that there is a better way to do things and get the same results.'

'So you would have taken Philippe for a coffee and then let him down gently, passed him a tissue and a week's wage for the inconvenience?'

'It's not just that; it's everything. It's like a dark cloud sweeps over a room when you enter it. How much more responsive people would be if they felt like they could approach you.'

'I don't want to be approached!' he yelled. He stepped forward, staring me down. 'Do not blow into this place and think that you know what's best; it will be done my way, or no way.'

I glowered back at him, hating every part of his stubborn, black soul. 'Yes, chef,' I said.

'If you worked in my hotel, you would be following in the footsteps of Philippe,' he warned.

'Well, what's stopping you? You fired him without so much as blinking.'

'I didn't make that call, Claire. Cecile did.'

'Then why didn't she fire him?'

'Because it was me who wanted to make a point.'

'It's always about the fear tactics with you, isn't it?'

His eyes bored into mine; his jaw was clenched so tight.

'Well, here's a newsflash, Monsieur Delarue,' I said, getting in his face. 'I am not afraid of you.'

'You won't be saying that after I am finished with this hotel.' His voice was dark, and the threat made my traitorous heart beat hard.

'This is not a Michelin-starred establishment,' I said.

'It most certainly is not.'

'And thank God for that,' I said, a bit too quickly. I saw a flicker of something in Louis's eyes, and although I was adamant not to be afraid of him, I'd obviously touched on something that hit a nerve in him. I knew that I had pressed back enough.

'Here,' I said, holding up the key. 'Rooms four, fourteen and twenty-three: you can call a staff meeting and rake us over the coals later if you like, you don't need me for that.'

He took the key from me, looking at it with interest as I made my way to the door.

'Does this mean I have won this round?'

I opened the door, pausing to look back at him. 'This is not a game,' I said.

Louis's mouth spread into wolfish smile. 'Well, as with everything, I guess we will have to agree to disagree about that.'

My answer to that was simple: I slammed the door behind me.

Chapter Twenty-One

had spent way too much time with the most infuriating human being – wait, in order to be called that he would at first have to be in fact human, and I wasn't quite sure he was. How could someone go from almost endearing and normal, to the egotistic monster who ruled the restaurant world with an iron fist so quickly?

With the fear of running my mouth off any more than I already had, I asked Cecile if I could go out for a bit. While Louis set about having one-on-one interviews with staff, I needed to slip into tourist mode. I wanted only to think about getting lost in this beautiful city. And I did just that, taking an outside table at the Café du Trocadéro and watching the world go by.

Nothing really seemed to trouble me until my mind drifted back to the hotel. I was clearly in over my head, and no amount of googling would get me up to speed on what was to come in the next few weeks. Clouds gathered in the sky and a light rain fell, but I was set perfectly under an awning so I welcomed the break in the weather. I didn't exclusively need sunshine to enjoy the solitude, I just needed to concentrate on inhaling and exhaling.

Cathy's words played in my head: *You could leave at any time.*

However true that was, there was no part of me that wanted to chuck in the towel yet; as strange as it was to argue with Louis, it also gave me a slight thrill to challenge him. I had never been able to challenge Liam, so after years of pent-up emotion I was finally able to open my mouth, even though it was by far my most lethal weapon and the very thing that got me into trouble the most. But I would not back down or run, I would see these weeks out even if it killed me – or Louis.

The café was in a large square that incorporated a number of museums and dominated by the Palais de Chaillot, a neo-Classical building dating from the 1937 Exposition Universelle, and designed in two wings with a gap between to frame views of the Eiffel Tower across the river. The palais incorporated the Théâtre National de Chaillot and four museums, although only two were open: the Musée de l'Homme and the Musée National de la Marine. As much as I wanted to explore them, I gathered my things and made my way across the curving intersection toward the Esplanáde du Trocadéro, which most people used as a platform for its great view of the Eiffel Tower.

Despite trying not to make the tower dominate my time in Paris since it linked me to the ghost of Liam, I had to admit that Trocadéro Square was pretty magnificent. On a clear day it would offer the perfect view of the tower: not too close, not too far. I even took the time to sit and enjoy the tower for a little while, not letting any of what had happened taint my experience.

Leaving the museums for another – rainy – day I descended a series of stairs away from the square, and walked through the beautiful gardens of the Jardins du Trocadéro, which led to the Pont d'léna on the Seine. The centrepiece of the gardens was the famous Fontaine de Varsovie, a long basin with twelve fountains creating columns of water twelve metres high, and another twenty-four smaller fountains and twenty powerful water cannons. Oh, how I wished the sun would come out. I stopped short of the Pont d'léna, thinking I had tested my emotions enough today. A strange power kept me to one side of the Seine; crossing over would be too hard and I wasn't quite ready to go there just yet.

By the time I had wandered back to the hotel I was completely zen. Something about the rain and the beautiful historical buildings all lined up like beautiful ladies had left me feeling completely sated, almost free. I carried the bits and pieces I'd got from the local store, feeling I could meet any challenge. Well, almost any.

Gaston met me at the front door with an anxious smile. 'Louis wants to meet with you.'

I sighed. 'Did he say why?'

'It's a part of the staff interviews. You're the last one. He's been waiting for you.'

I knew I should have ventured farther. 'So how did yours go?'

'It was good but . . . intense,' he said.

I laughed. 'Yep, sounds about right, where is he?'

'He's in the lounge,' Gaston said, before offering to take my bags.

'Oh, thanks, I'll grab them off you when I'm done.'

I walked through the foyer feeling strangely anxious, but not afraid, never afraid, remembering my declaration to Louis that he didn't have that effect on me. I said hello to Cecile as I passed. She was back to her normal, bashful self and I wondered how her interview went. She smiled and nodded her head toward the lounge.

Ugh, lucky last, I thought, rounding the corner to see Louis sitting on one of the blood-orange chairs, sipping on a coffee. He looked particularly menacing in his black suit; his gaze was on a paper he was reading, and despite me walking around the lounge to sit right before him, he never lifted his eyes once.

'How did you find the rooms?' I asked in an even voice.

'Dated, dirty and depressing.'

'See, you didn't need me to add to that experience.'

Louis closed the paper with a sigh. 'After I finish here with you, I am going to do an evaluation of the kitchen and the menu. I think that, as with everything, is probably in need of some work.'

'No doubt.' I swallowed hard – the restaurant was the most dreaded place of all. I could only hope he wouldn't fire

Gaspard and Francois as well – there would be no staff left. 'So have you worked on a solution for Philippe's replacement? Now that we are a person down there will need to be a—'

'The new replacement will start tomorrow morning.'

Okay, impressive.

'There will be coverage while staff get fitted for their new uniforms and my team will come in to strip rooms four, fourteen and twenty-three.'

Wow, he isn't mucking around.

This felt less like an interview and more like he was using me as a sounding board for his plans.

'So Cecile seems to believe that you are an excellent maître d', and do wonders for the front of house,' he said, looking at me pointedly.

I could feel myself running hot, shifting in my seat. I knew Cecile meant well, talking up my worth, but I had never been more serious than when I'd asked people to be honest; something told me someone like Louis had an excellent bullshit detector system going on.

'She is very kind. I'm all right.'

'"All right" is not good enough. I want the best.'

Well I certainly wasn't that. 'Things are a little different here to how they would be at home, so—'

'Keep your evening free tomorrow.'

'Um, okay,' I said, waiting for him to elaborate but he packed up the notepad and pen that sat on his side table. This meeting was over and I was ready to move, but didn't dare until Louis looked back at me with surprise that I was still sitting there.

'Is that all?' I asked.

'Oui,' he said.

At no stage had he asked me to be involved with the kitchen evaluation and I had no real interest in helping. As I walked away, I saw Louis make his way through the restaurant to the kitchen. I hadn't been there to suffer the wrath of the bedroom reviews and I wouldn't be there to see the shakedown of the kitchen; so far, so good. But when I returned to reception, curiosity got the better of me.

'Do you have any idea why he wants to keep my evening free tomorrow?'

Cecile shrugged. 'Uniform fittings?'

'Maybe, but I can't be sure; that wouldn't happen in the evening, surely?'

'I have never had any luxury fittings, so I cannot say.'

I smiled. 'Do you need me for anything else today?' I had no real hours or shifts, I was merely a shield for Louis Delarue damage control and even with that I was doing a terrible job.

'Just come down before breakfast starts and we can take it from there,' she said.

As far as I was concerned that sounded rather glorious, until the sound of swearing and the clanging of pots came from the kitchen.

'Oh God,' I said.

'What was that?' said Cecile.

'That, Cecile, is the sound of all hell breaking loose.' And with that I quickly grabbed my bags from Gaston and headed up to the sixth floor.

Not that I was afraid.

Chapter Twenty-Two

I had begun the day most pleasantly, chatting and pouring juice for the early-rising tourists. The restaurant wasn't a big space, and it seemed that the busiest time of day was breakfast, people filling their bellies up with sustenance before pounding the pavement to see the sights. I watched as an older couple from the US flipped through images on their expensive camera. If I thought my pronunciation of the local attractions was bad, theirs was downright woeful. Still, they were all set and excited for a new day's adventure, with their knee-high socks and bumbags. I kind of envied them – for their carefree spirit, not their bumbags.

Cathy had set up the station with cereals, juices and breads, doubling back with a fruit platter and setting it on the breakfast bench.

'Did you want me to help with anything?' I asked, looking over her shoulder to glance through the kitchen window.

'I wouldn't go in there if I were you, not just yet,' she warned.

My heart sank. 'Did the meeting with Louis not go so well?

Cathy shook her head. 'That would be an understatement,' she said quietly, peering over her shoulder as if double-checking no one was listening. 'He made Francois cry.'

'*What?* That's not cool,' I said, my heart aching for young Francois.

Cathy looked grim. I felt she was keeping something from me, that she was holding back on the dramatics, and that worried me.

'He wants me to keep my evening free, whatever that means,' I said. I was eagerly telling everyone what Louis had had said to me in the hope that maybe someone knew why, but no one did. They were too busy looking after their own areas of the hotel. The sudden dismissal of Philippe yesterday had really lit a fire underneath everyone.

Cathy's eyes shifted over my shoulder, a familiar glimmer of fear flashing in them as she quickly moved back to fuss over the breakfast bar. I turned, already prepared for what would face me, and sure enough, there he was, as if we had summoned him by some form of magic, all smart casual with a pin-striped blue shirt, a navy jacket and tan pants. He was dressed like he might be chartering a vessel to sail the Mediterranean; it was surely a different look for him, and much to my own horror, I was disappointed to find myself thinking he looked really handsome, as if he had stepped out of a Tommy Hilfiger catalogue.

Louis didn't wait to be seated, he just chose an empty two-seater table on the border between the restaurant and the lounge, the farthest away from the whispering tourists who were trying to pinpoint who he was. Then it registered on their faces. Just like Louis, I paid them no attention as I weaved my way through the tables, aiming to treat him just like anyone else.

'Coffee?' I asked, holding up the pot.

Louis's eyes shifted from the pot in my hand to my face. He seemed to be tossing up whether it might be poisoned or not. But he nodded his head and moved his arm away from his empty cup as I poured.

'Milk?' I asked.

'No, I take it black.'

Like your soul. 'Well, if you're sure.' *I can also make it with the tears of our kitchen staff.*

He looked annoyed, but then again, he always did. 'Are you ready for tonight?' He spoke as if I knew what he was referring to; naturally I had no idea.

'Are people getting fitted for uniforms tonight?' I asked as if it didn't really bother me whether I knew the answer or not. Maybe the interior decorator was stopping by, or the new staff member he organised to replace Philippe, or perhaps he was working on rejigging the menu? Whatever it was, clearing my calendar for the event at his request just made me even more curious, though I would never let on.

'Well, yes, they are but that is not why I am looking forward to tonight.' His blue eyes twinkled up at me as he blew on his coffee then sipped it. I could tell he really wanted me to ask more, but I stood my ground. *I am not taking the bait.*

I cleared my throat. 'Did you want some breakfast?' *Or are you still full from sucking the life force from people?* I tried to keep a straight face as he deliberated, looking into the depths of his black coffee.

'I think I will pass.'

I looked at the breakfast guests who were tucking into their plates, before turning my attention back to Louis, lowering my voice. 'It's not that bad.'

He breathed out a laugh. 'Do you always see things through rose-coloured glasses, Claire?'

There it was again, my name spoken like a caress, although I think it was just the accent that made everything sound sexier than it was. Gaspard could probably even make my name sound exotic. Then again, his sentences were usually finished with a hacking smoker's cough, so maybe not.

'I guess I am just an eternal optimist.'

Louis smiled, his fingers tracing the edge of his coffee cup. 'Maybe you're right then.'

This time I would take the bait. 'About what?'

He tilted his head back, swallowing the last of his coffee, putting the cup down and pushing his chair out. He stood, towering over me in his usual display of power.

'We don't have anything in common.'

'Said the pessimist,' I mused.

Louis shook his head, stepped around his chair and pushed it back in place.

'Said the realist.' And just like he had appeared in the restaurant, he was suddenly gone and I was still none the wiser as to what the day would bring.

Chapter Twenty-Three

Cecile fanned out the navy blue fabric on top of the reception counter.

'*Très magnifique*,' she cooed, brushing out the creases with her hands. 'Is it not the most beautiful colour?'

'It's lovely,' I agreed, running my hand over the soft fabric. The staff were going to look so sophisticated in their new uniforms and the ill-fitting burgundy uniforms would happily be cast aside. It felt strange getting excited over such a thing. I didn't even know if I was a part of the process of getting fitted for a uniform – I still in no way felt like an official staff member, more of a buffer to save them from the crazed outbursts of Louis.

On cue, I heard his voice as he walked through reception, yelling into his mobile in French before ending the call rather abruptly. He paused when his gaze landed on us. His eyes shifted to the fabric and he approached the counter, reaching out to feel it between his thumb and forefinger, a frown pinched at the bridge of his nose.

'*Très bien*,' he said under his breath.

'All you need to do is match the awnings outside and it will look amazing,' I said.

Louis turned, looking at me as if I was speaking a completely different language. Even Cecile seemed confused. Sometimes I really needed to just shut up.

'It's just that,' I babbled, 'the outside awnings and sign are a burgundy that matched the current uniforms.'

I had thought myself quite innovative and forward thinking; Louis's deadpan expression, on the other hand, said it all.

Cecile tried her best to lighten the moment. 'With hotels, once you create a clean spot it just snowballs to the next and to the next.' Her laughter was nervous.

But I was over his lordship's attitude. 'Don't you agree, Louis? That it makes sense to be cohesive?' I pressed, just wanting him to respond. In order for him to agree it would mean admitting that I'd had a good idea, and I couldn't see he would admit to that so freely. I waited for a reply.

'Is that before or after we refurbish the rooms, lounge, reception, restaurant and kitchen?' he asked, folding up the length of fabric.

Now I was the one who had nothing to say.

Louis turned to Cecile, handing her the fabric. 'Philippe's replacement will be here soon; perhaps Claire can cover reception while you take some time to speak with her.'

'Wait, what?' I squeaked. Reception – was he mad? I knew jack about reception, and I sure as hell wouldn't be able to speak any form of coherent French for any enquiries; guests were better left with the desk bell.

'Surely reception would be no problem for such an experienced maître d' as yourself?' he said. It infuriated me: the way he was always trying to catch people out.

I lifted my chin, feigning confidence. 'Take your time, Cecile, everything is under control.'

~

I was not in control, not in the slightest. While Cecile conducted a getting-to-know-you session in the office with Amelie – the tall, elegant Philippe replacement Louis had organised from his long list of connections; I was knocking over pen holders and wrestling with phone cords as I answered the reception phone.

'Bonjour, Hotel Trocadéro.' I tried to keep my voice from sounding manic. I closed my eyes, relieved by the sound of a thick American accent on the other end of the line.

'Oui, monsieur, I will have fresh towels sent up right away, your room number please?'

I scrawled 'room 12' on a scrap of paper and bid the caller a good day.

Okay, so that didn't kill me.

'Psst, Gaston,' I whispered, waving my arms theatrically, hoping to catch his attention, far too afraid to walk the dozen steps to ask him a question.

Gaston turned on my fifth wave, looking surprised as he left his post at the door and came to the desk.

'Room twelve wants fresh towels, what do I—'

'Leave it with me.' Gaston winked, picking up the phone and dialling a number so fast I barely had time to process it, then speaking even faster to the other person on the line in French before hanging up.

He beamed. 'All done.'

'Merci.' I sighed. 'Can you stand by in case I have a French-speaking emergency?'

Gaston laughed. 'I will be by the door keeping watch, call out if you need me.'

Mercifully Louis had an errand to run and wouldn't be witness to my potential meltdown at reception. The longer he stayed away the better; soon Cecile would return with her new protégé and all would be well with the world.

By the third enquiry I started to feel kind of badass about how I was rocking reception. Maybe I had missed my calling in life. I could be warm, welcoming and friendly. I could solve any guest's problem. On cue, the phone rang. I scooped it up in a timely fashion; bubbly and cheerful I ran through my spiel.

'Bonjour, Hotel Trocadéro, how may I help you?' I asked in a quasi-French accent that had me smiling to myself.

There was a hesitation on the other end of the line. 'Ah, yes, could you please put me through to Claire Shorten's room?'

All triumph, all certainty was wiped away as my mind struggled to adjust to what I'd heard as I blinked and looked at the receiver. I slowly pressed it against my ear again.

'Liam?'

'Claire?'

'What you doing ringing here?'

'What are you doing answering the phone?'

My mouth gaped, stopping myself from telling him I worked here. I didn't want him to know. I didn't want anyone to know. So far Hotel Trocadéro had been a kind of rehab for my broken heart, my sanctuary from the dealings of reality, and despite the lunacy and uncertainty of my situation, I felt alive; I felt like I was finding my way. Now I could sense myself unravelling, and it had only taken this phone call, that familiar voice. My stomach twisted with nausea, my mouth went dry and my legs began to tremble.

'What are you doing, Claire? Come home.'

'To what?' I scoffed. 'Have you managed to box up my things already?'

'Claire, please, it doesn't have to be like this. Come home and we can sit down and talk about it.'

'There is nothing to talk about, not any more.'

'Well, you can't stay in Paris forever. What are you doing for money?'

A darkness settled over me. Despite our relationship, his money had been his and mine had been mine. Other than the bills, there was nothing we really shared, not even our interests. It's amazing how hindsight can make you see so clearly.

'That's none of your concern.'

'Well, what am I supposed to tell your parents? I spoke to Sammi; she's worried about you.'

I wasn't ready for our break-up to become common knowledge, to be bombarded with endless questions and a new pressure to come home to Australia. I wanted none of it, and I certainly didn't need the likes of Liam guilt-tripping me into doing anything any more. I could feel the walls closing in, my sanctuary dissolving and worry and paranoia setting in.

'Go and water your pot plants, Liam, or maybe you don't need to do that any more. Has she moved in yet?'

Liam sighed wearily.

'Or are you going to open up both apartments into one big house? Oh, that sounds like a profitable venture,' I said, the words almost getting lodged in my throat as a mixture of anger and hurt raged inside me.

I heard Gaston cough behind me. 'Pardon, Claire?'

I held up my hand, now was not the time. I was on a roll of self-destruction as I turned from Gaston and stood further away, lowering my voice. 'Why did you call me, Liam?'

Had he changed his mind? Been lost without me? Was he kicking himself for ruining a good thing, dread filling up every ounce of his being? Perhaps he wanted nothing more than for me to come home and completely forget about that one time in Paris. I held my breath, waiting on him to answer with any one of those excellent reasons.

'Because I'm worried about you.'

I breathed out a laugh.

'Claire,' Gaston said softly again, but I couldn't acknowledge him, not now.

'Aside from that, why are you calling?'

There was a long, drawn-out silence, one that made the thundering of my heart pounding violently against my rib cage seem almost deafening.

'Liam?'

'I'm not doing this, not on the phone, Claire. Come home.'

Home sounded so intimate, so familiar, and yet didn't seem to apply, not to me, not any more.

'Liam, you broke up with me underneath the Eiffel Tower, there is nothing you could do that could top that.'

More silence.

Growing weary, if not more intrigued, I sighed, rubbing my eyes and trying to ignore Gaston's presence behind me.

'Liam, seriously just tell—'

'Veronica's pregnant.'

My world dropped away. The solid ground underneath my feet seemed like it was magnetised, wanting to swirl me into a soundless, black vortex of shock, disbelief and then anger. I didn't hear Liam continue, the receiver had dropped from my ear, and the muted sounds of my name being called made no sense. Inside I was shifting, turning, until I found a new strength by gripping the phone and crashing the receiver down violently, over and over again as I burst into tears.

'Fucking lying son of a bitch,' I wept, letting the phone fall off the hook to hopefully prevent him calling back. I spun around, having totally forgotten about the patiently waiting Gaston.

And there was the steely-eyed Louis Delarue, standing at Gaston's side, front row centre to my complete meltdown.

And if that wasn't bad enough, there was an entire camera crew filming me.

'You finished?' Louis said, his voice low, his stare hard. Gaston looked completely dismayed, mouthing 'Sorry' as he backed away to stand by the front door again.

Then, as Louis called me out for being the biggest phony and the most disastrous staff member he had ever had the displeasure of encountering, I stared vacantly, my cheeks flushed, my soul depleted. There was no room left in me to care about anything other than wanting to dissolve.

Just when I was about to tell Louis and his bloody nosy camera crew to get out of my face, the door to the office opened, laughter filtering out, as Cecile lead Amelie toward the reception.

'Oh, Claire, thank you so much for looking after the—' Cecile's words fell away, her eyes widening as she studied my face, turning to Louis and the camera crew then back again.

I swallowed, trying to keep my composure, trying to keep myself from crumpling into a ball. There was something oddly reassuring about the fact that Louis hadn't made me cry; well, not yet anyway.

'I said I didn't want to be on camera.' I spoke directly to Cecile, barely containing the rage that was bubbling underneath the surface.

'Of course, Louis knows that,' she said, her eyes filled with worry as she looked at Louis.

The man with the bulky camera on his shoulder shrugged arrogantly. 'We were told to film in reception.'

Louis Delarue said nothing, only stood there, his eyes fixed on me as if he was trying to solve the mysteries of the universe. His silence only made me more angry.

'Can I go now?' I asked Cecile, my voice low. It wasn't bad enough that my demeanour was completely flattened by what Liam had just told me, how he had asked me to come home – and for *that*. To drag out and ruin my life a little more. And now to add insult to injury, my entire meltdown was being witnessed by Louis and his bloody film crew.

'Oui, go rest, Claire. We will take over from here.'

I nodded, moving away from the counter, offering only a fleeting sad, apologetic smile to Amelie, who must have thought me a complete freak. I could still feel Louis's judgemental stare, the disappointment radiating off him as he no doubt waited for me to be completely out the way before he convinced Cecile that I was a hindrance to Hotel Trocadéro and to let me go.

I took in a deep breath. *Don't cry, don't cry . . . wait until you're inside the lift.*

The magical ding finally sounded and I dived into the small recess, urging the doors to close quickly enough to disguise meltdown round two. Just as I was about to give in to the misery, a hand plunged into the lift, preventing the door from closing, and making them shunt open. Louis stood there.

Oh God, he had come to fire me; apparently I didn't need to be absent for the conversation to take place, and apparently it was something that couldn't wait. They probably wanted my room for Amelie now, a true professional, not an imposter.

I braced myself for the words, thinking how I was actually quite relieved that it would be over soon, that I had given Paris a second chance, given it my all and it just hadn't worked out. Liam and I were over; my time at the Hotel Trocadéro was over. I was resigned to my fate. So when Louis wedged his foot against the concertina folds of the doors and smiled at me, I almost recoiled from the unexpectedness of it; not only was he going to fire me, but apparently he was going to enjoy it.

'Where are you going?' he asked.

My mouth gaped; I mean, surely it was obvious? Surely he didn't mean to torture me further? But his face seemed light, his demeanour carefree.

'I'm just going to—'

'Come with me.'

'What?' I said a bit too loudly.

'I said, come with me.'

'W-where?'

Louis shook his head. 'So many questions.'

'I don't like surprises,' I said, thinking how true that was under the circumstances. In fact, I really fucking despised being kept in the dark on any matter.

Louis seemed unperturbed. 'Meet me out front,' he said. 'It's the black Audi,' he said with a smirk as he stepped back, letting the door go. 'But something tells me you already know that.'

Chapter Twenty-Four

I had two choices: collapse into bed with the curtains drawn, or sate my curiosity and find out where Louis Delarue was taking me in his flash Audi. Was he taking me for a uniform fitting? That would be the only agenda that seemed to make sense right now, and based on that I was almost tempted to go with Plan A – almost.

I stopped by my room to pick up my bag and jacket and cleared away the smudges of my eye makeup in the lift's mirrored walls on my way back down to the lobby.

Cecile stopped still next to Amelie when she saw me. She seemed worried that I was back. It made me quite sad thinking she had to be different around me now that Amelie was here. I felt like a complete fool – what must they all think of me?

I approached the desk, clearing my throat. 'Do you know where Louis is taking me?' *A shallow grave somewhere in the French countryside?*

Cecile smiled. 'I think I have a pretty good idea.'

'Where?'

A car horn blasted from out the front, and we turned to the offending sound to see Louis's elbows resting on the windowsill, a pair of Ray-Bans over his eyes. The car was running, and a cheeky grin spread across his face.

Cecile laughed. 'Looks like you are about to find out.'

I swallowed, and walked to the car, my ballet flats clicking on the glossed reception floor as I approached my doom. I wove past the film crew, trying not to trip over a wayward cable that was strewn across the floor. I really couldn't wait to get out of here, I just wasn't so sure about the destination.

What are you doing? You are about to get into a car with a lunatic. You've just received the most crushing news of your life – why aren't you packing and going into witness protection so you can avoid the pity, the questions?

'Bonsoir,' Gaston said with a cheery smile, stepping up to the car and opening the passenger door for me. Was it my warped sense of reality right now or was everyone surprisingly happy and calm that I was about to get into the passenger seat with the devil? There was something unnerving about how happy Gaston was, but then what did I want him to be doing? Throwing himself across the bonnet screaming, 'Don't do it!'? I think I would've just liked to be reassured that wherever I was being taken, it wouldn't be too traumatic, despite the company.

I lacked the energy to do anything other than offer Gaston a weak smile as I slid into the Audi with its tan leather interior and new-car smell. This was definitely like no man's car I had ever been in before. There were no empty week-old Coke cans or screwed-up Macca's bags at my feet. It was like I was stepping into a whole new world: a grown-up world of riches. A world that had sharp, modern corners and elegant taste. The falling sun glinted off Louis's wristwatch as his arm rested on top of the steering wheel. His Ray-Bans disguised his blue eyes.

'Where are we going?'

'Noire,' he said without emotion, starting the car and glancing in his rear-view mirror.

I quickly grabbed for my seat belt, as I tried to decipher what 'Noire' meant – or did he say 'Nowhere'? His accent was pretty thick. My confusion must have seemed evident because Louis began to laugh as he pulled out and stepped on the accelerator, setting me back against the seat as he sped down the narrow avenue.

'You don't know what that is, do you?'

'Of course I do,' I lied.

Louis smiled widely. 'I like that you don't,' he said, taking a hairpin turn down another alley, shifting the gears like a racing-car driver. My hands gripped the edge of my seat as I tried not to look at the buildings that blurred by, making me feel nauseous. I wanted to yell at him to slow down, but somehow I didn't think telling Louis what to do would work, so instead I tried to distract myself by spreading my hands on the roof to brace myself as he came speeding up to a set of traffic lights at a busy intersection. There always seemed to be an insane amount of chaos on the roads. There were apparently no road rules, going by the way everyone was navigating the traffic. But Louis seemed to be a law unto himself.

I tried to busy myself by rolling the word 'Noire' around in my head. It sounded familiar: film noir? That was a thing, right? Were we going to see a film? That would be incredibly random, although me being in Louis's car was incredibly random, to say the least. It had occurred to me that maybe Louis had seen me upset, that maybe this was his attempt at getting me away from the hotel as a means to distract me, but then that would require some form of human emotion, and so far he had hardly said two words, let alone displayed any social graces. The most animated gesture had been him peeling off his sunnies and running his hand through his messy hair.

We cruised along, driving behind Palais de Chaillot before turning on to a beautiful tree-lined avenue where the sun tried to filter through its leafy canopies. We sped towards Avenue De New-York along the Siene. This part of the river wasn't riddled with vendors with their stands, catering for the strolling tourists, luring them from street corners with their crumpled maps trying to orientate themselves, but it did still have a spectacular view of the tower. In the sun's dying rays, the Eiffel Tower looked remarkable across the body of water. Maybe this was Louis's way of deliberately torturing me.

I'd thought that the expedition had only just begun, until Louis abruptly veered into a side street, parking alongside a collection of motorbikes. He killed the engine and looked at me expectantly. He seemed fascinated with the fact I appeared to be clinging onto life with white-knuckled intensity. I exhaled with relief that we had made it to our destination in one piece.

'Are you okay?'

'Oui,' I said with a sarcasm that only seemed to amuse him.

Opening his door, Louis moved out from behind the steering wheel with an air of gracefulness. I, on the other hand, clawed my way out of the passenger seat, struggling to stand on my wobbly legs. The ride had been so fast my brain was still catching up, my heart was still racing, my palms were clammy; I was probably pale from terror. The night air was cool on my cheeks as I braced myself against the car door, peering at Louis across its roof. He looked at me with a guarded interest.

'Where are we?' I asked, not recognising any landmarks aside from the river and tower across the way.

Louis's face seemed alight, like he was pleased that I had asked. He gave me a crooked smile.

'Welcome to Noire.'

Noire was definitely not a picture theatre. We entered via a rather inelegant back door from a side street, Louis holding the door open for me to walk through. When the aroma hit me, I knew exactly where I was. I didn't need to ask if this was Louis's famed restaurant, I had assumed so the moment he took off his jacket and hooked it near the back door. Louis was always self-assured – in his walk, the way he carried himself – but that was never more evident than when he had entered his little world, immersing himself in its militant chaos. He led me through one side of the galley-style kitchen and his presence inspired a definitive shift among his staff, a nervous energy, as heads lowered and chopping became faster and finer. The line of white-jacketed men with tall chef's hats busied themselves, the only sound in the kitchen that of creating. There was no smiling or laughing among the chefs; it was all business.

Louis vigorously shook the hand of a man who stood at the pass; he was smaller and younger than Louis, but his face bore lines of fatigue. They spoke in French, serious, concentrating, hands moving emphatically. It was hard to determine if the conversation was friendly until the man said something that had Louis smiling, almost laughing. The brotherly sparring seemed like it was something they always did.

The young chef's eyes turned to me, standing there awkwardly, not wanting to get in anyone's way.

'Claire, I want you to meet Jean-Pierre, my second-in-command.'

Jean-Pierre stepped forward, offering his hand to me. 'Except when he is off seeing to his celebrity chef duties.'

'*Va te faire foutre.*' Louis laughed, shoving at Jean-Pierre, who merely shook his head.

'Louis, don't swear in front of the lady.'

'Oh, it's okay, I don't speak French,' I said, enjoying the unusual sight of Louis bantering.

'Jean-Pierre, do you want to give Claire a tour?'

'Of course.' Jean-Pierre winked at me, sweeping his hand to the side, showing me the way. 'After you.'

Noire's tall bay windows overlooked the River Seine and the Eiffel Tower. The mauve and grey decor was ever so chic. In the dining room, lines of polished, sparkling glasses were being set by wait staff dressed impeccably in black, a regiment of soldiers who straightened cutlery and measured placements with precision.

Jean-Pierre took me out front, to look at the streetscape of the restaurant, which featured an illuminated sign: *noire*.

'How long have you worked here, Jean-Pierre?'

'Five years,' he said, his dark eyes gazing up at the lights of the building, a bizarre thing to be admiring when in the distance the Eiffel Tower lights had started to sparkle. It was hard not to be distracted by their beauty.

'And you like it here?' I didn't really expect a response, seeing as we both seemed distracted.

'Oui, cooking is my life,' he said.

'And working for Louis, that must take a lot of . . . patience.' I half laughed, expecting to hear him say that he was a pain in the arse, maybe, but that he respected him, or that it was a nightmare but he'd learnt so much.

But Jean-Pierre responded quite honestly. 'He is a good man.'

Nothing more, nothing less. My look of surprise inspired a cheeky smile from Jean-Pierre, who gazed back up at the sign with an element of pride.

'The problem with the passion and the beauty of Louis is his obsession with perfection,' he said thoughtfully. 'It takes a special kind of person. Being a head chef is physically difficult and mentally demanding – you have to be a little bit crazy.'

I smiled at that, thinking I could attest to the crazy. I walked over to the menu displayed behind glass, failing in my efforts to not be visibly shocked by the prices of the selections.

Jean-Pierre didn't miss a thing.

'Everything is beautifully cooked, beautifully presented, with no expense spared on the finest ingredients.'

'Amazing,' I breathed. 'So what's the meaning behind "Noire"?' I asked, feeling I could have honestly asked anything of Jean-Pierre and he would answer me in a very open way. It was a fascinating conversation to have with someone who probably knew Louis better than anyone. I felt like I was getting an insight into a whole other side of Louis, one that was far removed from his shouting television persona, and the more I dug, the more captivating the discovery.

'*Noire* means black; when Louis started up his own restaurant he was considered a bit of a dark horse in the culinary world – and a black sheep in his family, for becoming a chef.'

'How fitting,' I mused. 'So if I asked you to sum up Louis Delarue, what would you say?'

Jean-Pierre thought for a moment. 'He's a culinary sportsman.'

Oh. For someone who had so much to say, I was somewhat disappointed with his answer. I thought he might elaborate, seeing as he was looking at me with a little smirk.

'What?' I pressed.

'You like him.'

'What?' I cried. Where the hell had that come from?

'It's just you have spoken about nothing but Louis.'

Oh my God, had I?

'No, I just, I just – I'm working with him and I don't know what it is that makes him tick and he is terribly frustrating and confusing and I just never know where I stand with him.' As I stumbled over my manic reply, Jean-Pierre's amusement only seemed to grow as I babbled.

I was saved by an unexpected tapping on the glass of the bay window. Louis stood there, waving us inside.

Jean-Pierre acknowledged his summons with a nod. 'Ready?' he asked me.

I was slightly off balance. No, I wasn't ready. I was deeply disturbed by the conversation. I had wanted to talk more about what Jean-Pierre had implied, but that seemed a little too defensive, and besides, there was no time, we were heading through the front door and back to the kitchen.

Chapter Twenty-Five

All the chefs in the kitchen seemed pensive, slightly tense, as they waited for another fully booked night to kick off. It was the calm before the storm. Jean-Pierre said I was welcome to leave my coat and bag in the office for safe keeping, so I made my way tentatively to the back room. Rounding the corner, I slammed straight into Louis, who was coming out of the office.

'Sorry,' I said, almost dropping my belongings and stepping back. Louis's hand touched my upper arm as if he was afraid I might lose my feet, but it wasn't until I focused on him standing in front of me that I did feel I might actually lose my balance. Louis was dressed in a stark white, double-breasted jacket, dark pants, and had a blue and white striped apron in hand. Never had I seen him in anything other than his stylish suits; this was something else altogether.

'Claire?'

'You look beautiful,' I blurted, instantly cringing at the fact that, yes, I just said that out fucking loud. *I want to die.*

Louis's face registered his surprise. For the first time since I'd met him he seemed to be so taken aback he had no words of retaliation, no smartarse quip or response. But he didn't need one, because once he finally processed my mortifying words he did something so much worse than saying anything. He smirked, crookedly and smugly – he was saying 'I know' or 'You're only human'. He was so utterly infuriating that I was tempted to reach for an industrial frying pan and wipe the smile from his face.

I swallowed. 'I-I'm just leaving my things in the office, Jean-Pierre said that I could.'

Louis seemed confused, his eyes dropping to the jacket and bag in my hand. 'Why don't you just take it to your table?'

Now I was the one who was confused. 'My table?'

Louis sighed, taking my arm and practically frogmarched me back through the kitchen. It must have been funny, although none of the robotic chefs dared raise a smile, aside from Jean-Pierre, who looked on with interest.

'Mathias, show Mademoiselle Shorten to her table.' Louis motioned to the head waiter, who with a sharp nod swung into immediate action, leading me into the restaurant. I followed, looking over my shoulder to the pass where Louis stood, watching me go.

I don't know what I had expected exactly: at first maybe I had thought he had wanted to show me what a real restaurant looked like, and then seeing him in his chef finery – okay, I really didn't want to think about that. I cringed. I thought that maybe, since he seemed to be working tonight, I might be placed in the office out of the way or sat in a corner on a stool. So when Mathias led me to a beautiful circular white linen and crystal–clad table instead, pulling the plush chair out for me to sit, I was taken aback.

The kitchen and all that went on behind the scenes was displayed behind an enormous sheet of glass; it was like the chefs were on a stage and the diners were the audience. Patrons would probably have booked months in advance to secure a coveted window seat so as to overlook the sparkling Eiffel light show and the Seine, but I was more than pleased with my front-row seat to the action in the kitchen. The glass almost acted like a shield for the chefs, who seemed unperturbed by the fact that people were watching and there was no room for error. Except, as the wealthy, stylish women and jacketed men filtered into the restaurant, it appeared that no one seemed as invested as I was in observing the steely focus of Louis, or the sudden pinched, serious lines on Jean-Pierre's face as he shifted into his second-in-command role. It felt deliciously voyeuristic.

Mathias was an absolute star, speaking perfect English and delivering a wine menu with helpful recommendations. I swallowed deeply, ever aware of the price of everything, and the list of wines made my eyes blur. I wondered how it would be received if I just ordered water, and told Mathias I wasn't hungry, even if the traitorous rumble of my stomach said otherwise.

'Chef Delarue recommends 2011 Saumur "Clos des Carmes" Domaine Guiberteau.' Mathias offered the open wine bottle elegantly, his eyes looking at me questioningly. My eyes quickly returned to the menu, searching for the name on the wine list.

Holy shit. Yeah, I couldn't afford that, I most definitely couldn't afford the bottle, or the glass or even a sniff of such a wine. But before I could protest, my silence was taken as a yes and Mathias began to pour. I felt ill. I was definitely not eating tonight.

'Um, Mathias, maybe I should move out back; it's just that I don't feel very hungry and I think that the table should probably go to someone who is.'

Mathias looked uncomfortable, as if he wasn't really capable of dealing with such a request. 'No, mademoiselle, you are a guest of Chef Delarue; while you sit at his table, you can have anything you want.'

I squirmed in my chair. *Please don't make me say it out loud*, I thought, and as if by some magical form of telepathy, or maybe just because he was an excellent waiter, Mathias lowered his voice a little.

'Mademoiselle, chef has instructed there be no charge for your table tonight.'

'Sorry?'

Mathias smiled, taking the opportunity to top my glass up a little more. 'So, what will you be having tonight?'

I felt all kinds of strange. But mostly, I felt emotional. Course after delicious course began to arrive at my table. They were just like Jean-Pierre had described: beautifully cooked, beautifully presented. I know, because as I sipped my impossibly expensive wine I watched through the window into the kitchen. Louis was lit up like a god; the heat lamps reflecting off the stainless steel benches highlighting his angular face as he spoke to his team.

I was so conflicted because despite having been given the worst possible blow from Liam, here I was sitting in a Michelin-starred restaurant on the banks of the Seine, sipping wine and delving into culinary delights. I was completely lost in the bliss of it, watching Louis and Jean-Pierre in action, meticulously altering and analysing every plate that came to the pass. Louis worked his kitchen like a well-oiled machine: he yelled and they responded; he pushed and they delivered.

I couldn't help but be in awe of him. I didn't even resent the way I felt about him. Jean-Pierre's character assessment was right: Louis gave the best and expected the best, and that was the attitude he had brought to the Hotel Trocadéro each day, so when Gaspard's food was unseasoned, or the front reception was unmanned, then that simply wasn't good enough. He wasn't being a tyrant without reason, he had every reason, as well as the knowledge, to make a change. I suddenly felt mortified for having been so defiant toward his approach. I would definitely have to apologise – no, wait, he didn't like that. Well, I would just have to make it up to him in some way, not that I had a single clue how. I wasn't exactly capable of producing magnificent meals and bottles of wine worth hundreds of euros. Perhaps it was the wine that was influencing my rambling, fangirl thoughts now;

I decided it was time to lay off the good stuff and just settle down a bit, reaching instead for the glass of water.

Mathias appeared by my side again – he seemed to float on air, he was so graceful. I glanced up mid-sip, quickly swallowed and put the glass down.

'Mademoiselle, dessert will be served outside,' he said, looking delighted with the news he was delivering. I could almost feel my heart sink as I looked past him to the workings of the kitchen, hoping that Louis might make eye contact with me, but as had been the case throughout the night, his quicksilver eyes didn't lift to me. I really didn't want to leave my seat, but of course considering it was a seat I'd never thought would ever be mine in the first place, well, I wasn't exactly going to be a diva about it.

I smiled, placing the napkin from my lap on the table. 'Sounds perfect.'

Chapter Twenty-Six

In true Parisian style I sat with my back against the restaurant, the table to my side as I looked out onto the street; the shimmer of the Eiffel lights dancing before me made my heart feel full, which seemed rather appropriate, as it matched my belly. I couldn't comprehend what my meal had cost, and despite me ordering only one thing for myself, mysterious plates appeared at my table from Chef Louis and, oh, how glad I was that they had.

Lost in a numbness that was a combination of wine, the view and the cool night air, I jumped to attention when a plate of decadent chocolate delights was placed next to me. But it wasn't delivered by the usual black-clad arm of Mathias. As I looked up, my eyes met Louis's. The people at the surrounding tables were looking on with interest, murmuring to themselves at the presence of the man himself. And if that hadn't shocked me enough, Louis taking a seat in the vacant chair across from me, pressing his back against it and pushing out his long legs in front of him really had people gawping. He seemed tired, with dark circles under his eyes, his hair all tousled, and yet his chef's jacket was miraculously unstained.

Despite the continuous line of luxurious food that had come my way throughout the night, my mouth watered as I picked up my dessert fork. I felt all kinds of excited yet I was reluctant to spoil the gorgeous-looking dessert. The top layer of glossy tempered chocolate cracked under my fork, giving way to allow the tines to glide through the sumptuous gooey chocolate underneath. I smiled like a small child with a puppy and glanced at Louis, who was watching with great interest, a little smirk tugging at the corner of his mouth.

'Did you enjoy your meal?' he asked, resting his elbows on the table, which probably wasn't good etiquette but considering this was his kingdom, he could table dance if he wanted to and I think everyone would agree it was acceptable.

I savoured the velvety chocolate in my mouth, nodding and battling between wanting to take my time to enjoy it, yet eager to tell him just how incredible the night had been. And then it occurred to me, I didn't need to say sorry to him. I knew he didn't take kindly to the word. I did have another way of making it up to him, and that was to give credit where credit was due, and to generally just be a nicer, better person.

'I have never had such an incredible culinary experience. And I say "experience" because that's what it was; you took my taste buds on a journey and for one night you let me escape from reality – and to me, in this moment, that is just absolutely priceless. I know you don't like the word sorry, so I don't know how you feel about the words thank you, but I really don't care. Thank you, Louis, thank you for bringing me here, into your world. I will never forget this night. You have given me a new, beautiful memory of Paris, eating chocolate and watching the lights.' I saluted him with my fork and gestured toward the tower, my rambling speech fuelled by alcohol but my sincerity undiminished by it.

I thought that my heartfelt speech would have elicited some kind of emotion from him, but instead he looked at me as if filing my words away. Whether that meant dumping it into the useless-pieces-of-information section of his brain, it was hard to say. His non-response made me feel like a bit of a fool, so I quickly returned all my attention to my dessert.

Just shut up and eat, Claire!

'Do you want to go for a walk?'

～

It wasn't an instantaneous thing. I finished my dessert and then had to wait, and wait, and – my God – *wait* for the end of service. People rolled in and out long into the night; it became clear why everyone in the kitchen was so tired. Only after Louis had a debrief of sorts with his staff did he reemerge from behind the glass, spent but apparently in good spirits. By that time I had all but written off the walk and was sitting patiently, ready to go back to the hotel.

Louis stopped in front of me. 'You ready?'

'Oui,' I said with enthusiasm, standing and pulling on my jacket.

'Okay, let's go,' he said, leading me back to the kitchen, past the staff, who were busying themselves wiping down surfaces after a long day – to ready the kitchen for an early start, no doubt.

I paused, glancing around the industrial kitchen where all the magic had happened, and I was pleased to see Jean-Pierre.

'Bonsoir, Jean-Pierre. It was really nice to meet you,' I said, walking over and holding out my hand.

'Bonsoir, Claire. Keep him in line, yeah?' he said, offering a cheeky smile to Louis, who stood at the opposite end of the kitchen.

I laughed, ready to pull away, but was held in place by Jean-Pierre, who lowered his voice. 'He has never brought anyone here before. You must be something special.' Delighted by my apparent shock he let go of my hand, moving back down the bench. I wanted to ask him what he meant, ask him a million questions, but my thoughts were cut off by Louis's voice.

'Leave her alone, Jean-Pierre.'

'Oui, chef! She is all yours,' he said, winking at me. I had to gather myself quickly, hoping that Louis didn't see my cheeks burning, but as I turned to follow him out, I saw Louis had already disappeared from the kitchen.

I quickstepped to the back door where Louis's coat still hung; confused, I spun around. There he was in the back office, methodically unbuttoning his double-breasted chef's coat. The long line of his fingers tracing and unlooping the buttons made me hold my breath. He peeled off the coat, revealing a simple white T-shirt underneath. This usually wouldn't set my heart aflutter, but somehow there I was, the ultimate voyeur as I had been all night, except now Louis wasn't focused on the task at hand. So when his eyes lifted to mine and I was sprung ogling him, it felt like time stood still. Despite the feel of my cheeks turning red again, and my inner monologue screaming at me to *Look away, go outside and wait you massive pervert*, I stood frozen.

Louis, however, did move. He pulled the T-shirt over his head the way men always seemed to do, then threw the garment aside, revealing his tall, lean body. His shoulders were so square I wanted to run my hands along the lines of them, then down his biceps, which were curved in all the right places. My eyes were trailing along the very places that my mind was roaming and I quickly averted them before looking back at Louis's face, but it was too late. No matter how quickly my eyes had strayed he had caught it, and there was no undoing that damage. Strangely though, he didn't wear his usual cocky smirk; instead, his eyes burned, and his face held an almost similar expression to the one I had seen on him tonight, when he was working in his domain: an animalistic charge that came with his power. Seeing it again now excited me.

The sound of voices coming from the kitchen made me blink and break the connection between us. I moved to the back door, and headed outside, thinking some cool, fresh air was just what I needed – that and an ice-cold shower.

Chapter Twenty-Seven

I stood by Louis's car, my arms crossed as if to ward off a chill in the night air. Shifting from side to side restlessly, it was only when I heard the beep of the security lock did I look up to see Louis crossing the street, his hands thrust deep into the pockets of his dark coat, collar turned up like a French James Dean.

'Hey, do you mind if we head back? I'm kind of tired,' I said, feeling so lame. It's not like I had been the one slaving in a kitchen all night; all I had done was stuff my face.

If Louis was disappointed, he didn't show it. Not that he would be. God, he wasn't a sixteen-year-old girl – what would he care if I didn't want to walk with him? And, as suspected, he just shrugged one lazy shoulder.

'Let's go,' he said, opening up the driver's door and getting in behind the wheel.

If anything, I was the one feeling like a disappointed teenage girl. Christ, I really needed to clear my head, sober up a little and get some sleep. All these filtered Paris lights and moody, romantic restaurant settings were sending me loopy. I was clearly vulnerable.

And then it started to make sense. It was only several hours before that Liam had confirmed in the most brutal of ways his infidelity. It was one thing to break up with me but getting your mistress pregnant was something else altogether. And despite seeing Louis in a new light, one that gave me disturbing, tingling sensations, I had to shut that shit down. Classic rebound revenge sex was the worst idea imaginable and with someone like Louis? Definitely not, no way, no how. By the time I had belted myself back into his Audi I was thanking the gods we hadn't gone for that walk.

It was past midnight when Louis pulled up in front of our hotel; I caught myself smiling. It was like I was existing in some kind of parallel universe, one that had me riding in shiny black Audis and dining in Michelin-starred restaurants, not being dumped in the most romantic city in the world. I had to say, my situation was not awful.

I gathered my bag and my nerves after Louis's usual Formula 1 sprint back as Louis got out his side and walked around the front of the car to my door, opening it for me.

'I'm no Gaston, but I can open a door with the best of them.'

I laughed, pausing to look at this strange creature. He had gone from an amazing host, to silent, slightly awkward chauffeur to gentleman.

Who are you, Louis Delarue?

'Merci,' I said, sliding out of his car and standing next to him. Louis pushed through the door first, standing aside to hold it open for me. I could seriously get used to this side of him, I thought; the silence fell between us in a new, more comfortable way as we walked through the foyer to reception, long vacant now the staff had ended their shifts. The only person around was the night security guard manning the door, on standby should any dramas arise. I didn't even know his name; it wasn't like I made a habit of wandering the dimmed foyer at all hours of the night.

The material of Louis's coat brushed against my arm as we walked, and my skin tingled. It seemed so silly, reacting to such a small thing, but I wanted it to happen again. I didn't know if he had those same kind of ridiculous thoughts, but I seriously doubted it. As we approached the lift, Louis looked at me, really looked at me, and a slow, sexy smile formed, one that was contagious in its warmth, and that made me feel giddy at the thought of being locked in the small space of the lift with him. A series of insanely hot feelings flooded me in the anticipation until we turned the corner, and stopped dead in our tracks. There, slouched in one of the chairs in the lounge, looking bored and more miserable than ever, was *Liam*.

Chapter Twenty-Eight

'What are you doing here?'

Liam startled from his sleepy recline; his eyes brightened as he scrambled to stand.

'Claire!'

'Liam what—' I stood shocked – no, make that horrified – at seeing him stand before me.

'I had to come. I have to explain about . . .'

Liam's voice trailed off and we both turned to look at Louis, who was looking down at me without an ounce of amusement, judging me, and this rather awkward situation. He eventually turned his attention to Liam, whose eyes switched between us, wary. I didn't know if Liam recognised him, or if he was taken aback by me walking in with him. Whatever the emotion, Liam clamped it down and held out his hand.

'Liam Jackson,' he said, squaring his shoulders.

Louis had a particular way of making people feel small with a look – a look he was giving Liam now as he glanced at the outstretched hand, almost like he was confused by the offering. A few seconds passed, as Liam's hand hung in midair. I thought it might hang there forever, until Louis smirked.

'Forgive me if I don't shake hands,' he said dismissively before turning back to me. 'If I don't see you in the morning—'

'You will,' I said quickly, cutting him off. Of course he would.

He seemed unconvinced. '*Bonne nuit*,' he said, and to my surprise I remembered it meant goodnight and I smiled, always proud of any glimmer of understanding I had of the language.

'Goodnight,' I said.

For a long moment Louis looked into my eyes. I wished beyond anything that I could read his mind, because there was definitely something lingering there. For the first time, Louis Delarue was leaving something unsaid and walking away.

I was alone with Liam now and as I saw the lift doors close I so desperately wanted them to open again, for Louis to stay.

Under any other circumstance my heart might have been racing or butterflies might have fluttered in my tummy, and hope would have made tears well in my eyes at seeing Liam again, but I remembered the conversation of hours before and the way my heart had plummeted to the floor. There was no sentimentality in our reunion, only a bone-deep anger that made my hands clench at my sides.

Liam seemed nervous, watching me as if he had expected me to flee. The thought had crossed my mind.

'I got on the train as quickly as I could. I had to see you.'

I in no way wanted to invite him into my new world, or have this discussion in public. I turned, storming back through reception, doubling back the way I had come with Louis and passing the portly security guard, who watched with much interest. I pushed through the hotel door and was confronted by the shiny black Audi I had only just been in. It gave me a moment's pause as my mind returned to the night that had been, and how Louis had taken me away from my reality. For a few hours I had been distracted enough to forget. But now there was no forgetting, especially when Liam slowly reached for my arm.

'Claire, listen.'

'Don't you dare,' I said, pulling myself away and cutting him with a look that Louis would have been proud of. 'You don't get the right to ask me to listen, not any more, *not ever again*,' I shouted, my voice no doubt filtering up to the rooms above me. Could people hear me over the distant traffic noises? Could Louis hear? I doubted it.

'Claire, I came here to tell you—'

'It wasn't enough to hear it in my voice, you had to see it in my face? Well, here I am, memorise it because it's the last time you'll ever—'

'It's not mine, Claire!' he shouted. 'It's not my baby.'

I blinked. 'What?'

'It's not my baby because I have never slept with her.'

'B-but I thought—'

'She has a boyfriend . . . apparently.'

'So, you didn't . . .'

'No, of course not,' he said, stepping a little closer to me. 'When I realised that's what you thought I tried to explain, but you didn't give me the chance. Despite whatever problems we had, Claire, I would never cheat on you.'

The tiny shred of relief that flooded through me upon learning that Liam hadn't impregnated the idiotic plant waterer was short lived. 'That's the thing – I didn't think we had any problems.' Not until the second my world was turned upside down under the Eiffel Tower anyway.

Liam closed his eyes, as if summoning strength. 'Claire, please.'

'Oh no, wait, I do recall a problem: you apparently having a thing for the girl upstairs.'

Liam was fighting for patience, looking at me as if he wished he could gaffer tape my mouth closed. Yeah, good luck with that, buddy.

'So, what do you want, Liam? A medal for not succumbing to the desires out of a sense of loyalty to me? Forgive me if I don't swoon over you.'

'I'm not asking you to.'

'Well, what are you asking then?'

'God damn it, Claire, I'm asking for you!'

My eyes must have been blank; I *felt* blank, completely devoid of thought, my head empty in response to what he was saying. What the hell was he saying?

Liam cupped my face. 'Claire, I'm so sorry. You have to forgive me; you *have* to forgive me,' he pleaded. He brushed his mouth softly against mine and I was lost in his familiar warmth, overwhelmed with the unexpectedness of his confession, my heart spiking with the thrill of what was happening.

Liam wants me back.

He had made a mistake and he was here to claim what belonged to him, and he staked his claim by drawing me to him, kissing me hot and heavy like it had been between us at the very beginning. Grabbing at the fabric at his back, anchoring myself to the comfort of him, aware of nothing except the light dusting of rain that started to fall on us as we stood kissing under the hotel lights.

It couldn't get any better than this, the memory we were forming could be enough to erase all others, until Liam wrapped his arms around me and my head nestled in his shoulder and my eyes rested on the black Audi we stood next to.

My mind flashed back to the last time I stood in the rain in this very spot, beside the very same car that had revealed a pair of intense, quicksilver eyes that had me recoiling and wanting to be anywhere but here. Maybe it was the rain that reminded me of that day, the way I had walked from the bus stop to the hotel with numbness in the pit of my stomach, something I had never, ever wanted to feel again, and over the past few days, I hadn't. I had made sure of that by keeping myself busy and moving on from the pain of betrayal, a pain that had subsided until now. Liam pushed my hair back and looked down at me with such love in his eyes, the same eyes that had looked at me when he told me he had feelings for someone else. I wondered if he would be here now, standing before me, if that other woman wasn't pregnant with someone else's child. Was I the consolation prize because things had not worked out?

'I love you, Claire,' he said.

Such words should have been a dream come true – I had Liam back and now we could go home and forget Paris, forget the entire nightmare. It wouldn't be easy but we could get through this; in time, maybe it would make us even stronger as a couple. That's what Aunty Sue had said about her marriage, that Uncle Tom having an affair was the best thing that could ever have happened to them. I had always thought that was just ridiculous, and yet here I was. Standing before my boyfriend, trying to find the good in this situation. But as the rain fell harder, his touch left me cold and that very same numbness started growing inside me once more.

I stepped out of his hold.

'Claire, what's wrong?'

I wrapped my arms across my chest, blinking away the drops of rain. 'Go home, Liam.'

'But you're coming with me,' he said, confused by the sudden change in my demeanour.

I shook my head. 'No.'

'So . . . what? You going to stay here forever? Don't be ridiculous! You can't afford it.'

'I'll manage.'

Liam sighed, running his hand through his hair in frustration. 'Look, I get it, you want to punish me, but you can do that in London. You can give me the silent treatment, make me sleep on the couch . . . we'll move and start again, do whatever it takes. Just come back with me.'

It was a speech motivated by anger, not love. He had gone from pleading to annoyed, like he always did. It was like I was seeing the real him, the one that had always been there, the one I chose to put up with.

But not any more.

Chapter Twenty-Nine

Why wasn't I crying?

Was this normal? I had ended it – I had turned Liam away on my own terms. I had made a life-changing decision. Shouldn't I have felt some kind of pain? As I caught my dripping reflection in the yellow mirror of the lift it occurred to me that my heart had been broken and it was still imperfect and bitter about the world. I had chosen to try to heal it, to not have it stepped on again. So the feeling was . . . freedom. I had liberated myself in a way I had never done before and I felt giddy.

Liam's eyes had burned with rage as he'd asked me a question that really caught my attention.

'Is it because of him?' He'd gestured with his head to the hotel.

When my mouth opened but no words followed, he'd taken my shocked silence as the only thing he needed to know. He'd grunted, shaking his head as he backed away.

'Have a nice life, Claire,' he'd said, before walking into the night.

And I had returned to the hotel.

The doors to the lift opened on the sixth floor. Lost in my thoughts I cared little that I was dripping a trail over the plush carpet. Liam had thought I was staying because of Louis Delarue. It was almost laughable. But more worrying was the way my insides twisted at the very thought of that he might be right. It had horrified me even as it excited me. Yep, I was definitely broken.

Before taking another sodden step my eyes landed on the open balcony window and a familiar shadow, lazily leaning in the doorway, watching the cityscape. He didn't look around, too fascinated by the outside world. I slowly made my way over to stand beside him, following his gaze to the golden light filtering from the apartment across the street: an opulent space filled with people laughing and drinking champagne as Madeleine Peyroux crooned 'Dance Me to the End of Love'. I yearned to be a part of that world instead of standing here, cold and wet in the shadows.

Then Louis tore his eyes from the view and turned to look at me. Despite the dampened air and the breeze that blew through the open door, I didn't feel cold any more.

He didn't ask me about Liam, or about my dishevelled state, his eyes simply slid over my body, his mouth twitching with amusement before he looked into my eyes and, in true Louis fashion, titled his head toward the apartment across the street.

'Do you want to join the party?' he asked.

Confused, I looked across the way. 'What? Gatecrash their party?' I asked in dismay, trying to imagine the likes of Louis Delarue trying to slip into a party undetected.

Louis laughed; it was short and abrupt, an unexpected sound with its joyous notes, but more unexpected than the laugh was his hand reaching for mine to twirl me to the music.

'Not exactly,' he said, before pulling me into his arms as he took the lead. There on the landing of the sixth floor in the shadows we gatecrashed the party across the street and I could feel my spirits lift, laughing as Louis spun me once more and then dramatically dipped me so quickly I feared he might drop me. He didn't, he was far too strong for that. Breathless, my heart raced as he helped me stand, his hand still looped around my waist as we shifted to the sway of a Mélanie Laurent melody.

We were in our own world – even the outburst of laughter from across the street did little to break the spell. I was so lost in Louis that I was having trouble remembering to breathe. Until my eyes lowered and I saw dampness spreading across his jacket.

'I'm getting your suit wet,' I said, trying to step away.

Louis held me in place. 'I don't care,' he said, but I did. I had already ruined an expensive suit of Louis's and I didn't want it to become a habit.

'Hang on, I'll take off my jacket,' I said, but instead of letting me go, Louis swept his hand up under the material of my shoulders and pushed the damp garment back, drawing it down. His hands touched my cold skin, causing gooseflesh to prickle. My jacket fell into a clump on the floor. I could feel his laboured breaths blowing down on me as I stared at his chest. A voice inside my head told me not to look up, *Whatever you do, don't open yourself up to this man, don't think about the way his hands are moving their way back up your arms, lifting your hands to his shoulders, anchoring you in place.* I swallowed, trying to still my heartbeat, trying not to be distracted by the intense musky tone of his aftershave and trying not lean into his warmth. But when he stood there, unmoving, I ignored my inner voice and slowly lifted my eyes, and the instant I did I knew I was in serious trouble.

He searched my face, and then glanced at my mouth so briefly I might have imagined it, and just as his head began to lower, something inside me snapped.

'*Bonne nuit!*' I said very loudly and a little frantically, jumping back and turning to scuttle down the hall to my room.

Chapter Thirty

I fumbled through my bag – it was infuriatingly deep and impossible to locate a room key in an emergency, and this was definitely an emergency. I glanced up the hall to see Louis casually approaching. *Shit, come on, come on.*

It was too late, he had arrived at his door grinning like the Cheshire cat as he swung his key around his finger. I didn't have the time or patience to pay any attention to him since, as I searched, my mind was screaming, *I nearly kissed Louis Delarue . . . holy shit, I NEARLY KISSED LOUIS DELARUE!*

I upended my bag, and lipstick, compact, passport, tissues, purse and coins went flying.

'You forgot this.'

Louis dangled my jacket in front of me as I crouched on the floor. The thought of how it had come to be off in the first place tinged my cheeks with pink as I grabbed it from his hand. Only then did I feel the lump in the pocket of my jacket and discovered the key I had been looking for. *Ugh!*

I shoved my jacket and the junk back into my bag, thinking I really needed to calm down. *Be cool, Claire, nothing happened.* I had enough sense to know the difference between a good idea and a bad one, and no matter how tempting it was to erase the memory of Liam with a frivolous, meaningless conquest, I knew that I was most definitely not that kind of girl. I couldn't let such a fantasy drive me in anyway, even if the very thought gave me an unexpected thrill. I stood, hooked my bag over my shoulder and looked directly at a very amused-looking Louis, leaning with his back against his door, getting his own kind of thrill out of knowing I was frantic and fumbling because he had made me so. He was just the kind of man to enjoy making those around him squirm. *Cocky bastard.*

I shoved the key into the lock.

'Are you always running from something?'

I paused, his words raising the hairs on the back of my neck, not because he managed to push my buttons like no other man, but because there was a definite element of truth to them. I had run from my mundane existence in Melbourne to follow a boy and his dreams halfway around the world, and now I was running from that life too. I wasn't that girl any more, but now I didn't know who I was. Maybe I was a girl who should take risks, act out and not think twice about the repercussions – it had gotten me to the sixth floor after all, and the night had not been a total disaster. If I remembered rightly, I had had a nice time, and even more so in the arms of a man . . . they just didn't happen to be Liam's.

I turned, meeting Louis's eyes across the hall. There was a new voice inside my head, a new feeling building in me – it wasn't one of fear, or caution: it was one of adrenalin and sheer, mind-numbing stupidity that saw me drop my bag and take three short steps to push him hard against the door, grab the lapels of his jacket and pull his mouth to mine. It took him only a second to recover from his shock and slip his arms around me, pulling me against him and kissing me so feverishly I thought I was going to lose my mind. I opened my mouth to him, moaning softly, my hand flying up to glide through the thick curls of his hair. He spun me around and my back slammed into the door, driving the air from my lungs. The action only made me more determined to bring him close to me. As if reading my mind, Louis scooped me up in his arms as if I weighed nothing more than a feather. I wrapped my legs around him, feeling the hard length of him grind against me with the most delicious friction. My hands found their way under his jacket, my nails digging into his back through the thin fabric of his shirt as he nipped playfully at the nape of my neck, tasting and sucking on my skin, groaning in approval as I clamped my legs tighter, moving against him.

'We shouldn't be doing this,' I breathed, my eyes closed as if to deny what was happening, that Louis was not hard and wedged between my thighs.

'You want me to stop?' he whispered into my ear, biting the lobe and making me gasp. He pushed his hips forward, just in the right place. I opened my eyes just as his head pulled back a little, looking at me as if asking permission.

'Don't you dare.'

Louis smiled, seemingly pleased by my fervour as he once again lowered his mouth to mine, this time more slowly. His tongue entered my mouth much more tenderly, teasing, deepening our kiss in a way that drove me mad – in the best possible way. This was exactly what I had needed, to forget about my ordinary life and just live in the moment, and if that involved being fucked up against a door in Paris, then that was what I would do. Shutting my mind completely off, I lowered my hand to where Louis's belt looped through his trousers, yanking it free to access his fly. It's amazing what you can achieve quickly when you really want something; apparently I was far more desperate for what was inside Louis's pants than what had been at the bottom of my handbag.

Just as I lowered the zip, Louis let go of my legs and I slid back down the door with a yelp of surprise. Had he changed his mind? But before I could even worry further, Louis had spun me around, placing the palms of my hands on the glossy paint of his door; his back pressed against me, burning through my dampened top, as he kissed my neck. I went to move my hand to his soft hair, but he gripped my wrist and guided it back against the door.

'Don't move,' he whispered in my ear; the feel of his hot breath against my skin making my insides twist. There was something so insanely hot about being exposed like this, between our two worlds, neither inviting the other into their bed – we were in between, touching, tasting, testing one another. Louis's French mutterings only served to make me burn more for him, and damn him, he bloody knew it too.

Louis's hands moved along my bare thighs, lifting the fabric of my skirt, gathering the material to expose my underwear, then following the lacy edge of the waistband around to touch the skin below my navel. My hands were placed firmly on the door, anchoring me in place when all my knees wanted to do was give way. Louis used his foot to make me stand wider, to open myself up to him. I dropped my head back into the crook of his neck, his heavy breathing in my ear matching my pained gasps as his hand dipped lower, stealing inside the thin fabric to slip his fingers inside, one and then another, pressing his way into the most intimate part of me, working me slowly, then more frantically.

'Louis,' I gasped, almost as a plea as I worked my hips against his hand.

His other hand peeled down the front of my top, and one of my breasts spilled into his palm. He cupped me, squeezing the aching bud that was already hard from the chill of my damp clothes. I craned my head back, kissing Louis so passionately as his hands worked, drawing me closer and closer to the edge, an edge there was no coming back from – not that I really wanted to.

'Do you think about me being inside you?' His words were strained, his accent so thick I could have come just by hearing it.

'Yes,' I cried, breaking the rules and letting my hand fall from the door to clamp onto his forearm, pushing him deeper into me.

'Do you like that?' He breathed out a laugh, moving faster. Harder.

'Oh God, yes.'

I could feel his hardness pressing against my rump; I wanted to touch him, taste him, take him inside me, do all manner of wicked things with this man, but I was paralysed by my own ecstasy, as I started to come hard, unable to hold in my cry as I gripped the door and Louis's arm, rocking into his rhythm and melting from the mind-blowing pleasure that rolled through every part of my body. Louis didn't tell me to be quiet, he whispered words of encouragement as I fell apart, so completely and so loudly on the safety of the sixth floor, all until we heard the lift ding and the sound of doors gliding open.

Chapter Thirty-One

Holy shit.

Diving to my door, straightening my clothes and wrestling with the key that was still in the lock, this time I had no trouble letting myself in. I managed a glance back to see Louis looping the last of his belt back into place, pulling his jacket together as he waved at whoever had stepped out of the lift. Closing my door, I fell back onto it, breathing heavily, frightened and reeling from what had been the biggest, most shattering orgasm of my life.

I heard the muffled voices out in the hall, eternally grateful that Louis was the one that had distracted the intruder. The person didn't stay long, apparently delivering a message, and their footsteps faded back down the hall. I stayed with my ear pressed to the door, lingering until I heard the lift.

Should I open the door? Was Louis still out in the hall, waiting for me to reappear? I hadn't heard his door close. But if I opened mine, what would he think? Would it be weird if I didn't say goodnight? Or at least have some kind of exchange with him – his tongue had just been in my mouth, and the man just released years of pent-up tension with only his masterful fingertips. I wasn't sure what the Michelin-star equivalent for orgasms was, but he deserved at least three stars for making me come so hard – I had all but forgotten my own name.

Just as I wondered what I should do, I saw a shift of shadow move against the strip of light beneath my door and I held my breath. My heart was in my throat, and I felt giddy at the very thought of hearing him knock. I placed my hand on the door, ready to rip it open and drag him into my room and my bed without a moment's hesitation. I wanted more, I wanted *him,* if only for the night – I could be damned by the consequences later. I watched the shadow remain in front of my door, pause for a long moment, until the unexpected happened: the footsteps moved away, taking the shadow with them, and I heard Louis's door close.

He. Didn't. Knock.

I blinked, confused and completely and utterly deflated, as I gingerly twisted the handle and opened my door a crack, peering out into the empty hall and fixing my gaze on the infamous door that, much to my amazement, didn't bear the evidence of claw marks in the white paint. Just thinking about it made my cheeks flush in mortification. The way I had moaned and begged for more, the way I was so wanton and at his mercy. Who the hell was I? I quickly closed the door, snipping the chain across and suddenly thankful that

he hadn't knocked – he was probably recognising the inter-
lude for what it was.

A diabolical mistake.

~

I stood at the kitchen sink, violently scrubbing the last of the
pots in the ultimate black mood. Turns out I really wasn't
the kind of girl who was mentally equipped to deal with hot,
heavy and casual hallway hook-ups. I wasn't the kind who sent
boyfriends packing and then danced with mere acquaintances
in the moonlight. Far from it. How was I ever going to face
him? Had London not meant the possibility of seeing Liam
I would have been half tempted to flee back there, but that
would probably be exactly what Louis would expect, and I had
a bit more pride than that. Although having worked through
breakfast and lunch without so much as spotting him, it
seemed that I was not actually the one doing the avoiding.

Tasks complete, I longed for a walk, to take advantage
of the blue skies and sunshine that would hopefully lift my
mood, but as soon as I passed a smiling Gaston and stepped
out to the kerb I saw Louis's Audi, unmoved from last night.
I went to ask Gaston if he had seen him today, but thought
better of it. We should all be rejoicing that the lion was still
in his den; hopefully he would be there for the rest of his
stay. If he aimed to hide from me for the rest of his time here,
maybe I really had taken one for the team. My anger pushed
me down the street, and then ironically I was angry at myself
for being angry; I really couldn't win. I needed to escape.

Everyone in Paris has their own little corner of paradise, so where would I look to discover some much-needed space?

Hello, Galeries Lafayette! My own piece of heaven was on Boulevard Haussmann on the 9th arrondissement.

I entered the perfume and cosmetic area only to be instantly dazzled by a huge monitor showing the beautiful Charlize Theron sashaying down a hall of mirrors at Versailles Palace, advertising Dior. Sometimes you just want an experience, and for me, winding my way through the shoppers, craning my neck, was definitely an experience. I stopped under the magnificent leadlight dome and I got out my phone to capture what was absolutely an Instagram moment. Was there any better feeling than experiencing something for free? And to be honest, it really had to be – after I'd made my one allowance to actual retail therapy of course. Going to the Chanel counter, I chose a lipstick in my favourite shade and a decadent mascara, pushing my credit card quickly across the counter to the chic shop assistant, not wanting to think of the currency conversion too much. She swiped the card and placed my purchase into a dainty bag. This was happiness, and I would remember this feeling, savour it until my credit card statement came.

I had to keep moving, pushing through the crowds, feeling the heat from the enclosed spaces and the intense, brightly lit counters that were acting like a solarium. I tied my hair back, feeling flushed and overwhelmed as I skimmed my eyes over all the beautiful things I couldn't afford, from every designer you could think of: Tiffany, Dior, Chanel, Louis Vuitton.

Ugh, Louis. I really didn't need to be reminded of that name; after all, I had come here to escape. The memory of him pinning me against his door flashed through my mind, and if I wasn't hot before, I was now. I had to get some air. As I climbed each level by escalator, so did the temperature. When I mercifully reached the roof terrace on the seventh floor, any trace of uncertainty or discomfort was wiped away the instant I took in the panoramic city views. This had to be by far the best city-gazing hot spot I had managed to stumble on. Views of the Eiffel Tower, the Opéra Garnier and Sacre Coeur: I couldn't think of a better way to recharge my spirit and my soul, with boulevards and Haussmannian architecture spreading out before me, dramatic cloud formations overhead, and uninterrupted people-watching. I blinked against the wind that cooled my heated skin.

Yeah, I think I'm going to be okay.

Despite my earlier black mood, I did funnily enough feel a spring in my step, a lightness in my body, but as I made my way back to Hotel Trocadéro, I had an unnerving sense of something sweeping over me, and as each step brought me closer to the hotel, my mood darkened. Despite all my efforts to brainwash myself, there was no use. When I thought about last night with Louis . . . I really wanted to do it again.

Chapter Thirty-Two

The Hotel Trocadéro was a madhouse.

The dreaded television crew that I was avoiding at all costs was setting up for 'before' shots of the hotel and conducting on-camera staff interviews. I could only hope that they had received the memo to avoid the grumpy Australian lurking in the shadows.

I narrowly dodged a tradesman who blindly swung around from the back door of his van holding large tins of paint. He was too busy arguing with another tradie in his native tongue to see me. I kind of wished I had taken the chance to clear my head more seriously, because if I was looking for ongoing peace I was not going to be getting it here. I went to stand beside Gaston, who held the door open and out of the way.

'And so it begins.' He grinned, clearly excited about all that was happening.

'And where exactly do they begin?' I asked.

'They are starting by refurbishing the rooms.'

Of course. It was a part of the Louis Delarue experience.

'I pick my uniform up tomorrow.' Gaston's smile broadened. Never before had I seen such excitement over a uniform – he was positively adorable.

'I can't wait to see it. I bet it will look amazing.'

'Oui, it will match the awnings,' Gaston said, pointing above us. I looked up, confused, then paused, barely believing that I hadn't even noticed.

In my absence, the sign and exterior awnings had been replaced with a rich, lush-looking navy blue signage and canvas. It was a perfect match to the uniforms that would be worn by the hotel staff, but more than that it was an idea I had briefly mentioned, one that had been met with a brooding stare and much disinterest.

'But how did—'

'Monsieur Delarue was on the phone all morning.'

So he really hadn't moved, I thought, glancing at his car; despite the ounce of smugness I felt over the awnings, I would take this opportunity to get out while the going was good.

'Well, I'll see you later,' I said, smiling at Gaston, readying myself to go into the hotel.

'Ah, pardon, Claire, Louis has asked for all staff to meet in the restaurant at three o'clock.'

I skidded to a halt on the tiled floor, closing my eyes in dread as I prayed I had just misheard him. I turned.

'What for?' I asked, checking my wristwatch, my heart starting to pound. 'That's in five minutes.'

'Oui, so you have made it in excellent time,' said Gaston, always with the silver lining.

'That's debatable,' I mumbled, turning to drag my feet reluctantly into the restaurant, where, sure enough, the staff were seated around a table, looking just as unenthused and edgy as whenever they were summoned by Lord Louis. I, of course, was dreading it for a whole other reason.

I reluctantly took my seat next to Cathy, who shrugged her shoulders as if to say, 'Don't ask me'.

Unlike the staff who were intimidated by Louis, my attitude was more a deep-seated mortification. Every time I closed my eyes, I remembered how he had kissed me, as if he needed my air, so urgent was his searing kiss, the slow yet intent delving of his fingers gliding over my skin, and the way he had whispered dirty promises into my ear as he slid my panties aside.

'Earth to Claire.' A hand waved in front of my face and I blinked out of my heated memories to see Cecile sitting across from me, smiling.

'Sorry, I was a million miles away.' *Or in this case, on the sixth floor.*

'Where's Gaspard?' asked Cathy. The chef was the only one unaccounted for.

Oh no, he hasn't quit, has he? I thought. It wouldn't be in the least bit surprising if he had.

'He's been in the kitchen all afternoon with Louis,' said Francois. We all turned to look at the kitchen door, our eyes narrowed. We sat silently, waiting for bloodcurdling screams from within.

'All afternoon?' I asked in disbelief.

'Oui,' added Francois.

'Has anyone checked to see they are still alive?' said Cathy, her eyes wide with alarm.

Gaston, catching the end of the conversation, pulled out a chair and sat down next to Cecile. 'If they are not out by ten past, we will go and investigate.'

I was growing impatient. I was certainly not fussed about whether Louis and Gaspard were in there chasing each other around with wooden spoons. I really just wanted to slip away; would Louis even notice if I were here or not? I would probably be doing him a favour: we'd avoid any awkward exchanges, especially in front of the rest of the staff.

'Do we know what this is even all about?' I asked, crossing my arms, my foot jigging impatiently.

Before anyone could answer, the kitchen door swung open and out Louis strode, dressed in his crisp white double-breasted chef's jacket. He came to stand at the head of the table, tall, proud, ever so confident, even when his eyes turned to me; there was absolutely no chink in his armour, unlike my flushed cheeks and nervous shifting.

'Welcome to Gaston's restaurant,' he said, clapping and rubbing his hands together with excitement. 'Today we will be revealing a new-and-improved menu, with a new signature dish whose purpose will be to drive people through the doors just for a taste.'

By now everyone had gone from slumped and dismayed to sitting straight in their seats, interested. I found myself leaning on my elbows, listening intently, as the aromatic smells from the kitchen drifted into the restaurant with the swinging of the door.

Louis moved over to the sideboard near the kitchen door and picked up a stack of what looked like one-page menus printed on quality cardboard.

'These are in draft-form only,' he said, moving around the table, handing each person a menu until he came to me.

'I don't know about you,' he said, with a boyish grin, 'but I really love tasting new things.'

I glanced around the room to see if anyone had noticed his taunt, but everyone was too busy reading over the new menu. I was too busy following Louis as he paced, thoughtfully waiting for everyone to look over the selections. There was a long, drawn-out silence, but once all eyes had raised expectantly, Louis finally stopped pacing.

'So, what do we all think? Based on that menu, do you think you would want to come back for more?' he asked, before turning to me expectantly. 'What do you think, Claire, would you be happy to come back for seconds?'

His none-too-subtle innuendo was not lost on me. 'Well, that all depends on how hungry I am.'

'Say you're starving.'

'Starving?'

'Oui.'

'Well, I am also a mood eater, so it would have to depend on if I was in the mood for what was on offer.'

Louis's eyes twinkled with devilish intent, and I wondered if what we had said had made any sense to the others. They seemed a bit unnerved by my honesty.

'I guess we will just have to make a menu that is too good to refuse then,' he mused, his eyes resting squarely on me, and it felt like we were the only ones in the room.

I smiled as I leant my elbows on the table and looked at him pointedly. 'Oui, chef!'

Louis ignored my sarcastic reply and turned his attention back to the group.

'Let us begin.'

I tried to keep my face neutral as I quickly read over the simple yet mouthwatering selections that were inscribed on the expensive light blue card: grilled oysters, onion soup with shallots and cheese crisps; roast red-wine chicken; Provençal vegetable bake, and dark chocolate pudding. It all looked good enough to eat, and that was exactly the plan as the door to the kitchen swung open and a very smug-looking Gaspard carried a large silver tray to the table.

'Grilled oysters with a parsley crumb,' he announced, placing them onto the table.

'Fresh oysters,' Louis countered.

We all leaned in to look at the beautiful dish, before glancing up at a beaming Gaspard. He raised his arms as if conducting an orchestra.

'Bon appetit.'

The feast rolled on from buttermilk lamb with toasted buckwheat and herb salad to tomato and lentil millefuiles served with a delicious locally produced cider. The atmosphere had changed from one of extreme tension to one of merriment and, dare I say, joy. Each tempting morsel delivered to our table was met with appreciation and much fanfare. Gaspard refused our help, wanting to keep an element of surprise, not so secretly revelling in our delighted oohs and aahs when he placed the next sample on the table.

When the tasting was finished, we had a group discussion on what we liked and what we thought would build a well-rounded seasonal menu. For the first time, it felt like we were actually a team making group decisions. It occurred to me that Louis had chosen to stand, never to sit with us, an ever-watchful eye on our reactions and our conversation about his food selections. I could tell he was just as excited by our enthusiasm, I could see it in his eyes, although he had a better way of masking his emotions.

Louis finally gestured for Gaspard to join us at the table, while he leant against the breakfast buffet cabinet with his arms crossed, looking every bit the serious businessman.

'This will put us on the map,' said Cecile, beaming.

'I never thought I would be so excited about a carrot tarte tatin.' Cathy laughed.

Gaston slapped Gaspard on the shoulder. 'What do you think, Gaspard, can you pull it off when Louis goes home?'

'Of course, I have Francois; we will dominate the world.'

'Well, the kitchen anyway,' added Francois coyly.

'Nonsense, people will know our names.' Gaspard saluted Francois with his glass; I had never seen him so inspired. And I saw it for exactly what it was: Louis had torn down Gaspard to build him back up again, to inspire him to do better, and it had worked. I had believed Louis was bullying people for his own ego, but now I saw that it wasn't like that. He had run the kitchen at Noire like a well-oiled machine, he had garnered people's respect, and by doing so had built an empire. I had seen him in a completely new light, which kind of scared me; I really didn't need Louis to appear more attractive to me than he already was. That in itself was a very dangerous thing.

Sipping on my cider, I stole a glance at Louis, but somewhere between Gaspard joining the table and the banter, Louis had left us, the swinging kitchen door the only sign of his exit. I took a minute to think of an appropriate excuse to follow, considering myself a bit of genius as I casually started collecting the empty dishes.

'Let me help,' Cathy said.

'No, no, sit back, I've got this,' I insisted, glad that it didn't take too much to convince her to settle in her seat as I stacked the chocolate-smeared plates.

I pushed my back against the door and spun into the kitchen.

'Whoa!'

The menu was not the only thing that had been overhauled. The kitchen had also taken on a new look: gone were the battered old pots and cluttered utensil holders filling up the bench space. Despite the cooking that had just taken place, the kitchen had never looked cleaner. I didn't fool myself into thinking that Louis was back in the kitchen doing dishes – I am pretty sure that award-winning chefs didn't do their own dishes – but the woman elbow deep in soap suds took me somewhat by surprise.

'Oh, hello.'

The woman had short-cropped black hair and pretty heart-shaped face. She smiled, nodding her head. 'Bonjour.'

I walked over, feeling almost bad that I was adding to her pile as I placed down the plates next to her. 'I, um, is Louis here?'

The woman pointed to the back door; I wasn't sure if she even spoke English, but the finger point was pretty universal.

'Merci.' I smiled, feeling kind of foolish; it wasn't as though he could be many places back here – the cool room and the tiny back courtyard were pretty much it.

As I neared the back door I stopped, hearing voices from beyond – *Louis was not alone*. Now was not the time to talk to him, not that I exactly knew what had brought me back here, or what I had to say. 'Thanks for the screaming orgasm in the hallway' didn't seem appropriate.

Oh God. I cringed at the thought of what I had done. Was it possible to be mortified and yet still not regret something?

I backed away from the door, turning to see the watchful woman smiling at me.

'I'll catch up with him later,' I said casually. The woman laughed and shrugged, as if to say, 'I have no idea what you are talking about'.

Well, that makes two of us.

I was nearly home free when I heard the slamming of the screen door.

Shit.

'I was just bringing in some dirty dishes,' I said a bit too quickly, turning to see Louis and Jean-Pierre standing near the back door.

Jean-Pierre grinned. 'Bonjour, Claire.'

'Jean-Pierre, what are you doing here?' I asked, genuinely happy to see him.

He waved around at the tiny kitchen. 'You don't think Louis could manage all this on his own, do you?'

'I'm sure he's nothing without you,' I joked.

Louis cocked his brow. 'I am standing right here,' he said incredulously; it was a rare moment of the light-hearted joking I had seen between him and Jean-Pierre at Noire. I kind of hoped that Jean-Pierre could stay forever.

'Did you approve of the menu changes?' asked Jean-Pierre.

'It's amazing, but I don't think I could eat another thing.'

'Well, that's a shame; you won't be able to fit in Louis's world-class maçarons.'

My eyes widened. 'You make macarons?'

'Only the best,' he humbly confessed, then shrugged in that arrogant way of his.

It was like they had discovered my secret weakness and were testing me: there was always room for macarons. I adored the bite-sized meringues filled with ganache or buttercream. Damn the man if he didn't just make himself even more appealing to me.

'Are you going to make them now?' I asked, looking around for evidence of a baking session, hoping to see anything – egg whites, icing sugar, ground almonds, food colouring – anything.

'Not today. I have a few things to attend to,' he said, making my heart sink, when in all honesty I should have been relieved.

'Oh, okay, well, don't forget me when you do,' I said, looking at Louis for a few seconds, as if committing those eyes to memory, mostly because I loved the way they were looking at me: hard, and filled with hidden intent. It was the same way he had looked at me when he'd danced with me on the sixth-floor landing. I had thought that maybe I had imagined the change since he had taken me to Noire, but surely I hadn't; surely I wasn't imagining the tension between us now. I hoped I wasn't.

Louis came and stood next to me and peered through the restaurant window, a small smile on his face. Any other man would have asked if I had enjoyed the food, or if I thought the others had, but Louis seemed so self-assured in all that he did that he'd never need to ask for anyone's reassurance. He knew that it was good. Still, standing next to him, silence settling in the kitchen, I felt compelled to say something.

'The food really is lovely, Louis.'

His head turned, eyes boring into me as if he had mistaken what I had said. It did feel rather intimate and foreign to call him Louis, it was something I didn't think I had done before – at least, without being influenced by my anger. I knew I certainly hadn't ever given him a real compliment.

'You liked it?' he asked, actually asked, which made me smile; maybe he did need reassurance after all.

'It was my second favourite discovery of today.'

He frowned, troubled by what could have been better than his food. Then he shifted warily, perhaps worried that I had meant something else, something that wasn't exactly appropriate to mention in front of company. He glanced at Jean-Pierre and the dishwashing woman.

I smiled widely, loving the vulnerability in him, basking in the glory of making him uneasy for once. I couldn't help myself: I stepped forward without taking my eyes from his as I lowered my voice just to make him lean in a little.

'Those awnings made my day,' I said.

Louis laughed. He actually laughed. It was loud enough to get the attention of the staff in the restaurant. It was such a foreign sound.

He nodded his head. 'It was a good idea of mine, wasn't it?' he conceded.

I smiled. 'Ha! You can thank me later.'

Louis's brows rose into his hairline and it suddenly occurred to me how suggestive that must have sounded. 'In macarons,' I added, pushing my way into the restaurant with a big goofy grin and a little extra swagger in my hips.

Chapter Thirty-Three

The jig was up. My stint in the witness protection program in Paris was completely blown. I had known it the minute I received a panicked, all-capital email from my mother. Not that the capital letters were an indication of anything other than her not knowing how to turn the caps-lock button off – she was forever writing in shouty block letters – but who knows, maybe this time she meant it?

I JUST GOT OFF THE PHONE TO LIAM. ARE YOU ALL RIGHT? HE SAYS YOU HAVE BEEN IN PARIS ALL THIS TIME? WHY DIDN'T YOU TELL ME? PLEASE GIVE ME A CALL. I DON'T CARE WHAT TIME IT IS, LET ME KNOW YOU ARE OKAY. ARE YOU COMING HOME?

Every single email from my mum signed off with 'Are you coming home?' Crisis or not, it was always her hope that one day the answer would be yes – and it would some day, just not today. Trust Liam to run to my family, now that he could officially play the whole 'she dumped me' card. I had no doubt he hadn't gone into full detail about how I came to be in Paris, after all, he would play the victim for a little while longer. I decided to let him have his time; while they were fawning over him, they were more likely to leave me alone. I had hoped that a cheerful postcard from Paris would suffice, but as it turned out I was going to have to be a bit more diplomatic a lot sooner.

> *Hey Mum,*
> *Please don't worry, everything is fine. I am staying on in Paris because I have been given a tremendous opportunity too good to refuse. I didn't want to go into too much detail early on in case it didn't work out, but I am really enjoying my time here.*

I felt a strong urge to beg for funds like I was a teenager heading to a Blue Light Disco, but my twenty-five-year-old ego thought better of it. I really had to go talk to Cecile about my employment here; free board thus far had been awesome, but I hadn't been keeping stock of the minibar items I had been devouring. I mean, I was only human.

I signed off the email, hit send and closed my laptop, flinging myself back onto the bed, wondering what to do. With every noise I imagined I heard in the hall I craned my neck to listen more intently, but it was always nothing. I lay there, staring up at the ceiling, imagining what I might say to Louis if we just happened to bump into one another in the hall or the lift. It always ended up as a hot-and-heavy fantasy where there wasn't exactly that much talking. A new tension built inside me.

I cannot have these thoughts about Louis – I simply cannot! I grabbed at my pillow, shoving it over my face so as to muffle my screams of frustration.

It had been just so much easier when I was hating him, when he wasn't showing evidence of being a human being; when he didn't look at me the way he did now: a look that said that he was thinking about dirty things too. That was of no help whatsoever, neither was hearing the distant workings of the lift.

I pushed myself onto my elbows to listen more intently, and sure enough, I heard footsteps coming down the hall. My heart began to race as I jumped off the bed and padded barefoot to my door, plastering my ear to the cool, glossy surface to better make out the sounds from outside. Sure enough, the shadow appeared under my door again, a definite giveaway that not only was someone lingering outside in the hall, but they were doing it close to my door.

Oh my God, he is standing right there.

And just as I tried to keep my breaths even and silent, a loud thud sounded on the door, vibrating at my temple, causing me to jump back in fright.

Oh God, I wasn't prepared for this, dressed in my shorts and a baggy T; my hair was a mess, pinned up in a bun, and my face was makeup free. I was definitely not prepared for this.

'Just a minute,' I yelled, trying to keep my voice from sounding panicked as I quickly ran into the bathroom, yanking my hair painfully out of my bun and brushing the knots out. *Ouch, ouch, ouch.*

I had no time for much else except the light dab of some lip gloss and a spray and pirouette of Chanel Coco. I shoved my messy clothes and shoes into the cupboard and made my way back to the door.

'Coming,' I sing-songed, allowing myself a small moment of calm before unlocking and opening the door so quickly my hair whooshed backward.

'Bonjour!' I announced with a big smile, only for it to slide right off my face. Absolutely no one was there. I frowned as I ducked my head into the long, empty hall. Surely I hadn't imagined it – I'd felt the vibration of the knock against my head, and there is no way I had imagined that. And then before I could really begin to worry about my sanity my toe brushed against something and my eyes lowered to a small mint-green bag on the carpet. 'What the . . .'

I tentatively bent to pick up the elegant paper bag only to see exactly what it was. I grinned from ear to ear as I read the name across the bag. *Laduree,* only the most-loved and best-known seller of macarons in Paris.

I felt butterflies stir in my belly as I took a small card from the bag.

Let this be your favourite thing of today (until you try mine).

L

I took out the small floral box and squealed with delight when I opened it. Inside was a gorgeous rainbow treasure, and even as I eyed the delicious morsels of beauty, taking the raspberry macaron and biting into the light, slightly chewy yumminess, I couldn't help but think how wrong Louis was. Because my favourite part of the last twenty-four hours wasn't the awnings or the food, or the amazingly thoughtful macarons at my door.

It was actually none of those things, because hands down, my most favourite experience had been kissing him.

Chapter Thirty-Four

My hands covered my face, shielding my eyes from the screen. It was the easiest way to confess my sins, and aside from hearing my sister's audible gasp, I really didn't need to visualise Sammi's horrified expression. Still, I peeked through my fingers and sure enough, there she was on my laptop screen, her mouth agape, her head slowly shaking.

I lowered my hands, grabbing the pillow and hugging it to my chest like a small child as I winced. 'I know, I *know*.'

It took a little while for Sammi to gain her composure, tucking a strand of her long brown hair behind her ear. 'You know, when I said apologise, I actually meant *say* it, not dry hump him in a hotel hallway.'

I shoved the pillow over my face. 'I know!' I screamed, before dropping the pillow in my lap. 'It was just, you know, the rain, and the moonlight, the music, the dancing,' I explained. I hadn't stood a chance.

Sammi pouted. 'Yeah, curse Paris and all that romantic, moody lighting and magical ambience.' Her words dripped with sarcasm; even I had to admit this was pretty much a first-world problem.

'I was vulnerable,' I added, trying to build my case.

'And confused.'

'Yes!'

'And a little fragile.'

I nodded. 'Absolutely.'

'And horny.'

'Ye—What?!'

'Really, really horny.'

'Shut up!'

'Hey, you're only human – when Louis DelaHubba-Hubba rings the dinner bell, you come a-running.'

'Why do I tell you anything?'

'Because you want someone to tell you it's okay . . . and you really want permission to do it again.' Sammi grinned.

'I don't need your permission.'

'Well, you're in luck because . . . permission granted.' Sammi saluted like I was a brave soldier about to go into battle. 'You know, I think it would be really cool to have a world-famous chef as a brother-in-law. Think of all the family events he could cater – no more Mum's devilled eggs.'

We both shuddered at the memory of a classic Mum barbecue.

'He's a celebrity chef, Sammi, not a cater waiter.'

'A chef: yes; a celebrity: not so much. But, hey, you might be just what his ratings need!'

'Ratings?'

'God, how are you not up on this? Yeah, so, the word on the street – and by "street" I mean *Who* – is that *Renovation or Detonation* might be detonated. Kaput. No more. Apparently the ratings are dead in the water because Louis is too much of an enigma, or something. Doesn't engage with his fans, doesn't connect. Although, it sounds like he connected with you alright. Connected right on the—'

'Sammi!'

'Seriously, though, Claire, just live a little. You're in Paris. Walk in the rain, dance in the moonlight, kiss a sexy Frenchman; just promise me, *promise me*, you will leave there with no regrets.'

Against my better instinct my mouth twisted in amusement.

Sammi placed her hand on her heart. 'Now repeat after me.'

I rolled my eyes and mirrored her actions.

She cleared her throat. 'I, Claire Shorten.'

I laughed. 'I, Claire Shorten.'

'Will live each day as if it's my last.'

'Will live each day as if it's my last.'

'With not one tear shed, or one thought given to douchebag ex-boyfriends.'

'With not one tear shed, or one thought given to douchebag ex-boyfriends.'

'And I will enthusiastically accept all sexual advances from any men called Louis.'

I shook my head, giggling like I had when we were teenagers sharing a bedroom. 'You are mad!'

'Mad, and never wrong.'

'No, of course not,' I scoffed.

'Hey, I never liked Liam.'

I sighed. 'Yeah, well, that's true.'

'I mean, he had a cat, and pot plants . . . weird.' Sammi shuddered.

'Okay, Judgy McJudger from Judgement town, I'm going before the sun sets,' I said.

'Oh, oui, oui, show me what you're wearing.' Sammi clapped with excitement.

'Okay,' I said, picking up my laptop and placing it on the desk, then shimmying backward across the room and giving a twirl.

'What do you think?'

'Ooh la la, I love that skirt.'

I smoothed over the layered pastel pink fabric, before straightening the bow at my waist. 'It's rather fabulous.' I smiled, admiring the flow of the material that stopped just above my knees.

'You totally look like a local.'

'Right?' I swayed side to side, revelling in the swishing sound of the material.

'So, before you go, it would be remiss of me not to ask, because you know what Mum's like.'

I sat on the end of the bed, slipping on my ballet flats, knowing exactly where she was going with this.

'When are you coming home?'

I laughed at the predictability of the question. 'Tell her soon,' I said. 'First, I have to make sure I don't leave here with any regrets.' I gave Sammi a pointed look.

'Yes!' Sammi lifted her arms triumphantly. 'Vive la France.'

I breathed out a laugh. 'Goodbye, Sammi,' I said, pushing the laptop shut. 'Bloody lunatic.'

~

Maybe it was the sisterly pep talk, but I was feeling extra good as I double checked my hair in the reflected interior of the lift, pushing it over my shoulder. Reaching for my turquoise clutch, I searched for my lippy, checking it was the right shade. There were two things I could not face a day in Paris without: my 426 Roussy Chanel lipstick – or my 112 Temeraire Chanel lippy for night. A girl had to be prepared, I thought, gliding the silky pink stick along my bottom lip and pressing my lips together. Now I was ready, pushing the lid onto the tube just before the lift jolted violently to a stop. I glared up at the numbers, annoyed that someone was about to get on at level four, delaying me from my purpose.

I stepped aside, allowing room in the small space for the extra traveller. The door opened, assaulting me with light and the sound of drills, voices and chaos, but worse than all the loud drama was the fact I was confronted with the sight of Louis instructing a tradesman in French. He turned to step forward, and as his gaze landed on me, he placed his hand on the door to prevent it from shutting.

He liked what he saw, I could see it in the sparkle of his eyes as they landed on the pink bow at my waist. I stuck out my chin in a silent challenge, readying myself for him to say something suggestive about unwrapping his present, or a compliment of some kind, but instead he said, 'You look like a strawberry macaron.'

'What is it with you and macarons?' I said, jabbing the button to make the doors close.

He quickly stepped inside, laughing at my willingness to crush him. 'I take it you got the delivery, then?'

'I did, thank you,' I said, keeping my eyes on the floor numbers above the door, trying for the whole ice queen thing, not sure I was pulling it off.

'Where are you off to?' he asked.

'To get changed,' I deadpanned.

Louis breathed out a laugh. 'Always so serious.' He had his hands in his pockets, his head tilted to the side, looking over my attire again. 'Did you ever think that macarons are sweet, and beautiful?'

I looked at him. *Was he calling me beautiful?*

'You mean I don't look fat?'

Louis shook his head, as if he seriously didn't know what to do with me, then he bent to speak into my ear. 'What I meant is, you look good enough to taste.'

I swallowed, the feel of him so close to me, the heat from his body, the smell of him, I suddenly wanted to press the stop button on the lift so he could do exactly that. Damn him and his bloody sexy accent; I swear he could recite a shopping list to me and it would be a turn-on.

I cleared my throat, stepping to the side in the very limited space. 'Yes, well, I'm sure once is enough,' I said, hoping he'd rise to the bait, knowing there was no conviction in my words.

And before he could answer, the lift doors opened and I was out, drawing in a deep breath of fresh air to still my nerves.

Cecile looked up from her desk, her eyes brightening when she saw me. 'Oh, Claire, you look lovely!' she said.

I was about to respond when Louis joined me. 'Careful, Cecile, some people don't know how to take a compliment,' he warned.

'That's rich coming from someone who can't accept an apology,' I said incredulously.

Louis turned to face me. 'Why, Claire, are you offering me an apology?'

I shook my head. 'Like I said, once is enough for everything.'

Louis's eyes darkened, a wolfish smirk appearing on his face. 'Everything?'

'Everything,' I said, despite the fact my heart spiked its betrayal.

I could feel Cecile's eyes shifting between us, like she was watching some kind of raging tennis tournament.

'What are you doing now?' he asked, all hint of humour gone; the business-minded Louis was asking.

'Well, I was going to see if Gaspard and Francois needed me to help them with anything in the kitchen,' I lied. I had no intention of telling him I was off sightseeing, no doubt the workaholic in him would not approve of such luxury.

Louis rubbed the back of his neck. 'Well, good luck with that,' he said, spinning on his heel and heading for the hotel entrance.

'What's that supposed to mean?' I asked Cecile.

She smiled weakly, pointing over my shoulder with the pen she held; I turned to follow her eye line.

'You have got to be kidding me.'

Louis had completely shut down the kitchen – a large black tarp cordoned off the restaurant. I stood there, my head tilted thoughtfully, ever so tempted to pull back the tarp and sneak a peek; renovations had never been more exciting.

'Good luck keeping Gaspard away from this,' I murmured.

Cecile came to stand beside me. 'Well, that's where Louis has thought of everything.'

'Oh?'

'He has sent the kitchen staff to Noire for the week.'

'*Noire?*'

'Oui, to give them a chance to perfect their menu.'

'And what am I, chopped liver?'

She frowned as if she wasn't sure what I meant, but then she spoke and I knew she understood.

'I asked Louis if you wanted to go, but he said not to disturb you.'

'Oh, really?' I said, folding my arms, looking past her to where Louis stood out the front speaking to Gaston.

'To be honest, I thought you would have been relieved not to have to deal with Louis any more.'

It was a fair assumption; I had been less than thrilled about being thrown into the deep end as a kind of hostage negotiator, but ever since the bonding luncheon it was clear they didn't need me, and I didn't so much feel relief but a certain sense of sadness. I knew I wasn't a typical member of staff. I did the dishes, served coffee and juice through lunch, and delivered meals, but I felt like a complete phony, and as much as Cecile and Gaston and the kitchen crew made me feel like one of them, I knew Louis saw straight through me. That was, no doubt, why he wouldn't waste his money on fitting me with a uniform.

'But are you okay with that? I am more than happy to help – there are some pretty drastic changes going on, and it must be pretty overwhelming.'

Cecile smiled thoughtfully. 'It is, but for the first time in, well, forever, I feel like there has been a fire lit inside me. That I have been shown what is possible, and I have never felt so alive.'

I saw it in Cecile's eyes, a shimmering excitement I could never begrudge her.

'Well, for as long as I'm here you can call on me any time, I'm always happy to help.'

'And you are more than welcome to stay.'

I smiled; Cecile was sweet but not even I could push the friendship. 'That is very kind of you, but I'll be handing back the keys to the sixth floor very soon. You have been more than generous to me at a time when I needed it the most.'

'Claire, you stay as long as you want.'

'Well, you might want to run it by the owners before you go putting up Aussie tourists on the top floor.'

Cecile studied me as if she was waiting for me to say that I was kidding, but I was serious: no good could come of her boarding jilted, homeless tourists like me.

She broke into a broad smile. 'Claire . . . I am the owner.'

'What?'

'Well, my parents are, but I manage it as my own – they retired long ago.'

'Are you for real?'

'I was so desperate to make this hotel great again.'

'Cue Louis Delarue.'

'Crazy, huh?'

I shook my head, the fire that I saw in Cecile's eyes held a whole new meaning and I was seeing her in a completely new light. 'I'd say more like genius!'

Cecile straightened with pride, a new kind of confidence lifting her. And then I remembered, sometimes people just needed to be given permission that it was okay to take a risk, to throw caution to the wind and have no regrets.

I placed my hands on Cecile's shoulders. 'No matter where I am, kitchen or customer, I will do everything in my power to help this be the most amazing relaunch of Hotel Trocadéro you could ever hope for.'

'People are going to know our name.'

I smiled like the Cheshire Cat. 'Yes. Yes, they will.'

Chapter Thirty-Five

There's nothing more infuriating than having to chase after someone, and having to chase after someone with Louis's long strides, well, that was damn near impossible.

'Don't make me run!' I shouted, causing him to stop so suddenly I had trouble preventing myself from slamming into his back.

He sighed. 'What do you want, Claire?'

'I just wanted to – wait, where's your car?' I looked behind me, gaze trailing up the street to the front of the hotel where Louis's black Audi was usually parked. I turned back to him. 'You're walking?'

'I walk,' he said defensively.

I blinked. 'But where are you going?'

'To get some peace.'

'Oh, okay . . . can I come?'

Louis ran his hand through his hair in frustration.

'You asked me once, remember? To go for a walk.'

'Like a wise woman said, "Once is enough for everything."'

Okay, come on, Claire, turn on that cutesy charm I know you are capable of.

I glanced down coyly for a moment, biting my lip, before looking up at him from under my lowered eyelids. 'Everything?' I murmured.

Louis's eyes darkened, infused with a smouldering intent that had me feeling giddy, because it was a look I recognised. He stepped forward and lowered his head as if to whisper something in my ear. I kind of hoped that it would be something dirty and French, but he simply said, 'Everything,' before pulling away and walking down the street.

'God damn it, Louis!' I shouted, stamping my feet like a petulant child and waiting only seconds before picking up the hem of my skirt and beginning to chase him again.

Try as you might, you're not going to get away from me that easily, Louis Delarue.

~

In the end I followed Louis Delarue all the way to Café Du Trocadéro, where I sat with him at an outside table. The blisters on my feet aside, I was so glad that I had. Louis and I silently gazed at the Eiffel Tower against the background of a grey sky turning to pink. Well, I was gazing at Louis's head, which was buried in a menu. I couldn't believe it. *Forever the chef.*

'Do you still hate the view?' he asked, not looking up from his page.

'I never hated it! How could you, it's just so – well, look at it.'

Louis lifted his head from the menu, but remained silent, and I wondered if he looked at his surroundings like I did; did he see Paris for the magic it was?

'So you were saying?' he prompted.

I faced Louis, resting my elbows on the table so I could make eye contact with him. 'I heard about your ratings and I have an idea.'

He stared at me, not an ounce of excitement registering at my announcement. This was not going to be the easiest sell.

'You need to get with it, Louis.'

This piqued his interest; he turned to me, folding his arms across his chest.

'People don't want to wait for the next six-part series to come out in order to find out what's going on in your world. We are living in a downloadable generation – you have to give people what they want and you have to give it to them every day. Two, three, four times a day if need be.'

'Sounds exhausting,' Louis said.

I rolled my eyes. 'Get your mind out of the gutter, Delarue.'

Louis laughed, and the little outburst gave me hope, so I continued.

'Now, you're probably not going to like any of this, but sometimes it's a necessary evil, and I think that now, with the rejuvenation of Hotel Trocadéro, it is the best time to launch into a new phase.'

'Okay, you're scaring me.'

I stilled myself, linking my hands together and calmly resting them on the table. 'Facebook.'

'No.'

'Instagram.'

'Not going to happen.'

'Tumblr.'

'Whatever it is, no.'

'Twitter.'

'No fucking way.'

'Oh my god, you are such a dinosaur!'

'I like my privacy.'

'Oh, don't give me that shit; how many cooking shows, guest judging spots and reality TV shows do you do? You probably have your face on lunchboxes.'

'And I don't have time for anything else.'

'Make time. It's not just about you, it's for the good of the hotel too.'

'No.'

'I'll help you.'

Louis scoffed.

'You are such a child,' I said.

'I am not, times infinity, no returns.'

I stood up, scooping up my bag and pushing my chair aside.

Louis sighed. 'Where are you going?'

I made it barely three steps before spinning around and marching back to glare down at him.

'You are so incredibly selfish.'

'Selfish?'

'Oui, selfish. Cecile is the most caring, hardworking, good-hearted person I have ever met in my life. She has trusted you to tear apart her world and put it back together again, which is all fine and good but sometimes it takes more than money and an ego to give it your all, and most of the time I don't think you even give a shit about anyone or anything except yourself.'

I could tell I'd hit a nerve as soon as the words left my mouth, but I didn't regret it. He was running away, doing the exact same thing he had accused me of, except there was a very clear difference: I wasn't running, not any more. I was fighting for my place in this strange world, among a group of misfits where I still didn't belong, but I would see it through for as long as it took. In the span of a few minutes I had gone from being in awe of Louis, to realising he wasn't the man I thought he was at all.

He threw his napkin on the table and stood, glowering at me so hard I really wanted to step back, but I held my ground.

'I know more about this hotel than you could ever imagine. I have studied this hotel, dreamt about this hotel, poured money, my passion and my soul into this hotel, and what have you done? Besides nearly me against a door—'

Louis's words cut off as I slapped him across the face, so hard and so fast I shocked myself. I stood with my hand throbbing and my mouth agape. I wanted to be strong, but the tears of fury welled and threatened to flow the instant Louis's anguished eyes locked with mine.

I broke away from them, suddenly aware of the staring audience around us. I'd been so lost in the throes of anger it had never even occurred to me we were in public. I was mortified. I had to get out of there, and before I could even bring myself to look at Louis again, I did the very thing I had accused Louis of.

I ran away.

Chapter Thirty-Six

I pressed my knee on the top of my suitcase, trying to edge the zipper closed, giving it one last violent yank, only to hear the zip split.

'Oh no, no, no!' I started to cry, slumping to the floor and looking at the hopeless sight before me. There had been something strangely comforting about packing my bag, like I was shoving my world into it and setting it by the door, knowing that I could just roll away. Unless the fucking zip broke.

So much for an easy escape.

There was a solid knock on the door and a new hope rose inside me. Gaston was here to collect my bags and he would know of a solution. I really just had to calm down, I thought, taking in a deep breath and wiping my eyes. I would be out of here soon enough.

But after unlocking the door, I opened it to someone who was very much not Gaston.

'You're leaving,' Cecile said, more as an accusation than a question.

I sighed, leaving the door open and walking back into the room, waiting for her to follow. 'I have to go home,' I said, hoping she would just leave it at that.

'Why, has something happened?'

It was then I realised I didn't really have an answer for her, nothing that would be acceptable. What was I to say? 'I had a fight with Louis'? Even inside my head it seemed lame. So I tried with the truth, of sorts.

'I just think it's time to move on.'

'But what about the reveal, you have to stay for that, surely?'

My chest tightened at the thought of not being here for that, of not being able to see the look on everyone's faces as the black curtain was dropped, or not tasting the culinary delights made by a bunch of once-upon-a-time misfits in a formerly cramped, manky kitchen. It broke my heart to miss it, but I was tired, and being here wasn't healing me as I'd hoped it would. If I stayed, there was the chance that I would succumb to the likes of Louis, even though I had pretty much cemented the chances of him not wanting anything to do with me. And I knew that if I stayed he'd probably never speak to me again and that was too big a rejection to bear.

I was doing the rejecting first.

Cecile stepped forward. 'Can you at least wait until morning – sleep on it? And if you still feel the same way tomorrow, then go.'

I knew what she said was reasonable, but as I stood in my spacious apartment, I felt as if the walls were closing in on me.

'Besides,' she continued, 'everyone would be so upset if they weren't able to say goodbye to you properly.'

Yeah, well, almost everyone.

And just like I had conjured him up out of my imagination, Louis appeared in the doorway behind Cecile, looking serious and brooding. He never failed to make my stomach flip whenever his eyes connected with mine.

If I felt unnerved, then Cecile seemed damn right awkward. The tension between Louis and I was so thick, and she was standing right in the middle of it. She may have had no idea about the specifics but I think she was quickly catching on to the reasoning behind my decision.

'I just saw Gaston in the lift, he said he was coming to get your bags, but I said that he must be mistaken, Claire Shorten doesn't run away from a challenge,' he said, sauntering through the door and sitting on the edge of my bed.

He was the very reason I was running away. He was the biggest challenge of all.

'Claire is leaving in the morning,' Cecile blurted. My eyes bugged out at her as I tried to telepathically tell her to shut up.

Louis's mood darkened, his attention shifting to me, silently daring me to say it was true.

'Well, I better go tell Gaston what's going on,' said Cecile, eager to leave us to ourselves.

I really wished she wouldn't, but all too soon Cecile had made her way out the door, closing it behind her. The delicate click of it shutting sounded painfully loud.

The silence was broken by the sound of Louis rubbing the stubble on his jaw thoughtfully. 'I must say, you have one hell of a right hook,' he quipped. The acknowledgement almost made me feel better . . . almost.

'Well, even though you deserved it, I shouldn't have hit you, that was wrong.'

'Apology accepted.'

'Oh, I'm not sorry.'

Louis crossed his arms and looked up at me with a devious glint in his eyes. It was hard to believe that this was the man I had been screaming at only an hour before. It felt like this was always how we interacted: fight, fuck and flirt – usually minus the middle part – and then repeat. I swallowed, thinking about what came after fight, and the fact he was sitting on the edge of my bed.

'Well, I have to get up early in the morning so . . .'

'Oh, that's right, to head back to London,' he said, but there was nothing sincere in his words; if anything, he was mocking the shit out of me. Maybe a matching slap to the other side of his face might do him some good. 'You look at me like you want to do bad things to me,' he said.

'Well, don't get too excited, they're not the bad things you're thinking of.'

Louis laughed, then stood and approached me. I stepped back, only for my backside to hit the desk, leaving me no escape. He stopped before me, looking down on me, all traces of humour gone.

'And what am I thinking?'

'You're thinking of torturing me for a little longer, when I really need to go to bed.'

'Yeah, well, what's the saying? Fight or flight?'

I gripped the edge of the desk to stop my hands from trembling. 'If you tell me I am running away, I swear to—'

'I know you're not running away, well, not running away from here, anyway.' He looked up to the ceiling as if to indicate that he meant the hotel. 'But you are running away from something,' he said, stepping closer, his legs brushing against my knees. 'You're running away from me.'

He examined my face as if he was trying to unlock the mysteries of the universe. And the worst thing was, he wasn't that far from cracking the code – when he had voiced exactly what I was running from, my eyes had snapped up, giving myself away.

'Are you afraid of what I might take?' he asked, his thumb brushing my bottom lip.

Shaking my head ever so slightly, I swallowed my tears, cursing my weakness. 'I'm afraid of what you might give.'

Louis smiled. 'Don't be afraid of that.'

I could feel the rawness inside me, my emotions barely contained. This man caused a definite weakness in me. I could feel it in the way my body betrayed me, reacted to him, as his hands skimmed my thighs.

I swallowed, trying to keep my voice even. 'I'm leaving in the morning.'

Louis put his mouth to my shoulder, gently pressing one kiss, then another on my neck before straightening, his lips so close to mine.

'Well, we better make sure it's a goodbye you will never forget then,' he whispered.

I put my hand against his chest, and my eyes flicked to the hall, then back to his, a war raging inside me; this was my last night in Paris.

No regrets, remember, Claire.

And even though I'm pretty sure Louis was about to become my greatest regret of all, my resolve crumbled the moment he moved away.

I grabbed his arm. 'Wait . . .'

Louis stopped.

I breathed in. *Oh, God help me.*

'Lock the door.'

Chapter Thirty-Seven

Within a matter of seconds, Louis had locked the door and was lifting me up, pulling my top over my head and clearing the desk behind me. He pushed me down, the glossy wood cold on my back, a shock against the heat of my skin. It was short-lived as a new shock hit me, watching him hook my legs over his shoulders. He slid his hands along my thighs as he stared at me. My chest rose and fell rapidly, thrilled by the way he was looking at me like he wanted to devour me. Without breaking his heated stare, I slowly peeled my bra straps from my shoulders, one then the other, my breasts spilling free as I pulled my bra down to my navel, feeling a new confidence build as I bared myself to him.

'Better?'

Louise smiled. '*Beaucoup mieux.*' He leaned over me, kissing me softly on the lips before moving slowly down, inch by maddening inch, placing his hot mouth over the peak of my breast, then moving to the other. I arched my back, fighting the moan that wanted to escape. Looking down at

Louis's mouth tasting, nipping, sucking at my breast was the most erotic thing I had ever seen. And then he moved lower, kissing a trail down to my navel, so leisurely I thought I would go crazy.

He tilted his head to the side as he reached the loops of the bow at the front of my skirt, then glanced up at me, eyes shining with wicked intent.

'For me?' He laughed, slipping his fingers into the loops and unravelling the bow.

I giggled; his fingers skimming along my stomach were both pleasure and pain as he took his time unwrapping me.

A cheeky grin formed on his face as he straightened and stood before me like a god. Splayed out half naked before him, I felt so vulnerable, and yet so utterly sexy. No man had ever touched me the way he did, or even looked at me the way Louis was looking at me. His eyes raked over my body like I was the most beautiful woman he had ever seen, and whether or not that was true, little did it matter, because he made me believe it.

'We are going to do this properly,' he said; he slowly ran his hands along the outside of my thighs, hooking his fingers into the loosened waistband of my skirt.

I swallowed. 'Louis,' I breathed, half panicked, thinking about what he was about to do.

'The one thing you will learn about me, Claire,' he said quietly, as he took hold of the elastic of my skirt and panties and began to lower them down my thighs, exposing me fully to him in the most intimate of ways as he spread my legs apart, 'is that . . .'

He leant down and kissed my mouth.

He kissed my neck.

My breast.

My belly button.

My hip bone.

And then he paused, his breath heated against my thigh as he looked up me.

'I love a challenge too.' And with that he placed his mouth on me.

'Oh God.' My hands gripped the edge of the desk. I was wrong, so incredibly wrong, this was by far the most erotic thing I had ever experienced, watching the top of his head move as he pinned my thighs down so I was open to the slow, sensual working of his tongue gliding over me, sucking and circling with an intense pressure. I couldn't hold it in any more, and worse still, he didn't want me to. He pushed his finger inside me, sucking so hard I cried out, panting, and twisted and arched against the unbearable pleasure he was inflicting on me.

My hands lowered to grasp his hair, but he only held my thighs harder as he plunged his tongue deeper, tasting me, ensuring I was absolutely spent, and he must have known, felt it in the quiver of my thighs, the way my body had become languid and limp, and how my chest heaved as my mind struggled to catch up to my body, rippling in the aftershocks of my orgasm.

Louis crawled up my body, his arms resting on either side of my head, caging me in as he gazed down at me, his face flushed. There was an air of smugness in his crooked smile as he took in my flushed cheeks and completely sated, limp state.

He kissed me, soft but fleeting, as his hands skimmed the curves of my hips, down along my outer thighs and up again in a slow caress.

I looked down at him. 'This hardly seems fair.'

'Why do you say that?'

'Well, you've seen all of me, touched, tasted – that hardly seems fair.'

Louis smiled. 'What can I say? I am a very giving person.'

I twisted my fingers in the curl of his hair, looking into the depths of his blue eyes, getting lost in them. To hell with living safely, one night of passion with a man like Louis Delarue would be something I would be reminiscing for the rest of my days. It would be like that wrinkled old lady in *Titanic* banging on about the Heart of the Ocean while Celine Dion played in the background. So this might not be an epic love story, but there was no denying the way he made me feel, the way he touched me, whispered to me, urged me on into the most mind-altering pleasure I had ever experienced. Sure, he was an arrogant, bossy bastard most of the time, but in those fleeting moments where it was just us, succumbing to our needs, well, that was better than anything I could have ever hoped to find in Paris. I smiled up at him, propping myself up on my elbows, my long dark hair falling over my breasts.

'Well, maybe I should give something to you.'

A darkened fire flashed across Louis's face, which saw him pulling me up to sit on the desk. I suddenly felt exposed to him, wrapping my arms across my body to shield myself.

'What would you give to me?' he asked, his voice low, gravelly, his accent so thick and sexy I would almost agree to give him anything . . . almost.

I looked deep into his eyes, my hands moving to the buckle of his belt, flicking it undone and pulling it from its loops. My quick hands went to his fly, as I moved in to kiss his neck and whisper into his ear, 'I want to taste you.'

Louis swallowed hard and it made me smile against the curve of his neck, where I nipped at him gently, before kissing him in the same spot. I could feel the long line of him pressed against his pants as I ran my hand over the fabric.

'Claire.' He said my name as more of a warning, which was not the greatest idea, as it only encouraged me.

'Mmm,' I hummed into his neck, placing light, feathery kisses along his skin.

I had opened myself up to Louis, felt him, sampled him, but it wasn't enough, I wanted more, and the grinding against my thigh told me he wanted more too.

'Claire,' he said, his hands moving over mine, stopping them from breaching the line of his briefs.

'It's okay, I want to,' I said against his mouth before claiming it, leaving him with no doubt about what I wanted. And he almost let himself go with it, releasing my hand so I could reach down for him, caressing the long, hard length of him in long, slow strokes, again and again, revelling in the way his body reacted to my touch. The guttural French words that sounded so sexy as they came out of his mouth only encouraged me to move faster. I had never felt more powerful, taking control and pushing Louis to the brink of madness.

Until madness transcended into something else entirely, as Louis swore, pushed my hand away and took me in his arms to carry me to the bed.

When you imagine something often enough, there is always the fear of living the reality, of it not living up to what you've imagined, but sex with Louis? It was turning out exactly like I imagined: hot, heavy, hard. I pushed myself into him, like I pushed myself into his tongue. Meeting his thrusts, my hands splayed on the headboard, seeing his eyes fix on the place where we were joined, sliding in and out slowly, tauntingly at first, until it became too much for both of us. Louis shifted onto his knees, his hands gripping my hips as he drove into me with such force I felt a delicious kind of pain, the kind I revelled in knowing would be a dull ache between my thighs tomorrow, knowing who had made me feel it.

I lost myself so completely in him, my bones felt heavier, my feet dug into the mattress, and when my body began to tense he understood, pulling out of me and making me gasp in protest because I was empty of him. But not for long as he rolled on his back and guided me to straddle him. I positioned myself and sank slowly down on him, watching the rise and fall of his chest as I took control, loving the feeling of taking something from him, riding him in languid, deliberate circles to begin with, seeing him wince between agony and ecstasy as I rode him, faster and faster, his eyes still fixed on me. Sitting up, he brought his lips to mine, catching my sighs and moans and urging me on, faster, harder, in between delirious French words that only made me more wet, as he spoke the foreign sounds against my skin.

'Open your mouth,' he groaned and I did. He slid his tongue into my mouth to tangle with mine as he pushed up into me, building on a feeling that grew into something unbearable. My arms wrapped around his shoulders, my breasts pressed against his chest, my hot breaths blew into his face as I watched him watch me fall apart, moaning his name and begging for it to not stop, never to stop, until I couldn't take it any more and buried my face into the alcove of his neck, muffling my screams, coming so hard Louis had to hold me in place, allowing me to ride through the shockwaves. But only for a moment before he pulled out of me and manoeuvred me onto my knees and took me from behind, slamming into me, thoroughly fucking me until he came hard, shouting my name. It felt like a triumph, that I had made him come undone.

He slumped over me, pressing gentle kisses onto my shoulder as we both caught our breath. It was like we had been in battle; I could already feel the dull aches, and Louis bore half-moon indentations in his shoulders from my nails. I had hated him, hurt him because I was torn between the pleasure he was giving me and the fact I was getting something I wanted so badly, something I would never have again after tonight.

Louis pulled the cover over us and wrapped his arm around my waist like a lover and the mind-blowing pleasure that I had just experienced only filled me with sadness.

As if he sensed the shift in me, Louis cupped my chin and moved my face to his, his questioning quicksilver eyes looking down at me. He didn't ask me what was wrong or press for an answer, he simply kissed me, tenderly. I turned into him and let the warmth of his arms engulf me; he kissed my temple, whispering into my ear, '*Restez avec moi.*'

I pulled my head back, looking at him with a knowing smirk. 'More dirty talk?'

Louis shook his head, his eyes set hard, his expression serious. 'It means "stay with me".'

And just when I thought I couldn't take any more from this man, he went and blew my mind all over again.

Chapter Thirty-Eight

In the light of day, I didn't have the urge to run. I lay on my side, staring at Louis's profile. I had tried to sleep, but didn't really sleep so much as close my eyes, ever aware that he was next to me, breathing in that deep, rhythmic way people do when they are sleeping. I was far too wired for that, far too in shock that we had done what we had done, on the desk, in the bed, in the shower, against the wall.

Oh God. I slunk down into my blankets; there was something painfully different about the light of day all right. I sat up, squinting against the sun that peeked through the crack of the blinds in front of the bed. I grimaced, moving out from underneath the sheet ever so carefully to go to the bathroom, when Louis's hand snaked out, snaring my wrist and making me jump and squeal in fright.

'Ah ha!' he said, pulling me back into bed and using his brute force to tickle me into hysterics. 'You cannot leave until you pay the toll,' he said, pinning me to the mattress, his mischievous eyes flooded with a lightness I had never seen before. His stubble was thick, his hair in disarray; he looked seriously gorgeous. But he looked gorgeous whether he was well groomed, dressed smart casual or in work clothes – he was all man, and I could feel it with the hardened length of him digging into my belly.

The humour was not lost on him when my eyes dipped down and then up again with great interest. 'What's the toll then?' I teased, really hoping he was thinking what I was thinking.

Louis laughed. 'Such a one-track mind.'

'I don't know what you mean,' I lied, squirming a little, my hands still trapped under his strong hold.

'Do you want to know what the toll is?'

'Yes.'

'I don't know, do you think you can handle it?'

'Try me.'

'Okay,' he said, looking slightly worried for me, and I had almost bought into his ruse until he affectionately kissed me on the lips, lingering for a while before drawing away and taking great delight in watching me swoon.

'That's for trying to leave the bed; you won't believe what the toll is for leaving the room,' he mused.

'And what if I left the country?'

Something shuttered in Louis's eyes, but he didn't respond. If he wanted something serious he would have said so there and then. It wasn't like Louis was incapable of speaking his mind.

'You hungry?' he said, changing the subject, before letting me go and rolling off me, reaching for his pants.

I tried not to overthink his reaction, which was easy enough with my growling stomach as a distraction.

'Starving.'

'Leave it with me, I know a few people,' he said, pulling on his T-shirt and giving me a wink. He grabbed his jumper and shoes. 'Brunch on the balcony?'

'Oui!' I said with much enthusiasm. When Louis smiled it was the tooth-exposing kind; I had only ever seen it a few times, which really was a shame, it was certainly a rare and beautiful sight.

Hearing the door slam, I took a moment to roll over and squeal into my pillow, laughing and sitting myself up in bed, brushing my hair out of my eyes and shaking my head.

This cannot be happening.

~

I wasn't a chef, but I was pretty sure it didn't take an hour to boil an egg, or do whatever Louis had planned. I had showered, blowdried my hair, got dressed, unpacked, and now sat on the balcony, waiting.

An hour and forty-five minutes later, my leg jiggling kicked into gear. I had a million scenarios playing in my head. There had to be a perfectly logical explanation to this. Maybe he went to Noire for brunch; maybe he needed specific ingredients. I was foolish to think he could whip up just anything in this kitchen – it was closed, so surely he wouldn't be able to use it. Maybe he wasn't cooking, maybe he was just putting in an order somewhere.

Then where is he? It does not take two hours to get brunch.

Had he freaked out? Changed his mind?

Oh God, he's not coming. He's not coming.

And just as a ball of anxiety lodged in my throat, there was a knock on the door.

'Oh, thank God,' I sighed, clutching my heart and feeling instantly relieved. Louis was many things, but rejection such as that would be a very epic level of cruelty.

I went to the door, my heart racing, my stomach grumbling. 'About time, I'm bloody *star—*' I whipped open the door, my last word cutting off when my eyes landed on Cecile, standing there like she had the night before, only this time her demeanour was grim.

'Cecile?'

'Claire, you'd better come downstairs.'

~

I sat behind the desk in the tidy yet overcrowded office, my eyes ticking across the screen in disbelief. Watching the short clip run on a constant loop. I shook my head, spinning in my chair to where Louis stood in the corner, his brow furrowed, arms crossed, looking like he was a million miles away. Jean-Pierre was attentive though, waiting for me to say something.

'How?' I asked, turning back to the screen to see me, standing in front of Louis, before walking away and doubling back, shouting at him, him standing, us facing off before he starts yelling. My eyes dipped to see the video was muted, thank God. I really didn't need to hear it as well, especially seeing as Cecile and Gaston were standing by with matching grim expressions. And then of course it got worse, there was the money shot of me slapping Louis across the face. It looked bad; I didn't recognise that person, it made me feel ill to think I had behaved like that, and that people were witness to it.

'Somebody must have recognised Louis at the café, then of course add a bit of drama and a smart phone and the content can be uploaded in a matter of minutes,' said Jean-Pierre.

'Hence the thirty thousand views already,' added Gaston.

'Yeah, Louis Delarue is trending, and not in a good way.' Jean-Pierre rubbed at his face.

'What?' I said, a bit too loudly, blinking at the screen. I hadn't even thought about the views. 'Well, what are people saying?' I said, mainly to myself, as I started to scroll down, but Jean-Pierre stilled my hand over the mouse.

'Ah, I wouldn't do that if I were you.' He winced, which naturally only made me want to look all the more.

This could not be happening. To think of how hard I had tried to avoid the cameras altogether and there I was, larger than life, exposing myself in the worst possible light.

'So,' said Jean-Pierre, 'I would probably lay low for a while if I were you. We can't afford to have any negative press while we are trying to launch Hotel Trocadéro; in fact, I would probably put it off altogether until this all dies down.'

'That's a bit extreme, isn't it?' said Gaston.

Cecile shook her head. 'There's press out the front, and the phone hasn't stopped ringing.'

It broke my heart to see her so defeated, to go from renovation highs to total lockdown was too much. I sat up straight, ready to take on anyone. *What did I have to lose?*

'I'll front them. I don't care who they are.'

'Claire, I don't know what the press are like in Australia but they are pretty brutal here; if they take a dislike to what you are trying to achieve, they could destroy your career.'

I glanced at Louis, who still stared aimlessly off into space. I read the heartache on Cecile's face, the confusion on Gaston's and the understanding on Jean-Pierre's. Little did it matter whether they blamed me, because I blamed myself. I could have listened to Louis and his objection to joining any social media, instead of arguing the point with him like a spoilt child. I turned the screen away, not wanting to see any more.

'I am so sorry, everyone,' I said, my voice emotional as I tried to comprehend the ways in which this video going viral could impact Louis and the hotel.

I looked up at Cecile wanting her to know how sincere I was when I said what I had to. 'You just tell me what you want me to do and I'll do it.' If I had to face the media, conduct interviews, offer a public apology, I would do it without hesitation.

Cecile looked away. 'I think that you going back to London is probably for the best,' she said, her voice small and sad.

The words were like a physical blow, knocking all the wind from me. I lifted my chin, trying to think of all the things I would do in order to make it up to them. I just hadn't thought of Cecile asking me to leave.

I turned my gaze to Louis, and instead of demanding I stay, he was silent and thoughtful. I stood, walking past Jean-Pierre, caring little of the audience we had. I paused before Louis for a long moment.

'If you want me to go, I'll go,' I answered Cecile, but my focus remained on Louis, so when his eyes lifted to mine, and I saw that all the warmth and humour from the Louis I had known on the sixth floor was gone, replaced only by the cool, calm exterior of a businessman, my heart faltered. I held my breath as the silence lingered between us.

'Perhaps it would be for the best,' he said finally, without an ounce of emotion, like he was some kind of robot.

And instead of agreeing, I simply walked away from him, heading toward the office door, out into the hall and to the safety of the waiting lift.

I pressed the button to the sixth floor for what would be the very last time.

Chapter Thirty-Nine

I stood on the doorstep of an elegant, stark white terraced house in a quiet enclave just south of Kensington Gardens, my worldly belongings shoved into two garbage bags, one slung over my shoulder and the other on the ground by my side. I was told not to knock, not to ring the bell, just to stand there until the stroke of one o'clock and I would be allowed access. Contrary to how the cryptic text message sounded, I wasn't venturing into the witness program; instead, I was about to enter Kate Brown's home. Nobody visited Kate, ever. And now I was going to stay with her until I packed up my old life and returned to Australia.

As sure as the clock ticked over to one I heard the sound of elaborate deadbolts being unlocked behind the glossy black door, which then opened oh so slowly. I felt like I was about to step into a story reminiscent of *Alice in Wonderland*. A tall, blonde girl stood in the doorway, looking sullen and beautiful. Kate hadn't changed from school: her hair was just a bit longer and her personality as dry as a biscuit. She didn't embrace me like an old friend would, she merely looked at me with her big doe eyes and the corners of her mouth lifted slightly; it was impossible to tell if she was really struck with any kind of emotion.

'You must be desperate,' she said, her eyes never dipping to my garbage bags. Instead, she looked at my tousled locks – that would be the kind of thing Kate would notice. She wasn't being nasty; she was just being factual. There was a good reason that no one visited Kate, and it lived on the ground floor of a five-bedroom London terrace.

'How is Joy?' I asked, trying to seem light-hearted when referring to Kate's nasty grandmother. The fact that her name was actually Joy, well, the irony was lost on no one.

'She doesn't know you're here so you're going to have to be quiet,' she said, taking one of my garbage bags from me and motioning for me to follow her inside through the elegant entrance to the bottom of the staircase. I made sure to sneak up the stairs behind Kate, almost holding my breath. The house was thick with tension. Kate turned right into a huge, light-filled room that was almost a mini apartment all of its own, big enough for a lounge, bed, table: a little home away from home, or in this case, a home away from Joy.

Kate closed the door behind us softly, pausing and craning her neck as if to listen for something she might have expected to hear, but the house was silent, and only then did she seem to sag in relief.

'She's asleep,' she said, turning to me with a new light-ness in her expression, like she was seeing me for the first time. She placed her hands on her narrow hips, taking in my bloodshot eyes and sleep-deprived dark circles. 'Bad week?'

'A week I could handle – this seems to be a lifetime's worth of poor choices.'

'Sounds like it'll take a few bottles of wine to unpack all of that.'

I smiled, feeling finally at ease in Kate's upstairs hideaway. 'You know all the right things to say.'

'How about a hot shower while I hook you up to some wifi?'

'Kate, you are going to make some man very happy one day.'

She laughed. 'Well, don't listen to Joy because according to her I don't know how to do anything.'

~

The refuge in Kensington was a welcome distraction: two weeks of respite and I could feel myself forming a thicker exterior on my soul. Any time I saw a cooking show, or anything Paris affiliated, I shut it down. I kept right away from news columns, YouTube and every kind of social media. I guess I was sort of in the witness protection program, the one for the broken-hearted.

Ugh. Shut up, Claire.

Even I was sick of myself.

I sat crossed-legged on the rug, my laptop propped up on an ottoman so Sammi didn't have to be aware that today, like most days over the past fortnight, was no-pants Monday. My hair was swept up in a messy topknot, my daggy long nightshirt kept me cosy, and my fluffy bed socks were pulled up way too high. Avoiding Kate's frail yet feisty grandmother downstairs hadn't been a problem because I was in full-on hibernation mode. I didn't feel the urge to leave ever. Sometimes I caught Kate frowning at me from across the room, like last night when I cackled at *Four Weddings and a Funeral*, so engrossed half the popcorn I chucked into my mouth missed. It seemed that Kate was always hovering around me with a dustbuster.

'The thing is, Sammi, I feel great. Like this is who I am supposed to be in life, ya know?'

Sammi's face was screwed up. 'What, living like a hobo?'

I thought for a second. 'Yeah, I guess so.'

'So you find that this look is working for you then?' Sammi gave the impression she was glad to be thousands of miles away from me.

'I have been worried about materialism for so long, and it all means nothing. You know what? There was nothing wrong with Hotel Trocadéro the way it was. At least it had substance . . .'

Sammi sighed. 'Oh boy, here we go.'

'And then you bring in the cavalry trying to toff it up and it ruins everything.'

Twenty minutes later, and I felt like Sammi wasn't exactly invested in our conversation. 'And then he said, "Maybe it's for the best".' I made air quotes. 'Pfft, like he was doing me a favour or something, like *whatever.*' A splash of dip fell off my chip and landed on my top. 'Oh shit,' I said, scraping it off.

Kate plonked next to me. 'All right, that's it, I am calling for an intervention.'

'Oh, hallelujah!' cried Sammi. 'I was just about to pretend my internet was playing up.'

I frowned, thinking back over the last few days. 'Haven't you been having issues with your internet?'

Sammi tried to keep a straight face. 'Oh yeah, totally.'

'The thing is, Claire, we love you to death, but if you don't stop talking about Louis, I have gained permission from Sammi to euthanise you in your sleep, and don't think I'm not capable. I have been living with my Lucifer-reincarnated grandmother – I have thought about it.'

I looked from Kate to Sammi. 'I don't talk about him that much.'

'Are you fucking serious?' Sammi blurted. 'I feel like I'm the one who broke up with him.'

'I guess it's lucky that you didn't sleep with him, otherwise it would be ten times worse,' added Kate.

'Um, yeah, yeah, that would be really bad, huh?' I said, biting my lip and averting my eyes.

'Oh no, you didn't!' Sammi sing-songed.

Kate threw up her hands. 'Well, there it is, no wonder you're a basketcase. You have been ruined for all future men. You might as well just give up now because you are never going to get over this, ever.'

My fingers traced the loose thread from my bed socks and pulled it free, probably doing more damage rather than just leaving it alone: the story of my life. I could feel my vision blur as I shook my head, a wave of sadness overtaking my denial. I started to cry.

'I know, I know, I will never get over it. It's just that I thought I'd found who I was in Paris, but then it all ended and I feel like a hole has been punched through my chest, and it's hard to breathe. But if I talk about it, it kind of keeps it alive, it cements me in a time and place where I don't have to think about me sitting here, with my stubbly, unshaven legs and questionable hygiene.' I looked up to see Sammi's big, sad stare. 'I just feel lost, and there's nothing I can do about it,' I sobbed, losing myself to the comfort of Kate's embrace as she wrapped her arms around me.

'I'm so sorry, Claire.' I heard her voice crack. 'If you want to talk about him until you can't talk about him any more, we'll listen, won't we, Sammi?'

Sammi wiped away a stray tear, quickly gaining her composure. 'Absolutely, fire away.'

But funnily enough, now I had a captive audience, there was something in me holding back, as though I didn't have the urge to unload, as though I thought no good would come of it, and if I was going to move on, then I needed to find a different way of working through yet another change in my life.

I sniffed. 'Actually, I might have a shower, get with the times. Sammi, will you be around for a bit?'

'Sure.'

'Cool.' I nodded. 'Hey, and tell Mum I'm coming home.' I smiled weakly. 'I think it's time.'

That's what my head said anyway, now all I had to do was convince my heart.

Chapter Forty

In the scheme of things, a week can fly by when you're looking at real estate.

Sammi and I were rocking it old school, talking to each other on the phone while we browsed through real estate options in Melbourne. It was kind of weird not seeing Sammi's overly dramatic facial expressions, but I could still visualise them in my head clear as day.

'What about this one, Claire? One bed flat in Richmond, not far from the MCG, nice city views.'

Everything piqued my interest until I scrolled to the price bracket. 'Next.' I sighed, reducing the real estate screen and opening up Facebook; maybe there was a private rental group where I could make enquiries? This time next week I would be back at home, living in Mum's sewing room for all eternity if I didn't get a move on.

'God, you're so fussy,' said Sammi.

'No. I'm *broke*,' I corrected. It had been a while since I'd logged in to Facebook and my eyes skimmed over the page, annoyed about the layout change yet again; what was Zuckerberg up to now? There were dozens of notifications about my uncle's political views, my auntie's passive-aggressive memes about people who let you down in life, my younger cousin BJ's 'Like for an inbox' posts, whatever that meant. There was a plethora of thumbs up and someone had even . . .

'Oh my God.' I could feel the colour drain from my face. I lowered the phone as I stared at the screen. I blinked, confused by the distant high-pitched squeaking that was coming from the receiver. *Oh shit.*

I juggled the phone back to my ear again, still not taking my eyes away from the screen. 'Oh. My. God,' I repeated.

'What?' Sammi snapped. 'What are you going on about?'

I blinked a few more times, but the view was the same. 'Louis poked me.'

'Yeah, and I really don't need to keep hearing about it.'

'Not like that, you idiot, on Facebook . . . Louis Delarue poked me. He's not on Facebook; he doesn't do social media.'

'It's not a troll, is it?'

'I don't know.'

'Click on his name.'

I felt suddenly hot, and my hands were clammy as I scrolled the mouse up, hovering the cursor over his name. I almost wanted to close my eyes as I clicked, until his page appeared and my heart stopped.

'It's him; it's really him.'

I scrolled through his page, filled with before-and-after pics of the Hotel Trocadéro, pictures of Cecile at reception, dressed in her brand-new navy blue uniform. A picture of Gaston, opening the door with a beaming smile. The kitchen crew had expanded from three to six, all lined up in smart black double-breasted chef's jackets and tall hats. The refurbished rooms were unrecognisable; gone were the stained, threadbare carpets, tatty bed linen and mission-brown built-ins. Everything was white and fresh with accents of the same blue as the uniforms and awnings.

'Claire, what are you doing?'

'I'm just looking.'

'I don't like the sound of that.'

'No harm in looking – oh shit.' I clicked into Louis's 'About Me' section and there, right before me, was something I never thought I would see. Louis was on Twitter, Instagram, Tumblr, Blogger, Google Plus; he was linked in every way imaginable.

'Claire?'

'I'll call you back,' I said, hanging up before she had time to protest.

I took a deep breath and pushed out my chair, needing a moment to absorb what was in front of me. I reached for my mobile, tapping my Instagram app, something I hadn't done since I broke up with Liam, because frankly there had been nothing worth putting a filter on. But as I looked at my profile, my mouth gaped with the number of notifications I had received, the majority from @Lou_Dela.

My heart raced as I swiped my finger across the screen, only to find—

'Oh, wow!'

Shot after shot of the hotel, Noire, Louis's Audi, of food, of Paris, so many of Paris. There were no hashtags because I seriously wondered if he even knew what they were. I laughed, wiping away a stray tear, scrolling to the top of his profile.

'Holy shit!'

Louis had amassed 113,064 Instagram followers in less than a month. I knew it wasn't healthy but I skimmed through every one of his social pages: Facebook page, 1,528,619 likes; Twitter, 205,060 followers. And it wasn't just social pages – they were *well-maintained* social pages. Never would you see him snap a selfie and hashtag himself drinking wine smugly, that was just not his style, but as far as Instagram went he surely did have skills, and his tweets and responses to fans were also highly entertaining.

I went back to his Instagram, seeing the last photo he had tagged me in three days ago: a beautiful night shot of the Eiffel Tower in all its glittering splendour, taken from directly underneath, looking straight up through the centre of the structure. It made my heart ache, but never more so than when I read the caption of the photo. *Lights will show you the way home @Claire_shorten*

My chin trembled as I took in a deep breath. My head reeled from the emotions that were raging inside me. The shock, the amazement, but scariest of all – hope. My finger hovered over the screen before I pulled it away, and then back again hesitating while I thought long and hard about the ramifications of what I was about to do. Before I could talk myself out of it, my finger touched the screen, clicking on the heart.

Claire Shorten liked your photo.

Chapter Forty-One

It wasn't raining, which didn't really fit with my vision of how this would go when I'd planned it. In my head, I had been standing in the rain, looking up wistfully at the navy awnings of Hotel Trocadéro, dramatically screaming to the sky as lightning flashed across my face. Instead, the sun was streaming down on me and the skies had been a bright blue all day, affording me the pleasure of a good dose of Vitamin D as I strolled along the River Seine, past the quaint green wooden stalls that lined the river walk. It was times like this that I felt nothing but love for Paris, where no tainted memory could dull the sparkle; this was why I'd had to come, this was why I was here.

Having taken the early Eurostar to Paris, the mere thought of being both physically and emotionally baggageless by the day's end was something to truly be excited over. I had to be done with this weight that was lodged in my chest. Except for the Facebook poke and Instagram tags, there had been no word from Louis or Cecile. I had even gone as far as doing the one thing I had promised myself I would never do: I googled *Louis Delarue – Café de Trocadéro*, to see how viral the video had gone, but I couldn't find anything but photo stills of what took place and articles that described how a mystery woman had finally done what many had been dreaming of for years. There was also a mixture of comments from fans defending Louis and attacking me, to people defending me and attacking Louis. Five minutes of scrolling and I was done, and seriously reconsidering my need for closure.

But much to my own and even Kate's and Sammi's surprise, I'd known I had to come back. I had to seek closure before heading back to Melbourne. I wanted to be able to look at future travel shows on Paris and not cringe. I wanted to binge-watch *MasterChef* and not feel a burning contempt for anyone in a chef's uniform.

So I stood in the sunshine outside Hotel Trocadéro, summoning the courage to set one foot in front of the other, a task made so much simpler by the fact there wasn't a black Audi parked outside. That was something I wouldn't have to fear; Louis was long gone. But there was one thing I had decided on. After this trip was over and I was in Melbourne again, I wouldn't follow him on social media any more. There was just nothing healthy about it, and I knew that I would never truly heal if I didn't sever contact.

Christ, it felt like I was on a bloody seven-step program, although admittedly staying secretly at Kate's was pretty much what I imagined rehab to be like.

As I approached the glass door of the hotel it opened
for me, and a man who was not Gaston welcomed me with
his broad smile and sharp suit; he even had gloves on, very
shmick.

'Bonjour,' he said. 'Welcome to Hotel Trocadéro.'

'Merci,' I said. I was not prepared for Gaston not to be
here. Not a great start for my anxiety.

'Are you checking in, mademoiselle?' the suited man
asked.

'Oh no, I just . . .' I paused, my attention turning to
reception, a smile spreading across my face. 'No way!' I said,
turning to walk to the counter, and stand before Gaston, who
was at the printer, tall and proud, with an unmistakable new
accessory – a navy blue manager's jacket.

Gaston hadn't seen me, and I really wished at this point
that the bell hadn't been confiscated, so I cleared my throat.

'Pardon, monsieur, can I please speak with the manager
right away?'

Gaston turned, his eyes alight, an incredulous smile on
his face as he looked at me almost as if I was some kind of
mirage. He laughed, rounding the counter and crushing me
in his arms.

'Claire, what are you doing here?'

'Look at you!' I tugged at his jacket. 'This is amazing.'

Gaston straightened. 'No more dragging luggage.'

I couldn't believe that it had been less than a month – it
actually felt like years had passed – and maybe it was due

to the fact the hotel itself was so different. Gaston watched me take it all in.

'Do you want a tour?'

'Yes, please!'

Gaston bowed. 'Right this way.'

He showed me the refurbished guest rooms, with their new linen, towels, drapes, carpets, fresh paint and luxury products in the modernised bathrooms. It was like all the old horrors had been exorcised in all ways but one, as we headed back into the lift of death, which still managed to traumatise me, almost as much as glimpsing the number six button on the lift panel. I pushed that to the back of my mind. No good would come of it.

The lounge had also been refurbished with more classic chairs, the sofas reupholstered in navy and cream fabrics. A large plush rug lay on top of the newly installed herringbone flooring that shone beautifully under a sparkling chandelier.

'So beautiful.' Coming back had been the right thing to do, I knew that now.

'Well, if you like that, Claire, wait till you see this.'

Gaston seemed almost giddy as he led me to the restaurant. It had been nothing more than a black tarp to me the last time I saw it, and now, as Gaston led me through, I instantly felt my skin prickle into gooseflesh. And that was even before my eyes rested on the new, elegantly scripted signage.

Clare De Lune Restaurant.

Gaston stood next to me. 'We named it that because it reminded us of you. I mean, it's spelt differently but sounds the same, you know? It means "light of the moon".'

Taking in the crisp white linen, the fresh flowers and crystal flutes, my eyes filled with tears. The space was no bigger than before, but the warm blues and mood lighting made it unrecognisable.

'It's incredible.'

For the past few weeks I had thought that I'd been turned away from here, shamed and forgotten; now, my heart wanted to burst.

'I just wish I could have been here for the reveal.'

Gaston was confused. 'Reveal?'

My heart stopped. 'Oh God, that's right, the reveal was cancelled. Please tell me that it was rescheduled?'

Gaston laughed. 'Claire, we didn't need a reveal to let people know about Clare De Lune opening.'

'Really?'

He looked around, wary of others as he lowered his voice. 'You slapping Louis was the best thing that could have ever have happened to us.'

'Um, how do you figure that? It was awful.'

Gaston shook his head. 'People loved it: the post went viral and then everyone wanted to know the story behind it.'

'Oh God.'

'When you left we had a meeting. At the time we didn't know what to do with the restaurant reveal. Jean-Pierre thought about taking Louis's name off the project out of fear that it might harm the business, but after a couple of days the hype was escalating and people wanted to know about *you*, the mystery girl. Louis decided to weather the storm and get on social media; he rode the wave of interest, promoted the hotel, and now we are booked out for the summer. It's insane.'

'Louis, on social media . . . I still can't fathom that – he was so against it.'

'Yeah, well, he's changed in a lot of ways.'

My curiosity was piqued and I desperately wanted to know what he meant. But there was someone at reception.

'Pardon, Claire,' he said, making his way back behind the desk.

'Is Cecile around?' I called after him.

'Oui, I think she is in the office.'

I went to the office, expecting to see it exactly as it always was, small and cluttered. I knocked and pushed the door open, breathing out a laugh. 'I guess some things never change.'

But since Cecile wasn't in the office, I stepped back from the door, shutting it behind me, conscious of the time and needing to get back to catch my return train. I had been naive in my day-trip plans to think I could fit it all in. Really I needed a full day just to reacquaint myself with the hotel, and now it was too late. This time next week I would be home, and the possibility of coming back to Paris any time soon was – well, that was not going to happen.

As happy as I had been with what I'd found, and what I had learned, I felt like there was something missing. I really needed to see Cecile, and by some kind of magic she appeared, her heels clicking in the marbled foyer, her dark hair elegantly twisted into a French knot; her knee-length, figure-hugging, jet-black skirt the perfect base for the navy-blue tailored jacket that accentuated her petite waist. The white blouse with silken strips tied into a bow around her neck was elegant and feminine. She had never looked more radiant – or more surprised as she came to a standstill, mouth agape.

I shifted nervously; I couldn't tell if she was happy to see me, or if she was going to tell me to leave. For the first time I actually thought that coming here was a mistake, and all I wanted was for the ground to open up and devour me. Then the unexpected happened: Cecile walked forward and wrapped her arms tightly around me, instantly healing the ache inside my chest. This was what I had come back for; this was what I had needed.

I pulled back, crying despite my happiness. 'You mean you're not mad at me any more?'

Cecile laughed through her own tears. 'I could never be mad at you.'

I wanted to stay. I wanted to walk into the kitchen and see Gaspard at the helm, Francois by his side and Cathy owning the floor, but there was no time.

'Cecile, I have to go.' I winced.

'What? No, stay.'

'I really can't. I have to get back. I have to catch my train. Can you please tell everyone I said goodbye, and just thank them for everything?'

'Of course.'

I embraced her again. 'I am so proud of you, Cecile. Hotel Trocadéro is amazing, especially Clare De Lune.' I grinned.

'You can thank Louis for that.' She looked at me pointedly.

Hearing his name was like a physical blow. As much as I tried to convince myself that he was not a part of the ache inside me, I knew it was the biggest lie I had ever told myself. But I couldn't think about that, I had to go.

'Can you please call me a taxi for the station?'

'Oui, go sit, I will get one for you.'

'Merci.'

I paced along the reception, restless with the fear of being stranded in Paris. I really didn't want that to happen; my heart was closing off, getting itself ready to leave this place behind. And with every second that ticked by, my anxiety grew. Fifteen minutes passed, enough to duck into the kitchen and say my goodbyes to Gaspard, Francois and Cathy, which was the silver lining in a thickening dark cloud.

'Cecile, can you call another? It's been twenty minutes and I really have to—'

Gaston put down the phone. He nodded at me and Cecile. 'It's here.'

I blew out a deep breath, thanking the gods that I still might make my train.

Hugging them both goodbye, I ran through the foyer, pushing through the door myself because I was in too much of a hurry for the doorman's graces. The sun had gone down now, and the air was cool against my cheeks. I stood under the illuminated sign of the hotel, glancing down the street, panicked that Gaston had got it wrong, I couldn't see any ta—

I froze. Right before me, so blatantly shiny, sat a black Audi. My heart started to race. Was this some kind of cruel joke? But just as I began to edge forward, the window opened, just like it had the first time I met the pair of eyes that were looking at me now. Except this time they weren't mad, or questioning, they belonged to the Louis I had come to know on the sixth floor.

Just as I told myself to hold it together, I began to tremble; the ache in my heart was so intense I felt like I couldn't breathe. And then the car door opened, and there he was, towering over me. He looked past my shoulder, saluting through to the foyer.

I frowned, turning to see Cecile and Gaston smiling and giving Louis the thumbs up. They had ordered me a ride all right. *Traitors.*

Louis smirked. 'My people,' he quipped.

'I feel so betrayed right now.'

'Oh, don't be too hard on them. They've done well.'

'You asked them to look out for me?'

Louis's hands were in his pockets as he leant against his car. 'Every. Day.'

'You could have messaged me.'

Louis frowned. 'I poked you.'

'Sometimes, a poke is not enough.'

'I tagged you!'

I laughed. 'It's not enough.'

Louis sighed. 'Well, I guess I have a lot to learn.'

'Oui, chef, you do.'

Louis smiled. 'So you're headed back to London now?'

'If I make it.'

'Can I keep you if you don't?'

I laughed. 'I'm going home next week, back to Australia.'

Louis nodded thoughtfully, pushing himself off the car and walking in a circle around me. 'Well, I have a restaurant in London, but I don't have one in Australia.'

'Really?' I said, cocking my brow.

'And you know me . . . I do love a challenge,' he said.

'Me too.'

Louis turned to me and examined my face. 'Am I a big enough challenge for you?'

Having him so close made it hard to focus and I inhaled a deep breath. 'You are the most challenging man I know.'

I enjoyed the way Louis winced at my words, waiting for me to say whether that was a deal breaker or not. My mouth twitched and I stepped closer to him.

'Which means I might just have to slap you around every now and then.'

Louis burst out laughing, shaking his head and wrapping his arms around me, engulfing me in his warmth.

Maybe I was mad, but when it came to Louis Delarue, I wanted all the challenges. I wanted him, and he wanted me. I may have come to Paris and got completely lost, but somewhere in the dark I had found the light. As I stood in front of this beautiful, challenging man, I might not have known exactly where we were going, but I knew he would take me there, and I had never been so sure I wanted something in my existence.

Louis looked at me, brushing his knuckles against my cheek, a glimmer of worry flashing in his eyes as he read the thought process rolling through my mind. 'So is that oui?'

I leant into his touch; he felt my smile before it appeared as I turned my head to kiss the palm of his hand, then place it against the warmth of my heart, a heart that didn't ache any more. Looking up into his clear blue eyes, thinking how different they had been the first time we met on the kerbside what seemed like a lifetime ago.

'I say . . .' I paused, drawing out my answer and watching the emotion in his eyes as he waited intently for it.

I slowly stepped in to him, never once looking away as my mouth hovered close to his and I whispered, 'Challenge accepted.'

If you enjoyed *Paris Lights*, you'll lose yourself
completely in *New York Nights* and *London Bound*,
the second and third books in C.J. Duggan's
Heart of the City series.

 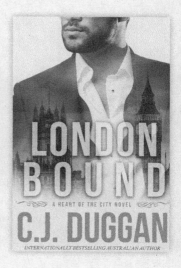

Read on for a sneak peek of *New York Nights* . . .

Chapter One

Since finishing school, all I'd wanted to do was travel and work with children, so au pairing was the perfect solution.

Or so I had thought.

Being an au pair is nothing like in *The Sound of Music*, though. To start with, I certainly wasn't a nun, I had zero musical abilities and I had failed sewing in high school. Plus, there was no handsome Captain von Trapp and no choreographed frolicking.

All that aside, it had sounded appealing. Sacrifice X amount of hours for childcare, then stroll through a foreign city in my downtime, immerse myself in the culture, learn another language, study maybe, truly find myself. All before falling in love with a wealthy, independent fisherman called Pascal who crafts small objects out of wood with his bare hands. Come nightfall, we'd make an incredible paella with the freshest of seafood while we sipped wine, arms linked, toasting to us. I mean, we all have to have goals, right?

The reality was somewhat different. The prospect of experiencing anything close to a handsome fisherman called Pascal was a world away when your days consisted of shampooing a toddler's hair or wiping the bottom of a five-year-old, while defrosting meat for an early dinner you would be eating with the children. It was very hard to feel like an adult when sitting at a tiny table with your knees up to your ears, trying to convince the children how delicious each mouthful was. 'Look, they're little trees, eat up your little trees,' I'd say, coaxing them to eat broccoli.

And as much as your employers made you a part of their family, there was never that feeling of freedom, the kind that let you wander into the lounge to flake out on the sofa and idly channel surf, or to fling open the fridge for an impromptu snack. There was no inviting friends over for dinner and definitely no bringing guys back.

I make it sound like it was all bad, but if the truth be known, for the past three years it had been my whole life. Now I sat, shoulders squared, on a plush white sofa, surrounded by white walls and fresh white flowers. Everything was white, save the glass-and-gold coffee table dividing me from them. 'Them' being Penny Worthington and her equally cold daughter, Emily Mayfair. Like her mother, Emily's smile didn't reach her eyes; there was no warmth there.

Emily swept her blonde bob from the side of her face in one elegant movement so she could look down at the papers she was holding, no doubt a background check on me they'd organised through a private detective. I wouldn't have put it past them.

'Won't be long now, we're just waiting on one other,' said Emily. Even her name sounded like she had married into money: her husband must be Lord Mayfair or something equally distinguished.

Their driver – yes, they had a driver – had picked me up from the Park Central Hotel and driven me to a beautiful brownstone in Turtle Bay Gardens, an enclave of row houses, gardens arranged to form a common space, with a four-metre-wide stone path down the centre and a fountain modelled after the Villa Medici in Tuscany, or so Dave the driver informed me; I was too busy looking up at the four-storey building with my mouth open. I'm not sure what I had expected; I had always thought of New York as cramped apartments with fire escapes, air-conditioner boxes hanging out of the windows.

'Oh, Emily, I think we'll just begin, you know what Dominique is like.'

Dominique? I was suddenly wondering who was interested in putting me on the stand. Was Emily the mother of the children I was meant to be caring for, or was the less-punctual Dominique the one? And more importantly, why was I about to be interviewed by *three* women? I took a sip of the water I was holding, which had been kindly provided by the maid. A driver and a maid: they made my previous employers, the rather self-sufficient Liebenbergs, look middle class. I chose to hold onto my glass of water for fear of leaving a condensation ring on the coffee table. I was certain that act alone would mean instant dismissal.

'So, Sarah Williams, tell us a bit about yourself,' Emily said, leafing through the pages before looking at me expectantly.

Oh God, how had I not prepared for perhaps the most obvious question of all? Somehow I'd thought there was actually no preparing for this kind of situation; I would simply wing it, turn on a bright and cheerful – not ditsy – façade and completely fake my confidence. I started by throwing caution to the wind and making eye contact with the maid, who promptly came forward and took away my empty glass. I was now free to place my hands in my lap and begin the Sarah Williams story. Until I was interrupted by a distant commotion: doors slamming and a loud voice out near the entrance.

Penny Worthington closed her eyes, apparently summoning the strength to remain calm. Emily sighed deeply as if the approaching footsteps grated to the bone. The maid prepared to throw herself into the path of the encroaching cyclone.

'Hello, Frieda, my love, how's that gorgeous man of yours?'

A loud and heavily pregnant blonde woman shimmied out of her jacket and handed it and her purse to a mortified-looking Frieda.

'He is well, thank you, Miss Dominique.'

'Frieda, how many times do I have to tell you? Call me Nikki. Every time you say Dominique it's like running your fingers down a blackboard.' Dominique, or rather Nikki,

brushed wisps of hair out of her face. She had nothing like
the elegance and poise of Penny and Emily, and for a moment
I thought surely, *surely*, they couldn't be related, but as soon
as Nikki turned I saw the same perfect nose and blue-grey
eyes. There was no mistaking that she was Penny's daughter.

'Hello, Mother.' She pecked Penny on the top of the
head. 'Sorry I'm late.' She waddled around the couch and
sat beside Emily.

'You're always late,' said Emily through pursed lips.

'Well, you're always in a bad mood, so neither one of us
can win. Ugh, Frieda, my love, can you please get me a water.
I am so fat.' She sighed, turning to look at me with a big,
genuine smile. 'And you must be Sarah?'

I knew within an instant of her turning that smile on
me that I loved her. Warmth and authenticity just radiated
from her.

I stood, leaning over to shake her hand so she didn't have
to bend over her belly. 'And you must be Nikki?' I said.

Her smile broadened as she looked at her sister and then
back at me. 'Oh, I like you, you don't miss a beat.'

I was flooded with relief, inwardly saying a prayer that it
was Nikki's children I would be caring for and not Emily's.
My eyes flicked to her belly, thinking maybe this was the
reason I had been called here so quickly; maybe Nikki, clearly
the black sheep of the family, needed help with her soon-to-
arrive baby.

'We haven't begun as yet, Dominique, we had just asked
Sarah to tell us about herself.'

Something told me there would be no way in hell Penny would resort to calling Dominique 'Nikki'.

'Oh, come on,' Nikki said, rolling her eyes, 'don't you know enough about the poor girl? How many more hurdles must she jump before you give her the job?'

Penny and Emily had matching glares, and it wasn't just because they had the same eyes, although that probably helped.

'Let me ask a question,' Nikki said, propping herself up with a cushion that definitely looked like it was more for show than actual use. 'What brought you here, Sarah?'

It was a question that was not easy to answer. Leaving the Liebenbergs' employment had not exactly been part of the plan, but neither was following them to Slovenia where they were opening a remote medical practice. Admitting as much, however, might make me seem unreliable, and an au pair is nothing if she isn't reliable; I would have to think of something better.

Nikki looked at me as if trying to tell me telepathically that she desperately wanted my answer to be perfect, so I answered honestly.

'I've dreamed of New York City all my life. The fact that something I love to do brought me here is a blessing and I know it. I am so grateful to Dr Liebenberg for setting up this interview for me; I know he is a very good friend of your family.'

Penny simply stared at me; there was a long, uncomfortable silence as I waited for her to say something, but she was giving me nothing. I cleared my throat and glanced at Nikki, who smiled and nodded, encouraging me to continue.

'The moment I stepped off the plane I knew that anything that lay ahead of me would be a challenge I'm willing to accept.' I looked directly at Penny and Emily. 'I feel I am more than ready for this new chapter of my life.'

'So you believe you can handle a challenge?' Emily asked, her perfectly sculpted brow curving with interest.

'I'm the eldest of four from a working-class family so I've been surrounded by children all my life. I don't shy away from anything, and my stomach doesn't turn, and the tears don't flow. I mean, I'm not a robot or anything, but I come from tough stock. I will love the children and I will care for them, I know this from working for the Liebenbergs. I cared for their boys, Alex and Oscar, since they were babies, which was definitely a challenge at times, but I loved my time there.'

'Dennis did provide a rather impressive recommendation for you,' Penny said finally. 'And I am going to be completely honest with you: if it wasn't for his recommendation, I seriously doubt I would have let you through the door.'

Okay, ouch.

'You see, I don't much care how many brothers and sisters you have – that really doesn't affect me one way or the other. Nor do I care for any girlish fantasies you have about traipsing around New York City. What I care about is you being fully present, in your mind, in your heart. That your dedication is solely to my grandchild.'

Bingo – grandchild, not children.

'You are to ask no questions, you are to simply do what is required and nothing more. If you are successful, you will be given a full induction on what is expected of you. You will sign a non-disclosure form.'

'And how am I to know if I am successful?' I asked, perhaps not as confidently as I would have liked.

'Well, we have a fair few questions to go through first,' said Emily in a no-nonsense, business-like tone.

'And another interview for you to complete,' said Penny.

'Another?' Nikki and Emily both looked at Penny, confusion creasing their brows. Well, creasing Nikki's anyway; something told me Botox was keeping the wrinkles at bay for Emily.

Penny gave her daughters a pointed look. 'Yes, another.'

'You don't mean—'

'Are you sure that's a good idea?' said Nikki, cutting off Emily's question.

Penny sighed.

'We can't hold off any longer, we have to get him involved.'

Their faces looked grim, worried. Like they were about to encounter the bogeyman. Their dread was palpable, and although I had just banged on about being able to handle anything, now I wasn't so sure.

'Get who involved?' I asked tentatively.

Penny's eyes cut sharply to mine, and I regretted my words immediately.

'First lesson to learn, Miss Williams: ask no questions.'

I glanced at Nikki, hoping to find some comfort in an eye roll or a wink, but I saw nothing more than her sad, worried expression, and my heart began to pound hard against my chest.

I swallowed, nodding my understanding even as I thought, *What the hell have I gotten myself into?*

Chapter Two

I t wasn't over. It would never be over and I would be hearing 'if you are successful' for the rest of my days. I went down the steps of the brownstone and made my way back to the car, feeling rather deflated despite the VIP experience. The driver was holding the car door open. Such a different world, I thought, as I smiled my thanks to him. Not really knowing the rules, I had tipped him on the way here, and at a guess I would tip him again on the way back. I was seriously going to run out of money at this rate. Maybe there was something in my NYC guide that would tell me if I even needed to tip private chauffeurs. I searched through the pocket guide, wondering how this could be my biggest drama right now.

Then the door opened. 'Slide over, sweetie.'

I did as the voice asked, juggling my book, too surprised to think. Then I recognised the body of Nikki as she slid in beside me.

'Where are you staying?' she asked, holding her belly and catching her breath.

'Park Central Hotel,' I said, looking at her, slightly worried we might be taking a detour to the hospital.

'Oh, nice. Hey, Dave, drop Sarah off first then drag me home, I know how much you love going to Brooklyn.'

A smiling pair of brown eyes flicked up in the rear-view mirror. 'I would drive to the ends of the earth for you, Nikki Fitzgerald.'

'Aw, bless,' she said, tilting her head and offering a high-wattage smile.

'You live in Brooklyn?' I asked.

'Much to my mother's disgust.' She laughed.

Silence fell as Dave indicated to pull out into the street.

'Hey, don't worry about that interview, it's just a process my mother and sister like to go through to ensure they are in control, when they're actually not. The job is yours.'

'You really think so?'

'They haven't even interviewed anyone else, and if the recommendation came from Dennis Liebenberg, you could be an axe murderer and they would be hard-pressed to go against it.'

'Well, I'm not an axe murderer so hopefully that will work in my favour too.'

'I should think so,' she said, examining me. 'I would pack my bags if I were you, I don't think you'll be staying at Park Central too much longer.' She turned away to look out her tinted window.

I was afraid to hope, but all I wanted to do was drill her with a thousand questions, all the ones I was forbidden to ask. Then I thought, if I was going to be the au pair to her baby, shouldn't she have a say?

'When are you due?'

Nikki sighed, her hand going to her belly. 'Never. I am never, ever having this baby. I feel like I have been pregnant for twelve months already.'

'Your first?'

Nikki burst out laughing. 'Oh no, but definitely my last; I have four more rugrats waiting for me back in Brooklyn. As much as my mother complains about my location, I am sure a big part of her is relieved that I don't visit with the grubby-fingered little munchkins often; I mean, you've seen how white that place is, that couch would be totally smashed within seconds.'

I actually wondered if Nikki had been adopted at birth, although there was no mistaking the physical resemblance. She had a warm, genuine aura about her; she had alleviated the thick tension the moment she entered the room. I really liked her, but I couldn't help but swallow at the thought of five children. Oh God, was I destined to become the au pair for them? Was this what all the cryptic interviews were about? Capture my interest and then hit me with the big reveal?

I cleared my throat, knowing I wasn't meant to ask questions, but I wouldn't sleep tonight unless I had a certain amount of clarity.

'So have you had au pairs before or is this your first time?'

Nikki looked at me and frowned. She really resembled her mother. Then her eyes widened and her face lightened as she broke into laughter. 'Oh God, no, I'm not hiring an au pair, oh gosh, no no no, I would never subject any poor soul to my brood. Oh, you poor thing, is that what you thought? No wonder you've gone white.' She continued to laugh, which really didn't make me feel any better, because that left a far worse alternative: I was going to be an au pair for Emily Mayfair – ice queen. I felt sick.

'Oh, okay, so how many children does Mrs Mayfair have?' I asked tentatively.

'Emily?'

I nodded.

'Emily has a boy and a girl, precious little poppets who have been sent away to the best boarding school that money can buy, so don't stress, my sister's au pair days are well and truly over.'

Now I was confused. Why was I even here? Who could I possibly be employed by? I knew they were being cryptic but this was just getting ridiculous. The no-questions rule be damned, I had to know.

'So you're thinking, why are you here?' Nikki said, as if reading my mind.

'Exactly.'

She smiled. 'Well, you're about to find out. Dave, can we take a detour to Lafayette, please?'

Lafayette Street is a major north–south road in New York City's Lower Manhattan. I didn't know anything about it beyond that, but I could sense some questions would be answered, or at least I was counting on it, seeing as Nikki, who had previously been quite open and forthright, had suddenly clammed up.

'Are you sure you want to make this detour?' Dave's eyes flicked up into the rear-view mirror again.

'Oh, it's okay, he's not there today,' she said, waving dismissively as she tapped away on her BlackBerry.

'And Mrs Worthington—'

'It will be our little secret.'

Dave began to mumble under his breath.

'Don't worry, Dave, she hasn't put a tracking device on your car . . . yet.' She said the last word under her breath, and as much as I was looking forward to the mystery being solved, I didn't want to get Dave fired.

I leant across the leather seat. 'You know, I think I'll just wait until tomorrow's interview. I mean, what's one more day anyway?'

'Absolutely not, I don't want anyone else for the job, and I certainly don't want you having a night to think about it and changing your mind.'

'Why would I change my mind?'

Dave's eyes flicked up again, meeting Nikki's briefly before she looked back out to the street. 'Oh, no reason,' she said in the most unconvincing of ways. Now I was worried; from the moment Dr Liebenberg had spoken of helping with a 'situation' it was obvious that I had flown over shark-infested waters into circumstances I was still not clear on. If I woke up in a bathtub of ice with my kidneys sold to the black market, I was going to be seriously pissed.

Acknowledgements

To Michael, for believing in and supporting everything I do with your unwavering love and understanding. For being patient with the stress I bring, with my deadlines and insanely odd hours. I know it's not easy, but you are the beautiful part of my reality and I wouldn't want to share it with anyone else.

To the entire Hachette family. It has been an absolute honour to continue to collaborate with such a reputable and prolific publishing team such as yours. Fiona Hazard, Kate Stevens – I have said it before and I will say it again: you ladies are a class act. Your passion, support and encouragement make working with you a sheer joy.

To Anita, Keary, Jess and Lilliana, for always pushing me and helping me to the finish line even when it seems impossible. Your friendship, patience and smarts are what help govern my success; I cherish each and every one of you.

To my amazing family and friends for putting up with my lockdowns and never-ending deadlines, for constantly reminding me of things I tend to forget; you remind me to live and be balanced, your love is the best anchor I could wish for.

To all the readers, bloggers, reviewers of my stories, for taking something away from my words and for loving and embracing the characters, for wanting to read Australian voices: our rich literary culture is worthy of any local or international platform. In a world that is often dark enough, it is a pleasure to inject it with a little bit of sunshine and a whole lot of passion.

And, of course, to Paris! For being such a gracious, inspiring host, you were everything I hoped you would be and so much more. *Je t'aime pour toujours.*

C.J. Duggan is the internationally bestselling author of the Summer, Paradise and Heart of the City series who lives with her husband in a rural border town of New South Wales. When she isn't writing books about swoon-worthy men you'll find her renovating her hundred-year-old Victorian homestead or annoying her local travel agent for a quote to escape the chaos.

CJDugganbooks.com
twitter.com/CJ_Duggan
facebook.com/CJDugganAuthor

Also by C.J. Duggan:

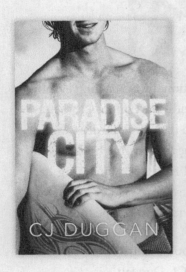 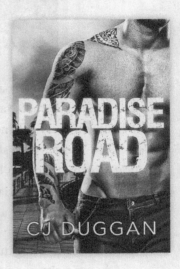

The Paradise series – sexy Australian new-adult romance full of sun, surf and steamy summer nights. There's bound to be trouble in Paradise . . .

BOOKS with HEART
Stories that make you feel

Books with Heart is an online place to chat about the authors
and the books that have captured your heart . . .
and to find new ones to do the same.

Join the conversation:
(f) /BooksWithHeartANZ • (y) @BooksWithHeart

··

Discover new books for **FREE** every month

··

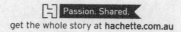

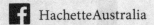
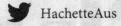
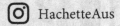
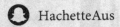